Shadow
in the Smoke

by

Jo A. Hiestand

The McLaren Mysteries

Shadow in the Smoke

Cover Art by *Angela Anderson*

The Wild Rose Press, Inc.
PO Box 708
Adams Basin, NY 14410-0708
Visit us at www.thewildrosepress.com

Publishing History: previously published by
L & L Dreamspell, 2012, as Torch Song
First Mainstream Mystery Edition, 2015
Print ISBN 978-1-5092-0362-8
Digital ISBN 978-1-5092-0363-5

The McLaren Mysteries
Published in the United States of America

"I'm sorry, Mrs. Ennis,
but even if I did take on your case, I don't think you could afford my fee."

"You haven't told me what it is."

He named his price, watching her intently.

"I'd double that if you could find Janet's killer." His right eyebrow rose in skepticism but she rushed on as he opened his mouth. "I'm serious. I've got the money. I can give you a check for the amount and you can cash it today, so you'll know it's good."

Recovering his composure, McLaren leaned back again. "It means that much to you, then."

"Yes. And it will to you, too."

"The money's nice, I admit, but—"

"Oh, I'm not referring to the money, Mr. McLaren, though I suppose that will be welcome."

"Then, what?"

"I meant coming up against your nemesis again and proving him wrong after all these years."

"My nemesis…"

"Yes. The man you tangled with, the man who's responsible for you leaving your police job last year. Charlie Harvester."

Praise for Jo A. Hiestand

With hints of the 1940s movie *Laura*, Michael McLaren is drawn with haunting music into the intricate path of attraction for a dead woman. It is easy to get caught up in the wonderful descriptions written by author Jo Hiestand, and then suddenly realize she just gave us a clue. Jo leads us along, following twists and turns, making us guess who the murderer is. I was so sure I knew who did it, and in the end, I was so wrong! *SHADOW IN THE SMOKE* is an excellent mystery and well worth reading.

~*Ann Collins, Librarian, Webster Groves Public Library*

~*~

LAST SEEN is another victory for Jo Hiestand. Well constructed, this murder mystery has all the twists and turns of a really good novel whilst managing to catch the very essence of Tutbury Castle and the area. Jo even manages to capture the competitive edge that can exist between Curators — sometimes!

~*Lesley Smith, Curator, Tutbury Castle*

~*~

COLD REVENGE is a mystery to sink your teeth into. Not only was the murder investigation top notch but also the peek into the life of the investigator added another layer to the mystery. A mystery worthy of sinking your teeth into; Cold Revenge is a keeper. This is my first Jo A. Hiestand book but it will not be my last.

~*Delane, Reviewer for Coffee Time Romance & More*

Dedication

For Don and Chris,
the photographer and the photographed.
Hope this continues to be fun for you both.

~*~

SHADOW IN THE SMOKE has a companion song. "Never Leave My Side" is available on a single-song CD recording. This torch song—lyrics by the author, melody composed and performed by Lola Hennicke Toben with piano, drums, and upright bass accompaniment—is available through the author's website:

http://www.johiestand.com/shadowinthesmoke.html

~*~

McLaren has his own website! Log on to learn about quirky British customs, interesting places to visit in the UK, cooking recipes, music anecdotes, and a calendar of appearances by the author.

http://www.mclaren-mysteries.com

Acknowledgments

Thank you to Detective-Superintendent David Doxey (ret.), Derbyshire Constabulary, who cast his eye upon the entire manuscript, correcting procedural problems and McLaren's tendency to wander at times; Detective-Sergeant Rob Church, Derbyshire Constabulary, who answered questions while anxiously awaiting Australia time; and long time St. Louis area Police Sergeant Paul Hornung, for suggesting sensible tweaks and catching the historical inconsistency.

A hardy handshake to Paul and Liz Davenport, who walked around Haddon Hall on my behalf. Thank you for the descriptions.

Thanks also to Arthur Oestereich, St. Louis-area Fire Marshal, for his help with fire properties and arson investigation. Also to Alison Moss, Head of Corporate Administration for the Derbyshire Fire and Rescue Service, for answers about legalities, firefighters' housing, shifts and service response time.

I thank Cindy Davis and Lori Graham of The Wild Rose Press for permitting a third McLaren case into the world.

Errors, if any exist, are solely mine.

~Jo A. Hiestand
St. Louis, June 2015

Cast of Characters

Michael McLaren: former police detective, Staffordshire Constabulary

Jamie Kydd: friend and police detective, Derbyshire Constabulary

Dena Ellison: McLaren's girlfriend

Gwen Hulme: McLaren's sister

Janet Ennis: singer, artist, caterer

Nora Ennis: Janet's mother

Stuart Ennis: Janet's father and Nora's ex-husband

Tom Murray: Janet's former boyfriend

Myles Tyson: Janet's fiancé

Dan Wilshaw: pianist in Janet's music trio

Ruth Wilshaw: Dan's wife

Ian O'Connor: bass player in Janet's music trio

Bruce Parrott: former drummer in Janet's music trio

Helene Brogan: Janet's catering business partner

Sean Fallon: Janet's former catering help

Kathryn Fallon: Sean's wife

Eva Lister: catering client

Corey Chappell: firefighter from Matlock Fire Services

Cheryl Kerrigan: Home Office forensic pathologist

Charlie Harvester: McLaren's former colleague, Derbyshire Constabulary

Chapter One

"I've explained to you several times—each instance you've been to see me, in fact—why your daughter's death is classified as an accident. I don't see what more you can accomplish by these semi-annual, if not more frequent, appeals." Charlie Harvester leaned back in his chair, signaling the end of the woman's visit. He glanced at her once more before gathering up the notepad and pen. Each occasion it was the same thing, and each conversion convinced him she was a mental case. Bonkers. No other word for it.

A sigh slipped between his lips. In all his years as a police officer, and even more so now as a detective-inspector, he'd never been subjected to such a leech. Or perhaps the better word for the woman was lunatic. She had to be, harping on about murder and arson and mysterious assailants. Sounded more like a movie than real life. The woman needed Pinewood Studios or the BBC film unit. Or a suite at the closest insane asylum. He sighed again, this time more audibly and conscious that she heard it. He made a habit of hiding his personal thoughts and feelings from the public, but he didn't care this time. He doubted if she'd remember the sigh or this visit by the time she got home.

Harvester closed the notepad cover and held it shut, tapping its bottom edge in a great show of Impatience and Dismissal. He looked at the woman now, his

1

lowered eyelids conveying both boredom and distain in one glance. Her face seemed to age more with every visit, the creases etching deeper into her pale skin, the gray streaks nearly engulfing her dark hair. She sat up straighter, as though it would show her determination more effectively. Harvester was not impressed. He stood up. If this didn't give her a nudge out the door he'd have to escort her.

"I don't come to harass the police," she said, her voice taking on a tinge of frustration. "I have the utmost respect for the Derbyshire Constabulary."

In spite of his feeling toward the woman, he couldn't keep a hint of a smile from turning up the corners of his mouth. He inclined his head toward her, as though he embodied the entire police force.

She continued, the gesture having no effect on her. "I'm here because I'm a mother who wants answers about my daughter's death. You can understand that, I'm sure."

"Mrs. Ennis." Harvester exhaled and looked at the wall clock opposite his desk. "I don't know what else I can say. You've visited the police stations in Buxton, Matlock, and Ashbourne. You've talked to inspectors, constables, and detectives so you know why we don't label her death as murder. I would think you would be happy to accept that. A murder has…well, it's much more upsetting than an accident."

"Upsetting is hardly the word I would have used, Mr. Harvester. Anyway, it's a matter of justice, isn't it? Someone killed my daughter and he should be made to pay for it. It's not so complicated."

"Look, Mrs. Ennis, I don't think this rehashing of the case is doing you any good. Besides wasting everyone's time, keeping it a matter of constant conversation prevents you from healing. Now, why don't you toddle off home, make yourself a nice hot cuppa, and let the matter lie." He bent forward, smiling, and patted her hand. It shook uncontrollably.

She removed her hand. "I may be an old age pensioner, Mr. Harvester, but I'm not senile."

Harvester shrugged and thrust his hand into his trousers pocket. "I didn't say that, Mrs. Ennis. I'm merely concerned for your emotional welfare. This can't be healthy, going over and over the case every few months, dredging up old memories. Five years is a long time to pursue an accident case. Why don't you give it a rest?"

"Five years is a long time, yes, but when it's murder—"

"This isn't doing either of us any good. We rehash the same things every time you come in. Look." He tapped the notepad as he brought it to his chest, cradling it. "Your daughter had been burning trash in the incinerator in the back garden of her house. People had been warned for months about the dangerous conditions for fires, ever since the drought began. It was a windy day but your daughter, evidently, had decided not to heed—" He stopped, deciding to rephrase the perceived slur. "She forgot about the high fire risk warning and the burn ban. No one is faulting her, Mrs. Ennis. It was an accident." He was aware of the word, the conclusion of the fire service report and the coroner's verdict at the inquest.

The thing is really the woman's problem, Harvester thought. How does she get the verdict overturned or the case reopened? It usually was a hell of a fight to get it done. He sniffed and wondered if he were getting a cold. Wouldn't doubt it. The woman increases my stress level every time she shows up, and stress triggers the onslaught of a cold. He glanced at her as he grabbed his handkerchief. What else could it be by an accident, the incinerator so close to the wooden outbuilding, the wind, the items within the structure that fueled the combustion? Plain as a pikestaff to anyone looking at this from a logical, unemotional viewpoint.

He smiled, trying to emulate the Constabulary publicity posters lining the lobby of the police station, the helpful, concerned bobby talking to the awestruck kid. Except Nora Ennis wasn't awestruck. Rather, she was frustrated and skeptical, even if she was in her seventies. Still, her mental confusion was evident, classifying her as a kid in his book. He glanced again at her gray hair—no matter its contemporary, short style it still spoke Age to him. Trying a different approach, he softened his voice. "I'm sorry your daughter tripped and was knocked unconscious, Mrs. Ennis. Dying like that…well, I know how horrific you imagine it was for her. But the postmortem examination found she died of smoke inhalation. She was unconscious," he repeated, hoping the finding would finally sink into the woman's brain. "She couldn't have known or felt anything. Now, I'm afraid I really must end our conversation. I have to meet with the Superintendent in a few minutes."

He flashed the smile again and he wondered if it would be more effective if his eyes showed some warmth.

"I honestly don't mean to belabor this," she said as Harvester moved toward the door, "but that indentation of the brain tissue… Even the pathologist said—"

Harvester pressed his lips together, as though mentally laboring over a response. Thrusting out his chin, he said rather slowly, "She tripped and fell, Mrs. Ennis. I'm sorry, but that's how it happened. I don't know why you're so keen to prove this was a case of murder. There was nothing under her fingernails to suggest a fight so she wasn't defending herself from your alleged attacker. There were no drag marks on the grass to indicate she had been taken to and shut up in her studio. She hit her head while trying to escape from the building when the fire got out of control. If you don't like it, I can't help it, but that is what happened."

"But the pathologist—"

"I really have to go."

"But why won't anyone look into this? Five years is a long time. There have been a lot of technical advancements, haven't there? DNA testing and such? Can't you look at the case again, sift through the fire debris?"

"Really, Mrs. Ennis—"

"Haven't you ever loved someone so much, Mr. Harvester? If you have, you wouldn't rest if this had happened to your family member."

Harvester's lips pressed together and his fingers gripped the edge of the notepad. His breathing rate increased in a series of audible exhales. In a barely audible voice, he said, "If you feel so keenly about this, you can always go elsewhere, but frankly, I don't see what that will gain you. The case is closed." The slamming door underscored his anger.

Chapter Two

"Do you know what it's like to lose a child to murder?" The woman sitting across from McLaren looked like she knew. Her wrinkled face held more than age; it appeared to hold defeat, grief and pain. And frustration. Her left hand shook slightly as she raised the teacup to her lips, a gesture McLaren thought bought her time or distanced her from the upsetting subject.

He shook his head, feeling inadequate. How could he talk to a parent about such a loss? He hadn't any kids. He hadn't even lost anyone in such a violent manner. Maybe she would do better going elsewhere, employing a real private investigator, someone with whom she might share a bond.

He suggested it, with an edge of hesitation to his voice. A rumble of thunder overhead seemed to echo his unspoken grumbling and prodded many of the tearoom's patrons to glance outside. "Not that I don't want to help you, Mrs. Ennis." McLaren watched her eyes for a glint of understanding. They were gray and lifeless, barely discernible against the tan curtains behind her. He let the waitress wheel the teacart past their table before adding, "I feel for you, for your loss. But five years—" He broke off, aware she was disappointed in his quick decision. Or was it cowardice? The thought shocked him, jolted him back to a scene last year when he had been a police detective.

When he had wavered for a moment, the irreversible decision to quit his job suddenly screamed louder in his ear than his anger to stand up for injustice. Ideals were marvelous beacons and goals, but the fundamentals of earning a living threatened to outshine his principles.

"Five years," she repeated, her voice flat and tired and sounding beyond her patience. "Too long, you're saying, however indirectly. Well, my daughter's been dead five years 28th of September and that's too long. And she was too young." The teacup rattled as she replaced it on the saucer and her head twitched again in a hint of disagreement.

Parkinson's disease, McLaren thought, watching her left hand shake. On top of everything else she had to contend with that.

"I sought you out on purpose." Nora Ennis picked up her handbag. She placed her palm on top of the table, ready to get up. "I was told that you helped people, that you fought injustice."

"I *do* fight injustice, Mrs. Ennis."

"But only when you don't have to work too hard."

McLaren reddened. Was the statement true? He didn't think so, otherwise he wouldn't have taken on the two previous cold cases of unsolved murders. But if he gave that impression now, to this woman who obviously needed him… Trying to patch up the misconception, he said, "Righting wrongs, however important that is, and however satisfying that is for me to accomplish, doesn't keep the roof over my head, Mrs. Ennis. I'm not a licensed private investigator. Digging into cold cases isn't my full time job. Please, sit back down. It's still raining."

He nodded toward the two women who passed

their table, their nylon jackets wet, their shoes leaving damp imprints on the carpet.

Nora Ennis relaxed her arm and sank back into her chair. The ding of the cash register rang into the air while she set her handbag on her lap. "But you do it, you have done it."

"I have. But I fell into the first one. The woman came to me."

"Rather like I'm doing now."

He nodded, feeling uncomfortable with the parallel cases.

"And you took that first case. Verity Dwyer told me you did."

"The lady from Noah's Ark animal shelter," he said, his mind flashing back to June. "You know her, I assume."

"We're friends, yes. She spoke highly of you, Mr. McLaren."

"Nice to hear. Yes, I did take that case. Though maybe I shouldn't have done."

"Why? Didn't you like being back at your old job, however unofficial it was?"

Images of Linnet Isherwood, the woman who had persuaded him to forsake his rock hammer, chisel and lonely patch of Derbyshire field, welled up in his mind. She had not only troubled to locate him but also had climbed a rather steep hill on a Sahara-like June day to ask for his help. McLaren nodded at the remembrance and wondered if he weren't trading Linnet Isherwood for Nora Ennis. Eyeing Nora, he said rather irritably, "We're not here to talk about my fling with playing Philip Marlowe, however brief or pleasant it was."

"You're right, we're not. And you've assured me

many times you're not an actual private eye. More of a concerned citizen." Nora Ennis smoothed out a wrinkle in the tablecloth, her gaze on her fingertips. Her voice sounded tired overall, but a softness had crept into her words. Hope?

"There are a lot of real private investigators in Manchester, Mrs. Ennis. In Sheffield, too, if that's closer to you. Why not rent one of them? Any one of them would be eager to take on your case. I don't know why you asked me, anyway, despite Verity Dwyer's glowing reference." This last was said with a hint of sarcasm coating his words. "I'm not a licensed private cop."

"But you've got the spark that the others lack." She opened her handbag. A crack of thunder accentuated her statement. "And even if you're merely a concerned citizen, you must admit you have the skill and experience that most of us lack. You've got your detective training to help you."

He noticed the hesitation before she spoke the last word, and guessed she'd really wanted to say 'me'. "What makes you so certain of that?"

"When you've lived as long as I have, Mr. McLaren—seventy-three years, in case it makes a difference to you—and experienced as much of humanity as I have…" She shrugged and watched his eyes. They were hazel in color and expressive, capable of conveying his thoughts and emotions. Which, at the moment, were annoyance and curiosity, in spite of his better judgment. And which also complemented his blue shirt. She broke her gaze and reached inside her bag. "What would it take to make my daughter's case your full time job right now?"

He ran his fingers through his short blond hair—a maverick display from his equally maverick Scandinavian grandmother—sank back into his chair, and snorted. This had the unpleasant ring of this past June. Here it was September, and through two cases and three months he had not altered his job choice or opinion about cold cases. He'd never get rich taking them on. And at age thirty-seven he'd lost the enthusiasm, or ignorance, of youth and knew he had to work hard for a living. Glancing at his watch, McLaren said, "I'm afraid it'd take more time and money."

"More time and money...than what? Than you've previously been paid?"

"Considering I got not a sausage from the last case I worked, that wouldn't be hard to top."

"Client couldn't pay you?"

"The client was my girlfriend and I took the case on as a favor."

"But too many favors don't keep the roof over your head."

"Like I say, Mrs. Ennis, it's no way to get rich."

"You haven't answered my question, Mr. McLaren." She paused, drawing a checkbook from her bag.

"About taking on your case."

"Yes. What about it?"

"I've got two jobs of work looming, Mrs. Ennis. I haven't time—"

"Two cases to investigate?" Her eyes suddenly sparked into life, bringing a suggestion of color to her ashen cheeks.

McLaren shook his head, annoyed by the subject. Slapping his fist on top of the chair arm he said, "Dry stone wall repairs. Near Bakewell." He was vague on purpose, not wanting her to come to his work site and pester him about the case.

"And these bits of repair will pay you more than taking on Janet's case."

He pulled in the corners of his mouth, annoyed at the woman and his attempt to rid himself of her. She had no right to question his choice of livelihood. Why should he alter anything to please her? He tugged at the knot of his plaid tie. It hadn't bothered him until now.

She must have sensed his building resentment or seen the glare in his eyes, for she said, "I *am* sorry, Mr. McLaren. That was uncalled for. But you can appreciate how I feel. I've been trying for five years to get my daughter's murder case opened again."

"Let me guess." He said it more sharply than he had intended, irritated with her, himself and the subject. "Our lads in blue won't listen to you."

"Nothing to make a song about, at least, no."

"Deaf ears." He leaned forward and picked up the bill for their tea. "I'm sorry, Mrs. Ennis, but even if I did take on your case, I don't think you could afford my fee."

"You haven't told me what it is."

He named his price, watching her intently.

"I'd double that if you could find Janet's killer." His right eyebrow rose in skepticism but she rushed on as he opened his mouth. "I'm serious. I've got the money. I can give you a check for the amount and you can cash it today, so you'll know it's good."

Recovering his composure, McLaren leaned back again. "It means that much to you, then."

"Yes. And it will to you, too."

"The money's nice, I admit, but—"

"Oh, I'm not referring to the money, Mr. McLaren, though I suppose that will be welcome."

"Then, what?"

"I meant coming up against your nemesis again and proving him wrong after all these years."

"My nemesis…"

"Yes. The man you tangled with, the man who's responsible for you leaving your police job last year. Charlie Harvester."

Chapter Three

"It couldn't have been very pleasant for you," Nora Ennis said as McLaren took a deep breath. He felt his heart was going to implode in his chest.

An eruption of thunder and lightning roared overhead, accentuating last June's roar of words and shouts now whirling in his head. Rain pelted the window beside their table, ran down the glass and collected in a stream on the outside sill before dripping onto the pavement. The water lay in wide puddles or ran across the concrete to deepen the streams beside the curb. A bus lumbered up the road, spraying the water high into the air. McLaren watched a rain drop slide down the windowpane and collect others to it before it, too, dropped and broke onto the sill.

"Harvester." McLaren managed to squeak out the distasteful name before his throat closed up. He turned back from the window and took a long sip of coffee before he could continue. "Harvester couldn't have worked on your daughter's original case. What's he got to do with this?"

She nodded, stating she was aware that five years ago Harvester, as well as McLaren, would have been in their early thirties. "I know Inspector Harvester wasn't the senior investigating officer on the case. Or should I more properly call him Detective-Inspector Harvester? It sounds more respectful."

"Of which neither you nor I concur with, am I right?" He gave her a knowing look, having heard the slight edge to her voice when she had said the copper's name.

"You haven't lost your detective skills, at any rate. Am I that transparent?"

"When it comes to Harvester, yes."

"You seem a capable man in many ways, Mr. McLaren. I know brawn doesn't necessarily equate to brains, but you're muscular, tall and well built. Surely you can handle…anything that comes your way without too much difficulty."

"I've had my tussles and have usually won, yes."

"And you can't be much of a dunce if you're a detective? I think I've found the man for the job."

McLaren colored slightly at the compliment and tried to gloss over it. "Right, then. You've done your research, got my interest and attention. And you've learned about my working relationship with my former colleague." He downed the last of his coffee and set the mug on the table with a thud. "What's your angle?"

"Nothing more than needing your help, Mr. McLaren. I told you about Janet—"

"You mentioned Harvester," he reminded her, rather gruffly. "He's obviously involved in the case, or you wouldn't have brought up his name. Not even as a lie to rope me into reviewing your daughter's murder. Since Harvester was with the Staffordshire Constabulary at the time your daughter died, and your case happened here in Derbyshire, in Darleycote, I believe you said. And the fire was investigated by the Derbyshire Constabulary…" He paused, letting the significance sink in. "Well, he can't have a tie to your case. At least none that waves as me."

"No, but he has something to do with it now, because he *is* with the Derbyshire CID at the moment." She paused, and McLaren looked at her. Laughter from a nearby table floated over to them, filling the silence in their conversation. McLaren nearly decided to tell Nora Ennis that he wasn't interested in the case, no matter if he would be able to escort Charlie Harvester to jail for something as trivial as littering, when Nora said, "He reviewed the case when I talked to him."

"And?"

"And he tossed it aside. He thinks I'm a nutter and should be in Bedlam."

"Besides the obvious that Harvester is..." He paused, embarrassed that he had nearly called Harvester a four-letter word in front of the woman. Swallowing quickly, he said, "that he's a nit and doesn't know his—" Heat flooded his cheeks, aware that his feelings were running wild and he was losing control of his better judgment. He exhaled heavily and flashed an apologetic grin before finishing. "And he doesn't know when to come in out of the rain... Why would he think you are anything other than a grieving mother?"

Nora glanced down at her trembling hands, squeezing them together. "I've been diagnosed with early stages of dementia." She said it so simply, so unemotionally, that McLaren nearly didn't catch the significance of her statement.

He mumbled his sympathy and asked if she had any family to help her.

"No. I had only the one child, Janet. I had her rather late in life, when I was thirty-eight, so perhaps she meant more to me that if I birthed her when I was in my twenties. That may be true of a lot of couples' feelings. I don't know. But my husband and I were thrilled that we had her at our ages."

"And your husband?" He glanced at her ring finger. It was bare.

"He divorced me soon after Janet's death."

"Sorry to hear that."

A flash of lightning lit up the sky across the street. Nora laid her checkbook on the table and opened it. "I've had nearly five years to get over it."

"But no one does completely."

"No, they don't. At least, I didn't. Do you want half your fee now? I don't know how this works, but I suppose a retainer of some amount is usual."

"I haven't said I'd take the case, Mrs. Ennis."

"Oh!" Her round eyes mirrored her surprise.

For an instant she looked incredibly young. A teenager, or a child, perhaps. Startled and slightly hurt, as though not receiving an expected gift.

Her hand went to the collar of her cardigan. "Sorry. I just assumed you'd take it on."

"You were telling me about Harvester and his dismissal of your case."

"That makes a difference to you?"

"I don't know until I hear it. Would you mind telling me?"

"Not at all." She laid the pen on the table, closed the checkbook and wrapped her hands around her teacup. The restaurant was not crowded, being a late Monday morning, and she spoke slowly, making certain she included all the pertinent details. "Every few months I go into the Buxton or Matlock police station to see if they've learned anything more about Janet's death. Buxton, because I live in Buxton, and Matlock because Darleycote—the village Janet lived in—is right outside Matlock. Just north of it."

"I know the spot, thanks."

"I don't nag them, please understand that, Mr. McLaren, but I feel I need to keep the pressure on them or else Janet's death could slip into a permanent cold case."

"Seems natural enough to me. So why does Harvester consider your inquiry a waste of time...for that's what it sounds like from your description."

"Mr. Harvester knows I have the beginnings of dementia. So he thinks, as I said, that I've lost my reasoning faculties and my memory."

"Just because a person has dementia—"

"But there's more, Mr. McLaren. Harvester deduced it, probably from my many visits to the station and from talking to him. He has dismissed me as having an obsession with the case and has hinted rather strongly that I've fabricated the whole thing."

"Impossible. If the police have a report and your daughter died—"

"But it's the *way* in which she died, and the verdict that labeled this case an accident, that has Harvester convinced I'm rattling on without good cause. That and the television film have made up his mind."

"What television film?"

"*Candidate for a Cold Case.*" The words came out slowly, hardly more than a mumble, and she blushed.

In the hesitation McLaren was aware of the music playing in the background. "Someone to Watch Over Me"—an old song. An omen? Did Janet need someone to watch over her? He watched Nora pull at the hem of her cardigan, smoothing out the bunched-up fabric. Was Nora the one who needed the protective glance?

"The film was on the telly some time ago. I don't even know if a DVD or anything is available. It was about a girl's death…very similar to Janet's case. Harvester knows the film and thinks I've confused the film with my daughter's death."

"Because you have dementia."

Nora nodded. She looked embarrassed to hand McLaren the same facts that had led Harvester to his conclusion.

"Doesn't surprise me that he wouldn't bother to investigate something so simple." McLaren felt the familiar tensing of his neck muscles and was aware his breathing had quickened. Every time he came in contact with Charlie Harvester, however remotely.

"He won't believe me, Mr. McLaren. In my working life I was a professor of anthropology. A rather good one, if I may repeat the opinions of my colleagues. I am the recipient of several honors and have written studies that are used in advanced degree courses at universities. Two years ago I finally retired but have tried to keep my mind active by being guest lecturer at universities and schools, and by serving as a guide on field trips to half a dozen countries."

"But all this made no difference to him," McLaren said, unable to speak Harvester's name. "Despite your intelligence and your obviously brilliant career."

"I brought a letter from my doctor, who explained my condition and assured Mr. Harvester that I am lucid and know what happened to Janet, but he won't listen or believe me. I don't know if he's too busy or what, but nothing seems to persuade him to look into the case."

"So you've come to me."

"The police and the firefighters were of the same opinion that day—that Janet burned household rubbish in the incinerator and the burning got out of control and set the artist studio on fire. But she didn't."

"You know this for a fact? Were you there?"

"I wasn't there, but I know my daughter. She would no more burn anything outside in unsafe, drought conditions than she would hold up a bank. It wasn't in her nature. You see, as a child and into her teen years Janet was a Girl Guide. She was also a nature lover, even as an adult. She cared for the earth and its wildlife. She would know better than to run such a risk. A fire in those conditions…it's inconceivable."

"And that's why you believe her death wasn't an accident. That someone else, perhaps, started that fire with her inside the studio."

Nora pulled a photograph from a battered manila envelope and handed it to McLaren. The glossy paper had lost some of its sheen in spots, probably from rubbing against the contents of the bag, and there were a few creases and damaged spots, but on the whole the photo had held up well. He found himself gazing at a thirty-something-year-old woman with dark brown eyes and shoulder-length brunette hair, a woman trapped at this moment in time, who'd forever retain her youthful appearance. The deep turquoise hue of her silky, full-skirted dress accented her eye color, and he felt drawn to her.

"This is Janet's publicity photo." Nora watched McLaren's face. "She dressed in 1940s clothing for many of her venues. It went well with the styles of songs she sang. Her fiancé, Myles Tyson, took the picture. Well, not officially her fiancé at that time…but later. He's a professional photographer. That's how they met, in fact. It's a very good likeness. I always thought it caught her kindness. Sometimes that's hard to see, isn't it? People usually are concerned that the photo show how beautiful or handsome they are. Not that Janet wasn't, but her kindness made her more beautiful. And I think it shines through here. But besides her talent, she was kind. Helped people all the time. Gave down-and-outers a hand up. She cared for people. But I guess that isn't what you need to know." She shook her head and laid her hand on top of McLaren's as he tried to return the photo. "Keep it. I've had it long enough. It needs to go to the man who will find the arsonist, her killer."

Chapter Four

That had been this morning. He was home now. The storm had spent itself, leaving a fresh washed scent in the air. Seated in his back room, with the late afternoon sunlight streaming through the windows, he tried to think rationally. Of course he didn't want to get mixed up in a repeat of the Linnet Isherwood case. But Nora Ennis did seem sincere. And totally cognizant despite the early dementia development. Was there really something he could investigate?

He took another sip of coffee before re-reading the notes she had given him. Janet Ennis' entire life had been reduced to one sheet of paper. Succinct, plain and short. Devoid of the colorful detail that makes life worth living. Settling back into the sofa, he grabbed the photographs. Nora had included a casual shot along with the professional portrait. The candid photo showed a confident, happy young woman of thirty-five, dressed in tired blue jeans, a maroon t-shirt and sandals. She sat on top of a low stone wall, a flower in her hand and held out, as if offering it to the photographer. McLaren laid that aside and picked up the second photo. The youthful face showed no signs of aging, so presumably the two had been taken about the same time. Janet still smiled, confident in her career, perhaps, and the underlying confidence shone from her eyes. But in the more formal, studio pose she seemed full of fire and ready to tackle anything.

McLaren sighed, the familiar feeling of infuriation creeping over him. He had stayed behind at the restaurant after Nora Ennis left, deliberating over whether or not it was wise after all to agree to take the case. He drank the coffee pot dry and, much to the waitress' annoyance, ordered another sandwich and hot tea. But he had remained at the table, dawdling over his meal and staring at Janet's soulful eyes. Not that a woman's eyes or beauty ever had any professional effect on him. He learned long ago not to get trapped by physical looks. But the story did intrigue him, especially when coupled with Harvester's refusal to look into the case again. Maybe Nora and Janet deserved a second chance.

Nora had known how to interest him, how to crack the core of his emotions. When he protested again that he had pending dry stone walls that needed fixing and that he was too old to be running around the county tracking down a murderer, she scoffed, replying that he couldn't be forty years old yet and that he was in better shape than most twenty year olds.

McLaren had admitted to her that he was thirty-seven and had enjoyed working on the last two cases he'd taken on. But he hadn't admitted that the surge of adrenaline he got from investigating made him feel more alive than anything else in his life at the moment. And, he confessed now, in the privacy of his home, he yearned for that feeling again.

"Then Janet's case should prove just as satisfactory to you as the others have," Nora had countered. "And as long as you're confessing, Mr. McLaren, I will open my soul to you. I know my dementia is worsening—my doctor has given me an idea of what to expect. That, coupled with the Parkinson's I have, doesn't paint a rosy future for me. Even if I escape the deterioration of memory and thought process that the later stages of Parkinson's bring, I believe Alzheimer's will claim me. I'm just selfish enough to want to see my daughter's killer caught while I am aware of the event. I can face whatever health future is in store for me if I know her killer has been brought to justice."

Which wasn't dementia talking at all, McLaren admitted to himself. So he told her he would investigate the case, hugging her as she stood up to leave and giving her a pep talk.

But now, seated in his back room, with the evening creeping over the landscape, he wondered if he shouldn't have looked into the case a bit before telling Nora he'd take it on. Were his hope-filled words more for her benefit or for his? Besides wanting to tangle with Harvester again, was he really motivated by the injustice Nora had received at Harvester's hands?

Yes, he told himself minutes later. He was incensed about the whole damned thing: about the coppers' indifference, about Harvester's martyred attitude, about a tragic end to a young life. About the five years of suffering Nora endured and no one caring enough to help her. So he jumped in, without fully knowing the details, ready to blow the cobwebs from the case and drag it in front of Harvester's nose. Ready to crack old alibis and stubborn heads, ready to bring justice to the two women.

He looked up from the paper before him, drawn suddenly to the photo on the wall opposite him. Dena, his girlfriend, smiled at him. Encouraging, believing in him, giving her blessing and telling him that he needed to do this. He smiled back, downed a quick swallow of coffee, then scanned the sheet of paper again.

The case boiled down to reports and rulings. Police and fire service investigation and reports, forensic chemists' decision, the coroner's inquest and the resulting verdict. No witnesses, no clear motive. So the ruling came down as death by accident, and the cops were standing by that. Case closed. The end.

But not so fast, McLaren thought as he read Nora's account. It didn't differ from the police report except with regards to the manner of death. The police favored accident; Nora and Janet's friends favored murder. The case may have never made it to a real jury but this self-proclaimed jury was hung.

The case story and details were becoming familiar as he re-read the story in the quiet of his house, imagining the scenario and placing Janet in it. It looked to be straight forward enough. She had been found dead in her artist's studio in the rear of her back garden. Myles Tyson had come over at eight for dinner that September Saturday, not certain if he'd be welcomed, since they'd had a tiff early that afternoon. He'd arrived with a bouquet, an apology and an explanation. He didn't get to offer any of them to her, though the police were interested in the latter.

The police questioned him, at first suspicious that he'd had something to do with the fire and Janet's death. But unless he was a superb actor, his grief seemed real enough, and he was not charged with anything.

McLaren leaned back, his head resting on the top edge of the sofa, and let the sheet of paper flutter onto the coffee table. His fingertips found the wooden and ceramic beads of his necklace and rolled them, much in the fashion of worry beads. He liked the feel of them and often toyed with them when he thought. Outdoor sounds of cawing rooks and barking dogs filtered through the half open window but McLaren didn't hear them. Rubbing his fingertips over his forehead he tried to remember what Nora told him. Not that it had been complicated or that he'd been pelted with information. But after Nora enlivened the conversation with Harvester's name, McLaren found it difficult to focus on anything else.

He sat up, downed the last of the coffee, Harvester's face shimmering before him in the growing dusk. This was a hell of a way to begin an investigation, he told himself. Prejudiced and focused on avenging himself on Harvester. Anyway, he didn't even know if I would investigate it. He had those two walls to fix near Bakewell, and he needed to paint the garage door this autumn. Besides, he'd like to spend the day with Dena, perhaps go 'round to Haddon Hall or Calke Abbey, have a picnic before the weather turned, see about a gig with his group at that fair… McLaren exhaled heavily and stood up, his gaze on the opposite wall where Dena seemed to mock him from her photograph. She'd know he was avoiding something if he rang her up and proposed a day out among the delights of Derbyshire. Not that he was devoid of a romantic gesture or candlelit dinner, but it happened so infrequently that the suggestion would have the whiff of a fishmonger because they'd spent the day together last Saturday.

McLaren's gaze drifted to the photo neighboring Dena's. He and a mate from early in both of their careers eyed him, laughing like a drain at his idea. He picked up the coffee mug and walked into the kitchen, scowling. Bloody marvelous. He couldn't even fool himself.

He fixed a salmon and cucumber sandwich, heated up a bowl of potato and leek soup and took his meal into the back room. He turned on the CD player, put on a recording of Chopin nocturnes, and sat down to eat. But several minutes later he put down his untasted sandwich, switched the CD for the one Nora Ennis gave him, brought along in the small, battered manila envelope because she'd been sure…or hopeful…of his help. He punched the Play button, not expecting much. After all, Janet Ennis wasn't a Name. She had dabbled in singing torch songs as she had everything else in her life, evidently. Singing was another creative outlet, along with her cooking and painting and gardening. But as the lyrics of the first song washed over McLaren, he found himself standing by the large back window, gazing out into the deepening dusk, listening to the smooth, warm voice. Janet was singing "The Very Thought of You" and the sound washed over him like liquid silk. They seemed to be alone in the room, her standing beside him and singing only for him. He turned, half expecting to see her sultry eyes and impish smile, disappointed when he didn't see her perched on the arm of the sofa or sitting beside the fireplace.

He shook his head, surprised he had such a strong reaction to a song and a woman he had never met, and wandered back into the kitchen for another cup of coffee. When he returned to the back room Janet was crooning "These Foolish Things."

You've got it right there. McLaren tilted back his

head in a long swallow. I'm too old to act so foolish… But the singer and the lyrics drew him again into her world and McLaren succumbed to the magic, sagging against the sofa cushions and imagining her leaning against a baby grand piano.

The voice lulled him to sleep, sweeping over him like warm waves of a tropical ocean. So it was with a start that he woke some time later, confused. She was singing a song he had never heard before. Of course he wasn't a student of the bluesy unrequited love songs, but he was a student of music. He'd have thought sometime in his nearly four decades of life he'd have heard of the title. He listened, the lyrics searing into his mind. When the song had finished, he got up, walked over to the stereo cabinet and started the song again. This time he heard it all the way through.

Where does the sun go
When it leaves the sky?
How do all the winds blow
Or a robin fly?
How can my poor heart beat
Now that you are gone,
Marking off Time's slow creep
To a lost-love song?
~*~
You promised me one single thing:
That you'd never leave my side.
~*~
Spring turns into summer
And still you are not here.
Time becomes the drummer,
Months fade into years.
This world spins through its seasons,

The stars traverse the sky.
You never told the reason,
Just left without good-bye.
~*~

You promised me one single thing:
That you'd never leave my side.
~*~

Just the other night I
Cried aloud your name.
I got no one to love and
I have got no one to blame.
Drowning in my memories
Is a painful way to die.
Throw a lifeline out to me
And never leave my side.
~*~

You promised me one single thing:
That you'd never leave my side.
~*~

He punched the Repeat button on the CD player, programming it to replay a dozen times, then reclaimed the sofa. He lost track of the repeat number as he fell asleep.

****

Tuesday morning woke McLaren with a murder of crows squawking outside the back room window. He blinked, momentarily floating in his dream. Then, as the birds' squabbling grew louder, he realized where he was, and that it was the next day. Standing, he stretched and watched the crows separate into two groups and fly off. Two ways of looking at every problem, he thought, grinning. He blew a kiss to Dena's photo and reminded himself that he was a lucky man to have the love of a woman who might have ended up with some bloke from her own social status. He gathered Janet's photos and case notes and put them back into the manila envelope. Then he took his shower, dressed in trousers and a short-sleeved polo shirt, and poured a cup of coffee before settling himself at his desk. He grabbed a piece of paper and a pen, then lifted the phone receiver and punched in the number for Jamie Kydd. His friend answered almost immediately.

"Mike! It's a little early for a beer but I'll make an exception for you." Jamie's voice sounded welcoming and eager to talk, his laugh reminding McLaren of previous evenings together at the pub.

"It's even early for me."

"Good."

Neither of them needed to elaborate on the jest. McLaren'd had too many months of depression in which he'd downed a beer or whiskey or gin at any hour, anything to help pass the time and dull his anger. Thankfully, he'd been strong enough to shake any drinking dependency that he'd developed. Quitting the job had swiftly turned into a double-edged sword.

"So," Jamie said, curiosity creeping into his voice. "What's this in aid of? You don't usually chat in the morning."

"Business, I'm afraid, though I'm not averse to that drink later this evening."

"It's a date. Now, what business, Mike? Police business, obviously, or you wouldn't be phoning the best copper in the Derbyshire Constabulary." Jamie laughed, and McLaren imagined his friend leaning back in his chair and propping his feet on the front edge of the desk. Jamie's voice broke through. "You have another case?"

McLaren grimaced, feeling foolish as he explained about Nora's quest to find Janet's murderer. "Am I grasping at straws, Jamie? Am I grabbing at something that's unsolvable just because I want to be back in detective work?"

"You're asking, not too subtly, if the investigating police screwed up the case. And if you have a chance to solve it even though they didn't."

"Yeah, I guess so."

"Harvester wasn't involved in the original investigation, Mike."

"Yeah, I know."

"So I have to assume that your desire to jump into this mess isn't a personal vendetta—other than showing him and others what a berk he is."

"Yeah."

"You want to find Janet Ennis' killer…if there is one."

McLaren nodded, his gaze fixed on the corner of his desk that held the small, framed photo of Dena.

"I don't know why you're asking me, Mike. You've made up your mind to go ahead with this thing, haven't you?"

"I guess so. Yes."

"So what did you *really* ring me about?"

"To see if you can locate some details on the case. I don't know anything other than what the victim's mother and the newspaper article related."

"Shouldn't be hard. I'll need some time to locate the file. It'll be in storage, unless it's sitting on Harvester's desk."

"Knowing him, and knowing what Nora Ennis had

to say about their latest talk, I doubt if Harvester drags the case notes out every time she pops by. He probably ignores that with the same ease he ignores her."

"Could be. Call me back in an hour, can you?" Without waiting for a reply, Jamie rang off.

McLaren filled the time by catching up on household chores. He washed the few dishes from his meals, made the bed and ran a small load of clothes in the washing machine. He tried to look up an article on the Internet, but was too impatient to sit, so he washed his car. He found himself listening to Nora's recital as he soaped up his Peugeot. She'd refrained from saying anything about Harvester's lack of professionalism, but she did comment on workplace egos and glass ceilings in general, and implied Charlie Harvester was just another ten pin to bowl down. She'd related her conflicting feelings, that she had the impression he suffered from short man syndrome, which might contribute to his inflated ego, that he liked to play up his power and intelligence, but that did little to calm her, for she felt overwhelmed at each visit to the station. McLaren agreed with Nora's assessment and felt frustrated that he could do nothing about it. He forced her out of his mind and whistled as he finished the car. By the time he'd coiled the garden hose, put away the sponge and soap, and towel-dried the car, the hour was over.

He went back into the house, dried his hands on a kitchen dishtowel, and phoned Jamie.

"Mike." Jamie glanced at his watch. "Even if you're not the world's best detective you're certainly punctual."

"To the minute. Do you have it?"

31

"It being the police report and not animal magnetism, I assume you mean. Okay, I'll let that pass. Give me a minute to get the file. I put it down when I got back here. The damned phone was ringing."

McLaren could hear a thud as Jamie laid the phone on the desk, then the tap of hard soled shoes diminish in volume. A faint rattle of metal against ceramic, followed by a thump and a muttered oath, then the hard soled shoes tapped louder and louder. There was a sharp rap and a dull sliding sound before the phone receiver rattled and Jamie spoke again in McLaren's ear.

"Damn. That file slid across the table…wait a minute while I…" He grunted as he reached for the manila folder. "Got it. Hold on…it just fell…got it," he said, sounding both breathless and aggravated. "Computers are our friends, I know, but the powers that be want it all backed up in reliable paper and filed away. For who knows what."

"For just this purpose. At least if someone comes in, your computer screen saver will cover up your nefarious deed."

Jamie said something uncomplimentary about people never appreciating other people, and read the case details to McLaren.

"Your Nora Ennis has been regular as clockwork, Mike, inquiring of various officers at Buxton, Ashbourne and Matlock police stations, wanting to know the status of the case."

"And told, in various ways, to leave them alone."

"That's about it. She's not missed a year, talking to inspectors, detectives and a chief inspector or two, when she can grab one. The last three times she's unfortunately wound up talking to Harvester."

"Poor woman. She should go to a different police station next time."

"She's gone to *you*, Mike," Jamie reminded him, then went on. "Janet Ennis died from smoke inhalation."

"Yeah, Nora told me. Damn."

"Yes. Nasty way to go."

"Horrific. I feel for Nora having to live with that memory. I assume the house wasn't damaged. The incinerator probably set back toward the rear of the property. Do you know where it was?" McLaren's eagerness came through in his voice.

"No. Well, not specifically. At the rear of the back garden, but, evidently, near enough to the little studio so it figured into the cause of the fire. By the way, her body was found in the debris of her studio. It was a small, detached, wooden building at the rear of the property. A sort of artist's studio. The assumption—"

"Sounds like Harvester had charge of the case. Assumption. What police officer assumes anything in an investigation?"

"The *assumption*," Jamie reiterated, "was that the fire began accidentally, spreading from rubbish she was burning in the incinerator, that it had been too near to the studio, and that the wind fanned the flames or burning rubbish onto the structure and it caught."

"She couldn't smell it? Well, I guess not, if she was burning rubbish. Probably thought it was part of that fire."

"Does sound bizarre, doesn't it? Especially from the viewpoint of hindsight."

"So she walks into her studio and sits there, leaving

the debris in the incinerator unattended and doesn't try to escape? Even Harvester, or whoever the SIO was at the time, would know that's implausible." In irritation he ran his fingers through his blond hair. "If she smelled the wooden structure on fire, surely she could get out. It wouldn't have erupted in flame all at once."

"Are you going to let me tell you or do you want to keep interrupting?"

"I'm waiting to be told but you aren't saying much."

"The *assumption*," Jamie said again, "was that she tripped in her hurry to escape, maybe fell into her table and bumped her head, and lay there unconscious."

"What does the postmortem report say? Is there evidence to support this? Even the SIO would want some medical statement to point a finger at that conclusion."

"Postmortem examination revealed a curved indentation of the soft brain tissue, consistent with something hitting the side of her head and producing an injury severe enough to cause her to lose consciousness."

"Gets better all the time, this."

"There are a lot of things in an artist's studio to hurt yourself on, Mike. Think about your own house, too. Besides the edge of a table, there are pieces of artwork, lamps, a small desk…"

"I get the picture."

"The SIO believes she panicked and tripped. There's no other explanation for the depression."

"Believes…"

"You can throw your classic blunt instrument into the ring, but the official police report rules out foul play. Inside the house, in the kitchen, the slow cooker was on. Cooking," he added before McLaren could make some snide comment. "A casserole, evidently for the evening meal. Lancashire hot pot, if you want details."

"The implication being that she put the food on to cook that morning and had an ordinary day before the studio fire."

"I always knew there was hope for you if you used your brain often enough."

"I use it more than some people I could name."

"There's nothing to suggest she was forced into the studio and then the structure set ablaze."

"So she's in the studio, merrily painting or whatever, the evening meal perking along in the slow cooker. If Myles wasn't lying when he said he was expected for dinner—"

"I doubt he was. The dining room table was set for two. Plates and utensils that implied a substantial meal, like dinner."

"Fine. Then Janet has the dinner cooking, she's painting until dinner or whenever. And she dies in a fire right before Myles comes over." His voice took on a hard edge. "I don't believe it."

"You're nearly quoting Janet's mother, Mike."

"Intelligent lady, no matter what Harvester thinks."

"The police report acknowledges the food in the slow cooker, that her body was found in the debris of her studio."

"Did our intelligent detectives learn how the structure started on fire? *Learn,* not *assume.*"

"The fire service investigated and believe it was an accident. They agree it looked as though she'd been burning rubbish or yard waste in the incinerator. They commented on it, Mike—loudly and often, angry that she hadn't used more common sense in placing the incinerator. It was too close to the studio, and being a windy day and of course everything parched from the drought—"

McLaren recalled the weather that long-ago summer. Not that he had memorized it, but because many trees had died on his family land. It had been professed that the country had suffered through the worst drought in one hundred years, so of course he'd recall it. The drought produced a record high temperature in July, with power cuts in areas of Central London. Add to that, the previous winter had been dry. What little precipitation that fell did nothing to replenish the desperately low water table levels. Consequently, vegetation died and severe fire conditions constantly threatened the country.

"Who called in the fire service?"

"Her bass player, Ian O'Connor. He played in her trio."

"He was over there too? What…for dinner along with Myles Tyson?"

"He wasn't invited for dinner. He's also her neighbor."

"Chummy arrangement."

Jamie sighed. "Ian rang her up at half past five. He talked to her for a minute or so."

McLaren made a notation on a sheet of paper. "Fine. O'Connor talks to Janet. I suppose it would be too coincidental if he actually saw something near the time of the fire."

"No one did. Janet's house sits apart from her

neighbors. It's at the end of the lane and, in addition to the drive and garage facing the street, has a back entrance…a small lane that twists through the wood. If you're thinking about murder, which I assume you are, it's a perfect entrance or exit for the killer, yes. And it was also why the fire may have started earlier than O'Connor finally saw it and phoned it in to the fire service."

"And that was…when?"

"It was near sunset. Around half past six. It's darker in the wood, too, so the flames from the studio were more visible than in bright sunlight."

"It could have been burning for a while if the house is as secluded as you say. Lucky for the killer."

"But there's no getting around the fact, Mike, that her body was found inside the burnt studio. A few feet of wall were standing but for the most part it was a complete loss."

"Fire brigade extinguish the blaze?"

"Rather promptly, I'd say. They got there close to six forty-five and found the studio pretty much demolished."

McLaren nodded, imagining the aftermath of the event. He'd seen a number of charred structures to feel the tragedy along with Nora. "The wooden structure burnt that quickly?"

"It had help, Mike. Paints, turpentine, paint thinner, canvas, wooden stretchers… You know. Artist's painting supplies."

"Hell."

"O'Connor said he smelled burning but he didn't think much of it because Janet burnt paper and cardboard and yard waste regularly in her incinerator.

He got worried, though, when he saw so much smoke and then the flames. That part was verified. The fire tender got there fifteen minutes after his call, coming from Matlock."

McLaren shook his head. "And when they did their probing about for hot spots in the debris they find Janet's body."

"Yeah. Around seven-fifteen, when things had cooled down a bit."

"Ever hear of a better stage for a murder, Jamie? Secluded house, private escape route, handy heat source and your choice of accelerant…plus the victim stumbling and hitting her head against something hard enough to cause unconsciousness?"

Chapter Five

The woman's barely conscious, Harvester thought as he walked upstairs to his office. Potty with a capital P. Why am I always stuck with seeing the nutter? His breathing sounded hollow on the hard floor, each rasp from his throat calling her name. He passed a poster reminding police personnel of the policy on harassment and bullying. What a laugh, he thought, glancing again at his watch. I doubt if the Police Federation would hear my grievance on Nora Ennis. She's been harassing anyone she can find to listen to her barmy story.

He opened the door to his office and switched on the overhead office light. The harsh, florescent light coated every item beneath it with a hint of blue. He'd been startled with it the first few days he'd had the office, but had quickly grown used to it. Paper appeared brighter under the light but it gave his brown hair a strange hue. Probably has something to do with its thinness and the light reflecting off my scalp. The tan, metal file cabinets showed not much difference in color, nor did the dark wooden desks that faced each other. He crossed the floor, eased out of his jacket and hung it over the back of his desk chair, then tossed the notepad onto the wooden windowsill. The pad skidded across the painted surface and came to rest against a flowerpot holding a dead jade plant. One of the larger, overhanging branches shook, sending a cascade of brown, shriveled leaves onto the top page. Loosening his tie, he checked his watch against the wall clock, and poured himself a cup of coffee. The beverage had no flavor and he muttered that his partner was as incompetent at coffee making as he was in interviewing suspects.

Harvester dumped a spoonful of sugar and some milk into the coffee—something he rarely did. Anything to give the black mess some flavor. He wandered to the window, opened it, and looked outside.

His section of Buxton spread out before him like a picture post card. Grand, stone houses stretched down Silverlands to the High Street. From his second-storey vantage point he could see the backs of the shops lining the main road. At right angles to this the upper portion of the town hall sat nearly silhouetted in the afternoon sky. Farther down the slope, out of his view, the seamless face of the Crescent would be lolling in early shadows. Tourists and office workers would be hurrying to finish their business before closing time, some going to the opera later that night, or to a pub or restaurant on the High Street, perhaps, or to an event in the garden. Harvester sniffed, suddenly feeling alone and unliked. When was the last time anyone had asked him for a night out?

He shifted his gaze from the High Street, feeling it healthier for his wellbeing. Across the road from the police station the football ground retained its blaze of brilliant green color despite the confetti-ing of red and yellow shed leaves around the perimeter. The leaves had taken on their autumnal hues weeks ago and many trees were already bare. A whiff of dry leaves assaulted his nostrils and for a moment, he recalled his son,

Emory, grinning at him from where he sat in a pile of debris. He rolled in the castoffs and laughed as the dead leaves cracked. Harvester had leaned on his rake, pretending to be irritated at having to redo his work. But his son's play was infectious and Harvester joined Emory in jumping into the pile...

That had been last autumn, Harvester realized with a shock. His time with Emory was so short, so restricted by the divorce settlement. He had lived—existed, actually—through the ensuing nine lonely years more like a robot than a human being. He hadn't the makeup either for waking in or going home to an empty house. It was like he was punishing himself. If it continued much longer, he knew he would be as barmy as Nora Ennis.

Talk of the devil...

Harvester turned his head to follow Nora's progress across the car park. Her stooped, small figure seemed tinier viewed from the elevation of his office. Not exactly like an ant crawling over the land, but not exactly like a real person. Nothing extraordinary would have attracted his attention or cemented his view on her. Her gait was like that of many older people, slow and slightly unsteady. But Nora's walk had a directness to it, a determination, as though she had a time limit or an appointment. As she got into her car and started its engine, Harvester sniffed. Not only was the woman a nutter, she also was obsessed by the old case. Maybe she heard her daughter talking to her in her head.

He picked up the pad of paper and leafed through the notes he'd taken during the meeting with the Superintendent. Seconds later he was absorbed in the police federation assignment. He settled into his desk chair, having had enough of Nora Ennis and her hallucinations.

Chapter Six

"Does stretch the limitation of believability," Jamie conceded. "Plus, the postmortem examination revealed the head indentation to be concave, resulting from a round surface."

"Leaves out the edge of the door or table, then."

"I'm getting that whiff of fish you're smelling, Mike." He swallowed a mouthful of tea before continuing. "But there were objects in the studio, according to statements and remnants found in the fire debris, that might have caused the wound."

"What, for instance?"

"The edge of her desk chair as well as the top of a stool had rounded edges. A heavy cast iron sculpture that sat on the corner of her desk was one of those modern, abstract things."

"Round or curved, I take it."

"The point is, Mike, that she could've fallen, hit her head on one of these objects, and been struck unconscious. Not out of the realms of possibility."

"I'm trying to keep an open mind."

"Should be easy."

"So, the bass-playing neighbor talks to her at half past five. I don't suppose he can be wrong about the time," McLaren suggested.

"His mobile phone record confirms the time."

"So we have the phone company as witness. Right.

Janet's alive at five-thirty. But she's dead at six forty-five when the fire brigade and the police arrive. Any more help from the postmortem report?"

"That's about as accurate as you're going to get with time of death. The fire...well, that's what the postmortem established."

"Then we're focusing on someone who had a seventy-five minute opportunity to kill Janet and torch the studio. Any observant neighbor see a vehicle in front of Janet's house, or a non-resident walking near her house?"

"You don't really want to know."

"Everyone was inside, watching the telly, eating dinner. Bloody helpful."

"That's part of the problem. But, as I said, there is another way to get to her."

"Through the forest behind her house." He could imagine how dark the wood might be at night. The cluster of trees, dense and obliterating much of the moonlight, might be a criminal's best friend.

"Could anything have been secreted in the studio to make it the target of arson, Mike?"

"That's what I was wondering. Why would someone torch it?"

"Was she blackmailing someone and had the evidence in there? You know, like maybe she was thinking it wasn't as obvious a place, her studio. She keeps the photograph or tape recording or whatever there 'cause most anyone would think she'd secrete it in her house."

"I suppose our brilliant SIO—who was it, anyway?"

"Edwards. Bill Edwards. Know him?"

"Yeah. Efficient Eddie. So Edwards didn't have a theory, I take it."

"Actually, he did. No, don't groan, Mike. It makes sense."

"To someone in Bedlam, perhaps."

"But it throws out your arson theory."

"I'm all ears."

"As I mentioned, her small incinerator for yard waste is close to the shed. The incinerator was one of those things made from chicken wire. O'Connor, the neighbor, says Janet used to burn a lot of paper in it."

"Fascinating."

"Well, Edwards figures that with the extremely dry conditions of the grass and other vegetation, due to the drought, if a gust of wind came up as is usual before an approaching rain storm, well, the shed could have caught fire accidentally. Pieces of paper or embers blowing over to the building, if she had the incinerator too close, would catch the studio on fire."

McLaren paused, picturing the scene in his mind. It was vivid enough, with the acrid smoke odor and the wind fanning the leaves, pushing them across the lawn. Perhaps there had been curtains at the studio windows, waving from the breeze. Embers and bits of partially burnt paper tumbled over the ground, their life blown away from the gusts. He rubbed his forehead and sketched a few curled leaves on the open page of his notepad. "Was there an approaching rain storm?"

"Nothing to write home about. The weather service report confirmed that it rained for about a half hour later that evening, but it obviously didn't break the drought."

"Yes. It all does sound logical, doesn't it? And

convenient if someone wanted to make it look like an accident."

"But why?"

"All will be revealed in good order, Jamie. I need a copy of Edwards' report. Plus reports by the H.O. Forensic chemist. Oh, and the fire service report."

"Were you this greedy as a child around Christmas time?"

"You able to lay your hands on any photos of the crime scene or house or yard without getting caught?"

"Got 'em right here."

"I'll also need a copy of the plan drawn up by the police artist, Jamie. I need to know what I'm looking at."

"You want me to email all this to your mobile or computer? Where are you, anyway?"

"About to go to Janet's house to look around. Don't worry," he said as Jamie protested. "I have the blessing of the new owners. Email all that. I can get them on my laptop. I want a larger image than the phone will afford."

"You're getting old, mate."

"No. I want to see the details. Thanks."

McLaren next rang up Cheryl Kerrigan, the Home Office Pathologist. Though not strictly orthodox procedure, he hoped she would tell him about the postmortem examination. As the phone rang, he said a prayer that she had been the pathologist on the case.

Her greeting on hearing his voice was close to making his day. He smiled and asked if she could do him a favor.

"They're adding up, you know," she said, the good

humor behind her words.

"You're obviously keeping score."

"I have to. I know you won't. What do you want?"

"It's not exactly kosher…"

"If I guess wrong you don't owe me a steak dinner. A PM report."

"I won't ask what restaurant you'd like to go to."

"Do you know the date or the victim's name?"

He told her, then said, "You performed that post mortem examination, I hope."

"Meaning you won't feel so guilty about me losing my job if I get caught giving you this information."

"That's as good a reply as any."

As he waited for her to look up the report he imagined her office. He'd been in it many times on various cases and had always wondered how she managed to work in such a sterile environment. White and shiny chrome weren't his first choice of a color scheme conducive to thinking. But he'd take that and like it if he had a choice between that and sharing a comfy office with Harvester. He had just about figured out how to brick Harvester into the office corner when Cheryl returned with the report. Her voice fragmented Harvester and the fantasy office.

"You've got more luck than anyone I've ever seen, Michael McLaren. Yes, I recall the incident now. A thirty-five year old female found in the debris of an artist's studio. What do you want to know…mechanism of death? I suppose you know the police and firefighters labeled it an accident, for lack of conclusive evidence otherwise."

"Yeah."

"But you're evidently working for someone who

wants the case looked at again."

"Another good guess."

"I can't afford to guess. It's too risky. All right, let's see." She mumbled beneath her breath, pausing to read parts of the report aloud. "She suffered a depression to the right side of her head, just above the ear. The wound was consistent with a rounded object about the size of a tennis ball. The firefighters found her lying on her left side, wound-side-up, which is normal if someone suffered a forceful blow like that, forceful enough to knock them down. People usually fall so that the wound is not touching the floor."

"No suspicions there, in other words."

"No. The leucocytes—white blood cells—of a burned, living person travel to the site of the injury. They produce an inflammation—hyperemia—and blistering that is quite usual. Under lab tests, we look for a positive protein reaction. However, if a *deceased* person is burned, the burns normally are hard and yellow. There is little, if any, blistering, and liquid that might be present will not give the protein effect."

"So, you found—"

"She died from smoke inhalation, as is standard with someone unconscious in a fire."

"Tough."

"Yes. She had a concentration of CO in her blood, which also underscores she died in the fire."

"Carbon monoxide."

"The opposite being that a body devoid of CO should raise red flags in the postmortem exam."

"Suggesting some sort of treachery or violence occurred before death and she died before the fire."

"As good a finger-pointer as any, Mike."

"And this head depression…"

"I'd say the blow could produce a concussion and unconsciousness."

"The blow… You mean someone struck her?"

"That's possible, certainly. But it's also just as possible that it was an accident, that the head injury occurred if she fell of her own accord, falling backward and slightly to the side. There was an iron sculpture in the studio, and some of her furniture had solid, rounded edges. If she fell against any of those objects, that may also have caused the head injury."

"So you didn't think it particularly suspicious to find that head wound."

"Not at all. Not with the items in her studio. I thought it unlikely it was murder or foul play."

"Did you match that sculpture or the furniture to the head depression? You'd know then if she fell or was struck." He didn't say it, but he couldn't see someone slamming Janet's head against the edge of the desk. If anything, the murderer would pick up the sculpture or something else small and strike her.

"I tried."

"Sounds as though you couldn't come up with a particular item."

"The wound slightly matched the microphone in her studio. I found one section that fit the ball end, but the iron sculpture also had a similarly sized ball, which also matched. There was a smaller straight section of one millimeter which didn't correspond with anything that might have been in the studio."

"At least nothing that anyone remembered as normally being there."

"True." Cheryl yawned, apologized, and explained

that she'd had a late night. "Anyway, whether the fire consumed that object, or your murderer took it with him, I don't know. But that, in part, is why the coroner made his decision. I couldn't be conclusive it was foul play or accident, Mike."

"You said the skull was indented. Anything else?"

"There was a curved indentation of the soft brain tissue. Bearing in mind the overall circumstances, Mike, you shouldn't be surprised that the coroner recorded an open verdict."

"Bloody helpful."

"The official police statement ran something like 'We've gone as far as we can, and without further evidence, we cannot take the investigation further.'"

"That's safe."

"Mike, forget I was the Home Office Forensic Pathologist performing that PM examination. *No* senior investigating officer, I don't care what rank he is, would go against the opinion of the H.O. Forensic Pathologist. If the SIO doesn't like *and* trust that there are grounds for believing the report may be wrong, *then* you might consider a second opinion. You might then go for a second post mortem examination with a different H.O. forensic pathologist. But in all my years working in this job, I've never even heard of that happening."

"So you're saying I should take this as read."

"Not because I did the examination, Mike."

"Because the coroner's verdict has pretty much stalled the investigation."

The silence lay between them as McLaren thought of the fire and its consequences.

Finally, Cheryl said, "She couldn't have suffered,

Mike. She wasn't cognizant. That should bring you some peace, if that's what you're thinking about."

"That's what I'm thinking about. Thanks."

McLaren took the back roads as he drove to Janet's house in the village of Darleycote. A few puddles remained from yesterday's rain; the water sprawled within deep ruts along the verge or in small depressions in the road. Several tree branches had fallen from the wind and lay like strange deer antlers among the lifeless leaves and other debris of the wood. The tree branches and trunks held the darker colors of brown and black where the bark was still damp. McLaren breathed deeply of the scents, thinking it one of the best fragrances he knew.

His tires splashed through puddles and threw water onto the windscreen. He ran the windscreen wipers until he emerged onto a dry section of road and smiled when the sun poked through a line of gray clouds. The house, if he remembered the directions correctly, was only minutes away.

Nora Ennis had assured him that the present homeowners gave their blessing to any investigation, official or unofficial, and wouldn't mind him poking about in the back garden or the wood that nestled up to their property line. They even gave permission to peer through the windows into the kitchen. Anything to help solve the murder, they had said, and McLaren wished there were more people like them.

He punched the Play button on his car's CD player, and as he turned onto the road outside his driveway he was singing along with his folk group, adding harmony to his lead in "The Meeting of the Waters."

Darleycote was nearly straight south of his home outside Somerley in Derbyshire's High Peak District. It would have been faster to zip down the A6 to Matlock and then drive the short distance north to the village. But the warm autumn sun and the feeling of hope mixed in his heart, and McLaren had no desire to dispense with either too quickly. So he took the B6049 south, connected up with the A623 and meandered down several more B roads to Darleycote.

As he turned onto the B5057 and approached the village the CD track changed to "Nut Brown Maiden," and McLaren was into the first verse before he realized he was thinking of Janet:

Her eye so brightly beaming,
Her look so frank and free
In waking or in dreaming
Is evermore with me.

Evermore with me, he thought as he parked the car outside her former house and gazed at the structure. Her photo had that effect on him last night. Her singing did, too. Would she to be with him always, a companion while he grew old, married to him spiritually and emotionally even when he was married to Dena? Could he keep the feeling a secret, or would Dena find out? Perhaps he should stop now, abandon the case and save his sanity, for that's what he feared might happen...

He turned off the car's engine and sat for a moment letting the song play itself out. Janet's voice crept into the vocals, overpowering his voice at times, providing a soft background at others. He stared at the house sitting at 191 Paddington Lane. A tan stone building, it mirrored the architectural style and 18th century age of its neighbors farther up the lane. Her house sat in the back, as Jamie had said, on an elevated plot, hugged by trees and nearly dissolving into the wood. A blaze of reds, yellows, and oranges from autumn chrysanthemums and ornamental grasses ran across the length of the house's foundation, waking up the drab stone and injecting a spark of normality into the strange visit. Even as the CD clicked off at the end, Janet's voice still echoed the words…in waking or in dreaming is evermore with me. He closed his eyes for a moment, lost in the velvety richness of her voice, the hint that he was losing his mind. Of course he had never met her, never knew her. She had died five years ago, when she was thirty-five and he was in his early thirties. But she seemed as real to him as if she stood by her door, inviting him inside.

A quick search on the Internet via his iPad gave him additional information about the case. A photo of the house and back garden sprang into vivid life on the computer screen. As though not trusting the newspaper article, McLaren glanced at the house's façade. The two matched. He read the rest of the article, jotting down notes in his small notebook, then shoved the notebook into his trousers pocket.

He opened his email and found that he had received the police photos and sketches of the house and crime scene. He studied them closely, noting areas that he had questioned when he had first read Nora's account. The various reports he had requested had also arrived. All except the fire report, which Jamie suggested might be on Harvester's desk, since he'd just spoken with Nora Ennis. McLaren spent nearly a half hour reading the emailed reports and jotting down notes in his notepad, then logged off and set down the tablet.

The CD clicked to another song. Before the music could start, McLaren turned the key in the ignition, shutting off the power to the player, and got out of the car. He walked up the hill and around to the back garden, his mind now focused on the crime.

Although Nora had said the current owners would welcome him, he knocked on the back door. No one appeared. He scribbled a note announcing his investigation on a notebook page and placed it on the back step, using a stone as a paperweight. Then he followed the path into the forest.

The wood held the dampness of yesterday's storm, not just in the bark of the trees but also in the sogginess of the moss. It held his shoe imprints as he walked along the path. It wasn't used much, he thought. Seedlings of pine and oak had sprouted and now stood a foot tall beside their mighty parents. Ferns glistened bright green or pale yellow in the light and cast off occasional droplets of water in the slight breeze. McLaren rubbed against an exuberant fern and looked down on feeling the wetness seep through his trouser leg. He shook off any excess and stepped over a rotting log. The trail was littered with broken boughs, and lichen and mushrooms had taken hold of the dead limbs and shade-wrapped rocks.

He stopped several yards inside the wood, turned, and looked back at the house. Of course he knew he wouldn't find anything after five years. And the death had occurred inside the studio. But he needed to stand within the fringe of trees, bracken, and ferns, looking back at the house, imagining what had happened there. Besides, the murderer may have used this path as an escape route.

That Janet had met a violent death, he didn't doubt. But would she not have smelled the studio burning? Even if she had chosen to burn rubbish that day, the smell of paper and cardboard and gardening waste would be different from a painted wooden structure. She had to have known the building was on fire. Had she stumbled, as the police report suggested? McLaren needed to find out.

Minutes later—he didn't know how long—he walked over to where he supposed the studio had been. Farther back in the garden, farther up the hill, its roof probably had been barely discernable to O'Connor. Despite the present owners' effort, there was a depression in the soil. About four times the size of a large tool shed, he thought. The area had not been built up, but held an ornamental statue, flowers and a teak bench. More of a monument to Janet, he thought, than a relaxing spot in the garden.

He stood in the depression and looked at the house and the site of the fire.

For the briefest of seconds when McLaren read Nora's report he'd hoped someone else had died in the fire and that Janet was in hospital, suffering from amnesia. But dental records confirmed it was her body in the fire, and his hope that she would heal and return to torch singing had died.

He walked back to his car and turned off the CD player, driving to Matlock in silence.

Chapter Seven

Nora stood in the strong afternoon sunlight slanting through her kitchen window. The day had been tiring even with the euphoria of engaging Michael McLaren's investigative services. Most any activity was fatiguing these days. The hope McLaren gave her when he accepted the check now lapsed into exhaustion, draining her physically, mentally and emotionally.

The screech of the kettle broke her reverie. She poured the boiling water into the teapot and noted the time. She was a stickler for proper steeping of tea. There were few things in life she could control or make to perfection, but the brewing of tea was one, and she reveled in that ability.

Janet had been another perfect creation. Not that Nora or her husband had had one hundred percent control in forming Janet's character and morals—Janet hadn't been a puppet or a doll that they had fabricated from man-made materials—but she had emulated her parents' values and taken their life lessons to heart. The result had been a beautiful woman who had attracted many friends and who had influenced others with her convictions.

The steeping time being up, Nora drew the teabag from the pot and set it on a saucer. She poured the tea into a mug and added sugar and milk to the hot liquid. She settled the tea things onto a metal tray, added a plate of chocolate biscuits, and carried them into the front room.

The room, designed to catch the morning sunlight, held the chill of dusky afternoon and her burgeoning concern that McLaren might give her the same account that the police had: accidental death. She rubbed her arms and knotted the silk scarf around her neck, but the cold still clung. Is it cold, she wondered, getting up and walking to the fireplace, or is it my inner self warning me about a possible disappointment? But Verity Dwyer had recommended him without hesitation. The man had such a fine track record while in the police force and now, on his own. He can't let me down... She gazed at her daughter's photograph on the mantel and said a quick prayer. Surely, with God's help, McLaren would succeed.

She grabbed the mug of hot tea and cupped her hands around it, but it did not relieve the chill deep within her. Perhaps it's the décor, she thought, giving the room's interior a good look. It could hardly be said to be cheery. The dark hues of the walls and furniture didn't help with psychological warmth, the pieces old and handed down from Victorian-age ancestors. She made a mental note to change the wallpaper to a lighter design next spring—it might help lessen her depression—turned on the electric fire, and settled back into the sofa.

The heat from the tea and the fire melted some of her body-numbing weariness but something picked at her mind, making her feel unusually anxious. She got up, went to the stereo system, and put on Janet's CD recording. Seconds later, her daughter's voice filled the room and Nora's soul. She returned to the sofa and lost herself in "The Very Thought of You."

Had it been just a terrible accident, Nora thought, staring at Janet's photograph. Am I pestering the police for no reason? Have I grown into an old woman who has nothing better to do with her remaining years than to fabricate fanciful scenarios and bend the ears of anyone I can corner?

She leaned back and closed her eyes. "Stormy Weather" eased into the room and Nora realized she was thinking about Charlie Harvester. The man irritated her, angered her at times. Like a permanent dark cloud hovering on the horizon, endangering the picnic. His flippant treatment of her distress probably was the most infuriating, though. And disrespectful. That arrogant smirk that he tried unsuccessfully to hide nearly goaded her at times into smacking him across his mouth. And that frightened her. She'd never been a violent person. Even immediately after Janet's death, when her grief threatened to consume her sanity and cloister her from the world. She had struggled through each day, feeling as though she'd never escape the blackness engulfing her, as though her heart would implode from pain.

But the agony had lessened—everyone told her it would—yet the resolve still burned as fiercely as ever. Perhaps more fervently after each encounter with Charlie Harvester. The poster child of the quintessential 1960s cop who lauded his macho make-up and perhaps leaned slightly toward racism and sexism. Just one of the boys, flexing his Paleolithic muscles. Girlie pictures on the office walls and loud laughs at off-color jokes.

As if access to Nora's thoughts, Janet crooned "I Wanna Be Around," bringing a startlingly real quality to Nora's mounting anger. "Sing it, Janet," she said, her voice barely audible against Janet's deep-throated taunt. "Give that man the same thing he's wishing to give me." Nora stared at Janet's photograph, reassuring herself of her surroundings. The familiarity of the room soothed her fast-beating heart, but Janet's face confused her, the features slipping into the late afternoon shadows now filling the room.

Nora blinked, uncertain of the time or how long she'd been sitting. The clock did nothing to lessen her confusion. She couldn't remember when she'd come into the room...and was that a new photo of Janet? Her wedding picture, maybe? Why had Janet changed from her white dress for the photo, and where was Tom? He should be in the photo. Janet's dark brown eyes seemed to stare from the picture, alive when the rest of the face was little more than a shadowy oval. It wasn't the picture she remembered. What had happened to Janet's braids and Girl Guide uniform? What year was it?

Janet's rendition of "Crazy" pulled Nora through the years. She lay suspended in a nebulous half-world of past and future, faces and voices and music tornadic in its intensity.

"Janet, where are you?"

"Hide and seek, Mum. Come and find me!"

"I can't see you—you're in the shadows."

"Better in the shadows than in the fire. I'm a shadow in the smoke, Mum."

Nora blinked, confused. "But you sing torch songs, darling. That's part of the fire."

"They only burn the heart, though. The pain is in losing the man you love."

"Tom loved you, didn't he?"

"It died as I died."

"I loved you."

"And I loved you, but it's not the same, mum. It's not like a man's love."

"There's one here who doesn't love you, Janet. Do you know Charlie Harvester? He won't seek you, even though I've asked."

"Michael McLaren can find me, Mum. Leave me to him."

"But if you're hiding…"

"Fire doesn't consume everything. McLaren will seek where others won't."

"I hear the fire bell, darling. It's coming for you. Don't go…"

A ringing, insistent and shrill, broke through the cacophony. A hand seemed to reach out to her and pull her back to her front room. She swept her fingers across the sofa cushion, as if the tactile action anchored her in the present. Another jab of the sound woke her sufficiently for her to reach for the phone on the side table.

"Hello? Yes? Janet?"

A brief hesitation greeted her questions and she repeated Janet's name. The caller cleared his throat, as though unsure of his answer.

"Mrs. Ennis?" He paused again. "I apologize if I've dialed a wrong number. I'm trying to get ahold of Nora Ennis. Is this she?"

Nora replied, her voice cracking and the tone uneven. "Janet? Have you come home?"

"Mrs. Ennis, this is Mike McLaren. You spoke to me yesterday about taking on your daughter's case. Do you remember?"

"Remember…"

"We met at a restaurant and you told me about Janet. You asked me to—" He took a deep breath and went on. "You wanted me to find out what happened to her."

"You're not Janet? This isn't Stuart, then… You want to come back?"

It was McLaren's turn to ask the question. "Stuart? I'm sorry—"

"You were so bitter after Janet's death. Have you decided to come back to me, to be a family again?"

Stuart. Nora's ex-husband. McLaren swallowed slowly. "No, Mrs. Ennis. This isn't Stuart. It's Mike McLaren. Perhaps I should call back some other time…"

"Mike…" Her voice betrayed her disappointment.

He tried again. "Yes, Mike McLaren. I'm the ex-police officer you spoke with about Janet, about helping you get to the truth about Janet."

"Not Janet. Oh. You're not playing a prank on me. Janet likes to play games. Hide and Seek, Ghost in the Graveyard, Manhunt… But those are running games. We're not running right now." She looked around the room, frowning. "I don't know exactly… I'm inside."

"Your house, perhaps? You're in your house, listening to Janet's CD."

"Yes. My house. And you are?"

"Michael McLaren, Mrs. Ennis. We talked yesterday about Janet. About me looking into what happened."

A slow intake of breath, followed by a mumbled phrase, and then Nora said, "Oh, yes. Mr. McLaren. We did talk. I-I'm sorry. I must have fallen asleep. I fixed a pot of tea and put on Janet's CD…" He didn't care about that, Nora told herself. He'd phoned to tell me something. She nodded, crossed the room and switched off the CD. "There, that's better. Now I can hear you properly." She sat down and changed the wireless phone receiver to her other ear. "I'm sorry if I was a bit confused. Talking to you and listening to Janet's CD…"

"Too many memories," he finished for her.

"I-I suppose so."

"Bound to be."

"I shouldn't have done that. It doesn't help my— well, I struggle to know what's real and what is just my…my wishes. I do apologize."

"That's all right, Mrs. Ennis. I called to ask you a question, if you have a moment."

"Certainly. I'll help however I can. You know that."

"Right. I'd like to know if you have a fire report. I know it's a bit unusual, because insurance companies normally request the document. But I thought, well, under the circumstances of Janet's case—"

"I have one, Mr. McLaren. I had to pay for it, of course, but I knew almost from the first of the police investigation that things were going wrong. So I got the fire report. Do you need to see it?"

"Not right now. But I would like to know if the attending firefighters' names are listed."

"If you can wait a moment." She put down the receiver and returned minutes later somewhat out of breath, but giving him the names. "Does this help you, then?"

"I won't know until I talk to them, but I'll let you know as soon as I have something to relate."

"And there's something else, if you have a minute."

"Sure. What?"

"I don't know if it means anything, but I could never find one of Janet's coats after-afterward. I looked all through her house. I know she didn't give it away because it was her favorite. I asked at the cleaners."

"What kind of coat?"

"A blue ski jacket. One of those down-filled things. It has dark red chevrons on the sleeves. I thought she might be mending it because it has a small rip on the right side hip area, but it wasn't with her sewing. Do you think that means anything?"

"I'll keep it in mind," he said. "Thanks for the information, Mrs. Ennis." He bid her good night, as Nora hung up.

Chapter Eight

McLaren flipped the mobile closed and sat in his idling car. It swayed as a lorry carrying tractor tires passed him on the A632. Nora's confusion worried him. Even if her dementia had worsened, would listening to one of Janet's recordings tip her into such bewilderment? He hated to give Harvester even the slightest acknowledgment, but perhaps he had read Nora's true nature. Perhaps Harvester was right about her mental state. Despite the police report of finding Janet's body in the debris, perhaps Nora had embroidered the incident from that television film, turning a plain accident into a fictitious murder.

He lowered his head and silently cursed his timing. Did she lapse into her yesterdays each night at this time? Had her memory finally broken? He wished his sister or fiancé had been handling the call. Women were so much better at this than men. Well, at least than he.

He opened his mobile and punched in a phone number. A rich, smooth voice answered his call and for an instant he thought he had joined Nora Ennis in her fantasy world. He stuttered his name and asked to speak to Helene Brogan.

"This is she." The voice waited for him to continue.

He explained that Nora had given him Helene's name and phone number, and asked if it would be convenient if he came over now to talk to her.

"About what?" Helene asked.

"I'd rather not talk about it more than necessary over the phone. Would ten minutes or so be all right to see you?"

"You sound like you're on my doorstep. Yes, fine. Come over. I assume you know where the house is."

He thanked her, rang off and in twelve minutes was sitting in Helene Brogan's house.

"Janet and I owned a catering business together." Helene settled McLaren in the front room. It seemed to be comprised of windows, framed photos, awards, and vases of flowers. She offered him tea, but he declined, needing to make the visit less of a social call.

"Interesting business, running a catering concern. A lot of hard work at odd hours, I expect."

"Yes, but we loved it." Her blue eyes sparkled, intense deep color heightened by the shaft of sunlight that fell at her feet. "But more than that," she continued as she took a chair opposite him, "we'd been friends since we met in school at age six. We'd had twenty-six years of friendship before Janet died. That was a terrible day for me, her death."

"I expect it was hard to lose a friend. Nora Ennis said you were in the same Girl Guides troop, too."

Helene sniffed and nodded. She ran the palm of her right hand over her brown silk trousers. "Camping trips were the best. I think that's where Janet's environmental outlook was born. She was a staunch lover of wildlife and the land, and carried that into her life beyond the Guide years."

"That's what I'd like to talk to you about, Ms. Brogan. You were friends for a long time and you probably knew her better than most people. I need to know about Janet."

"*About* her?" Helene's voice sharpened. "Like what? You're a private investigator, you said."

"Not exactly. I'm helping Janet's family."

"Like a detective."

"A private citizen looking into the events surrounding Janet's death."

"Same thing, isn't it? A private investigator."

"Actually, no. I'm not licensed. I'm inquiring strictly on my own."

"Sounds commendable. So, you've no real authority, then."

McLaren's pulse throbbed in his throat. The sentence was becoming too common, the assumption that he could be dismissed and sent packing having an annoying ring. He swallowed, hoping his cheeks wouldn't flush, and forced a brightness into his tone. "I didn't know I needed authority to bring justice to someone who was wronged."

Helene laughed, a quick ripple of light. "Then we're of the same mind. What do you want to know about Janet?"

McLaren asked if she thought it probable that Janet would do outdoor burning on the day of her death.

"I remember that day." Helene's voice slipped back into its no-nonsense tone. "Of course due to Janet's death, but also due to that awful weather spell we all endured. Horrible drought, fire alerts going up all the time. Made people afraid to do anything like that outside. I even thought twice about accepting event orders that entailed grilling outdoors, worried about a bit of hot ash settling in the dry grass and starting a fire.

Terrible."

"Was Janet of the same opinion, do you know?"

"Would she burn an incinerator full of rubbish, is what you're asking."

"Yes. It seems to be a crucial point."

"Now that you've asked, and thinking back to that day, I must say I do recall thinking it odd at the time."

"Because the rubbish burning was out of character for her?"

"I don't believe she would have done that. She *was* very conscious of the environment—this was five years ago, Mr. McLaren, before all this 'green' awareness really became the thing to do."

"Janet was a recycler, I take it."

"More than that. She didn't use pesticides in her garden and she ate only organically grown foods. I think that's one reason we went into the catering business together. We had the same outlook on food and cooking, and we offered a rather unique menu to clients."

"A step above the usual sandwiches and sausage rolls at receptions."

"Nothing wrong with sandwiches and sausage rolls, but we wanted to give our patrons something a bit more wholesome. And we proved we could do that without it being a slab of tofu and a box of biscuits on a white plate."

"So, you don't believe Janet would have had that fire going, then."

Helene rearranged the neckline of her beige silk shirt before answering. "It's my opinion. Nothing that would have much weight in court, if it came to that. But he would stake everything he owned that she wouldn't be burning anything. She'd not risk a fire. She wouldn't want to damage the habitat or the wildlife…or destroy the woods, either. She was aware of things like that. Any help?"

"As you said, won't really stand up in court, but it's giving me an idea."

"A good one, I hope."

"I guess we'll know in not too many more days." He thanked her and jogged back to his car, his mind racing.

****

McLaren spent several hours talking to people about the firefighters who had attended the scene. He concentrated on the residences near the fire station, Matlock having a crewed station whose firefighters live in houses neighboring the facility. After ending their day shift, they could still respond to any incident that came up. Summoned by a pager, they were never more than minutes away from the station. It was a good system, giving Matlock's residents twenty-four hour fire protection.

Some people were reluctant to talk about their neighbors, but one man's name cropped up constantly. And although having done nothing criminal—at least nothing the neighbors or McLaren could discover— Corey Chappell seemed to have one event in his past that would provide McLaren with the carrot to prod Corey into talking, should he prove reticent.

McLaren found Corey at his home near the Matlock fire station. The firefighter stood in the doorway, filling it with his massive shoulders. McLaren's name and purpose for his visit had no effect on Corey's demeanor. He crossed his arms over his chest in a silent dare.

"I don't know how you found out about me being on duty at that fire," Corey said, eyeing McLaren suspiciously. "None of that is public knowledge. Now, bugger off. I'm busy."

"Too busy to help with a death inquiry?"

"Yeah. Too busy. That was a long time ago, mate. The case is closed, or didn't you hear that?"

"A lot of folks may think it's closed but I'm opening it."

"And you're part of the police?" He snorted, aware of McLaren's position. "Hardly. Nosey-parker is more like it. A 'has been.' Washed up but still yearning to play cops and robbers like in the old days. Well, I'm having none of it, mate, so hop it."

"I can't appeal to your better nature, then?"

"You don't appeal to me at all." Corey laughed, a great blast of noise that roared past McLaren in one swift exhale.

"That's too bad," McLaren said, sighing in apparent disappointment. "I was hoping you'd help me."

"If it helps you get off my premises I'll tell you that I'm one second away from calling the police on you. What's so funny, mate? Think I won't call the cops?"

"You won't. Not right now, at least."

"Oh? You want to listen?"

"You won't because I'm about to phone Derbyshire County Council."

At the mention of the man's employer, Corey paused in his half turn. Facing McLaren once more, he said, "What's the Council to do with anything?"

"You've got a nice job, haven't you?" McLaren said, eyeing the house and the fire station. "A bit of excitement to break up the monotony that claims so many people. Nice place to live, too. Too bad if you'd have to leave your career."

"You're daft, man. Now, like I said before, on your bike."

"You're more accommodating with Olivia."

He took a step toward McLaren, his eyes narrowing. "How do you know about Olivia?"

"As I said, Mr. Chappell, I'm doing an investigation."

"I wouldn't have thought my private life would be connected to a five year old fire."

"Many things in life are connected."

"Yeah, well, I doubt if the Council will be interested in Olivia. Now, like I said before, hop it."

"If the Council won't listen, maybe your wife will. Shall we find out? She inside?"

Corey blanched and stared at McLaren. He glanced over his shoulder, at the front room, then stepped outside and eased the door shut. In the quiet the roar of a motorcycle zooming along the main road floated to them. Corey stood with his back against the door, his hands thrust into his jeans pockets. "What's this about Olivia, then? If you're going to drag her into anything…"

"Oh, I think you know."

"The hell I do. You're the one who comes around here throwing out her name like it should mean something to me."

"It'll mean much more if I have to talk to your wife."

Corey raised his arm and pointed at McLaren. "That's the second time you mentioned her. Now, what's this in aid of?"

"You don't really want me to talk to her, do you? I mean…" he glanced at the exterior of the house, "why spoil your life when this can be avoided?"

"Yeah? Like what?"

"Well, it'd be a shame if I had to tell your wife that a…how would you like to label it…a *casual relationship* has developed between a firefighter and the named female. The same female who happens to have a daughter who plays on the same netball team as *your* daughter. It would be a pity if your wife received an anonymous call about that. She'd probably be none too pleased. Nor would Olivia's husband, I'm guessing. Now—" he leaned forward, the grin off his face "—do we understand each other? Are you going to talk to me about the fire at Janet Ennis' house?"

Chapter Nine

"That's blackmail." Corey uttered the words barely above a whisper.

"That's how you term it. I think of it as helping Janet's mother find answers to questions that have plagued her for five years."

"You're getting dangerously close to ruining my life, McLaren."

"Nora's life has already been ruined by Janet's death, and Janet's life has certainly been…ruined, if you want to call it that." He grabbed his car key in readiness to leave. "It's your decision, Chappell. I need your answer."

"But if my wife or my mates at the station find out I've talked to you…"

"You're wasting my time, Chappell. I don't give a damn about the Council, your wife or your mates. You got yourself into this situation in the first place. You knew you were playing with fire by having an affair with this woman." He took a step toward Corey, and looked down at the man. "You're pathetic. You obviously are more concerned about your damned reputation than with your wife or daughter's feelings. I'd almost feel sorry for you if I weren't so disgusted. A man who won't help a mother discover what happened to her daughter…" He started to leave but Corey grabbed McLaren's arm. McLaren tried to shake off the grip but Corey squeezed tighter.

"Please. McLaren! Don't go. I-I didn't mean to be such a…" He snorted as McLaren looked at him. "I'm not such a damned sissy. Or a berk. I'm sorry. Please. Can't I help?"

McLaren considered his actions against the man's future, then nodded.

Corey relaxed his grip and let his arm drop to his side. "What do you want to know?"

"First, I'd like to know if you suspected arson. Any niggle of doubt, no matter how small or infrequent, that the fire wasn't an accident."

"The studio held a lot of accelerants—well, it would, since it was used for her art work."

"Things like artist paint?"

"Sure. Also turpentine. But she'd have that for cleaning her brushes, wouldn't she? We discovered a fair amount of burnt wood in one corner of the building, but that turned out to be easels and wedged stretchers for her painting canvases."

"When you arrived, the fire was still burning."

"Yes. A wooden structure like that burns quickly. We wasted no time in getting there after receiving the phone call. I don't know the length of time, but I can't remember any call ever creating a response problem. But even with our prompt arrival, the place was well on its way to being destroyed."

"Being there more or less early on, do you recall the color of the smoke?"

Corey nodded. Smoke color indicated what substance was burning. "Surprised I do, actually."

"Why is that?"

"Well, it wasn't anything that seemed odd. It was a

wooden structure. We had gray smoke and yellow and red flames. Ordinary. There was a small amount of black smoke, but we concluded that the paints and turpentine caused that. There wasn't a huge cloud of black smoke, if that's what you're wanting to know. Nothing to suggest any petroleum product was sprinkled about as an accelerant."

"How about smoke patterns?"

"We'd usually look for those, sure. Around windows and doors to see if they were open to advance oxygen through the structure. But the building was a near loss. No windows or door were left standing."

McLaren nodded, his mind racing. "Any unusual odor?"

Corey shook his head, exhaling loudly. "Sorry. No help there. If there was, I didn't notice it. Just what you'd expect—paint and turpentine and charred wood."

"Did you make a search for faulty electric wiring or electrical equipment? Maybe Janet had an electric kettle for brewing tea, or maybe she was burning candles. Lots of women do, I know."

"You're looking for cause."

"Yes. Something had to have started this thing."

"We sifted through the rubble, as we do at every incident site. Nothing seemed suspicious. She had two lamps, I remember, and one of those portable CD players. We found no evidence of candles or cigarettes, although there was a small portable electric heater, microphone, computer, two-burner hot plate, small refrigerator and a two-drawer filing cabinet. They were all badly melted, of course, but none of the electrical objects proved to be faulty."

"And I assume from what you said about the

remnants of the structure that you couldn't determine if there had been multiple flash points."

"Basically we had half of one wall—the east wall, the average height on that remnant was four and a half feet. The adjoining wall, the north wall was in slightly better condition but still only about five feet of that remained. The other two walls had burnt down to the foundation or near to it. As I said, McLaren, it was a wooden structure filled with paint, turpentine, canvas, cotton rags and paper. We didn't expect much to be left after we extinguished the fire."

"But on those two walls you found no multiple flash points or evidence of several points of origin."

"You *want* this to be a case of arson?" Corey's left eyebrow shot up, mirroring his astonishment.

"No. That would indicate Janet had an enemy—or was mentally unstable if she set it herself." He paused, his mind replaying his recent conversation with Nora. Mental illness didn't run in families, did it? Taking a deep breath, McLaren clenched his left fist and tapped it against his right palm. What did he want this to be? Would he feel better, would Nora feel better, if he uncovered evidence of arson? Would it make everything worse if this led to murder? He flashed a grin at Corey and said rather slowly, "No. I'm not keen to prove arson, but I've been retained by Janet's mother to find out everything I can about this fire and about her death. I need to learn all I can so I can eliminate or focus on one specific thread."

"Sure. Of course. Didn't mean to get all…well, it's a tough subject to talk about, isn't it? Especially when someone dies in a fire."

"Where did you find Janet's body?"

"Where did we find—"

"In the studio, I know, but was it near the door, like she'd been trying to get out but the door was blocked, maybe? Or by a window? Did she have her mobile in her hand?"

"I can tell you, she gave me a start."

"Oh?"

"Not the position or condition of her body, but finding her there. The studio wasn't that big. Size of a large room. Twenty one by thirty feet."

"That is large."

"Well, it would be, wouldn't it, if it's an artist studio. Needed space for her supplies and to work in."

"So you found her…"

"Near the center of the room. More away from the entry than toward it. She faced away from the door, too. Like she wasn't even conscious of the fire or had tried to get out. I thought that a bit odd, but if she had been unconscious she wouldn't have known about the fire. Her body was in the classic pugilist pose. You know what that means?"

"Fists clenched, arms raised and knees toward the chest." McLaren looked away from Corey, suddenly queasy. Recalling Janet's face from the photo and remembering her singing…well, she had been real. He had talked about her to Nora and Helene, he had seen her house, stood in the forest and seen where she had worked as an artist. To even hint at her any other way repulsed him.

"I know what you're thinking."

"Zero in on one of them, then."

"This happened five years ago, so how can I remember it so exactly and you be sure what I'm telling you is accurate."

"That had crossed my mind."

"I remember because we found Janet's body in the rubble. I remember because the weather had been so hellish and when we got to the blaze we were scared shitless that the forest would catch on fire. I remember because I heard a recording of one of Janet's songs a month later and thought what a hell of a waste that such talent was lost." He clenched his hands together until the skin of his knuckles shone white in the sunlight. "When you've got all that dumped on you from one incident, you don't easily forget. Like you probably remember some murder cases you worked on."

"You're right. Some things do engrave themselves on the mind." And emotions, McLaren wanted to add. He still could not shake the image of that hanged man. The corpse, stiff with rigor mortis, slowly swung from the rope, easing into and out of the half-light of the basement. He had been so careful, climbing on the ladder in order to cut the rope. The body swayed, and in so doing, one of its rigid arms touched McLaren on his shoulder. He had yelped and jumped, nearly falling off the ladder in his fright. The purpled and swollen flesh, so upsetting later in the light from the police work lamps, had been terrifying in the gloom. McLaren doubted he would ever forget the sight or the touch of the dead man.

But that ten years ago. Corey and McLaren stood in the quiet, each occupied with his thoughts. The shadows of early afternoon had lengthened in the time they'd been talking, and the eastern section of the garden sat in a patch of ochre-hued light.

Corey said slowly, thinking, "We didn't discover

anything odd in the debris. I know that for a fact. I would have remembered after discovering…well, after we found her body. It would've made an impression on me. But nothing screamed that it had been arson."

"Did Nora supply you with a list of things that would've been in the studio?"

"No. We had no reason to suspect arson, as I said."

"So you don't know if anything was moved into or out of the studio before the fire."

Corey frowned and tapped the back of his hand against his lips. "You're hinting that someone moved something important into the studio and set fire to the place to collect insurance money."

"Or moved something out to save it from the blaze so it wouldn't be missed…and *then* got the insurance for the so-called missing item."

"Mrs. Ennis didn't mention a specific item. And she would have done if it were important. We were there; she could have asked us to search for a particular thing." He looked at McLaren, his eyebrows lowered. "If what you've just said is right, if that did happen, well, who would that insurance fraud benefit?"

"Right now I'd say the mother, the fiancé or the ex-boy friend."

"Sounds like something the police would've found out."

"Maybe their incompetence stopped them."

****

Myles Tyson, Janet's fiancé, apologized for being late. "To tell you the truth—" he sat across from McLaren in the pub "—I got lost. When you said The King's Head for some reason I envisioned The King's Arms and went there. I finally realized my mistake after sitting there for fifteen minutes. I'm sorry for keeping you waiting." He took a breath and ordered a cup of coffee from the waitress.

McLaren took a few seconds to evaluate the man. Myles looked to be in his early forties. There seemed to be nothing remarkable about him—medium height, brown hair and eyes, not particularly muscular or handsome. But how muscular did he need to be to carry around photographic equipment? His hair had started to recede at his temples and was flecked with gray. Otherwise, he had no obvious signs of aging; age spots didn't mar his large, tanned hands or face. McLaren settled down to the task at hand, leaving the mystery of attraction between the sexes to another time.

"That's quite all right, Mr. Tyson." McLaren picked up his mug of coffee. "I suggested this because it was close to your house and I thought I could grab a late lunch at the same time."

"Sure. Right." Myles looked around the room, nodding. The main crush of the lunchtime crowd had cleared out, leaving only a handful of diners within the pub's white plastered interior. A pinball machine blinked in vibrant neon in the corner, humming as it waited for a player. "So," Myles said, his gaze still on the expectant machine. "How can I help?"

McLaren explained the situation and ended with "Do you know anyone who might have wanted Janet dead?"

Myles' eyes widened and his cheeks flooded with color. He stared at McLaren, shaking his head. "No, uh, no. Of course not."

"Of course not...what? Of course you don't know anyone like that, or of course no one would want to kill

Janet?"

"Why, uh, yes. Both." He broke off, thanking the waitress for the coffee, and took a sip. "Maybe I should've ordered a stiff whisky." It came out as a jest, but his expression suggested he meant it. "Everyone loved Janet. What harm had she ever done to anyone?"

"That's what I'm trying to find out."

"She wasn't a pushy person. She didn't try to walk over people to attain her goals. She was a caterer and a singer. Both occupations can be cutthroat, but Janet wasn't of that ilk. She took her careers almost casually, not expecting too much, just having a grand time with life."

"Were there jealousies? A singer, perhaps, who was covetous of Janet's success, or a prestigious catering event Janet got instead of some other company? Feelings run high in things like that."

Myles shook his head again, this time more emphatically. "No. She wasn't like that. Sure, she wanted to be successful—who wouldn't after all the work and hours she put into it? But she didn't walk over people. She kept her eyes and mind focused on the future and kept moving ahead."

"What about her former catering employee? Mightn't he have been angry with her? Losing a job doesn't exactly call for roses on the boss' birthday."

"I don't know about that. I mean, I know she fired him—Nora said as much, and Janet even mentioned it. But I don't know how he felt. He left work that day without uttering threats, if that means anything."

"You'd been engaged…how long?"

"We were engaged in August."

"So, approximately one month, then. Had you

known each other long before that? I know you were her photographer, but I mean were you friends before you became her photographer?"

"We knew each other, sure. I did a few odd photo shoots before she employed me as her full time photographer."

"Like, when another photographer couldn't accommodate her?"

"Yes. I never did any food shots, though. That's a completely different type of photographic skill. I just did shoots for her CD cover, website, posters for the clubs she'd appear at—things like that. You get to know someone pretty well and pretty quickly when you're photographing them. We were friends for about a year, I guess, before the engagement."

As Dena and I were friends before our engagement... The thought popped into McLaren's mind without him willing it, thrusting Dena's face into the conversation with Myles. McLaren pulled in his bottom lip, annoyed that his mind wandered in the midst of a serious interview, and focused on the photographer. "In that year did Janet ever talk to you about Tom Murray?"

"Her former boy friend? Sure. But she wouldn't pour out her heart to me, if that's what you're after. I wasn't a diary or a priest. She never said a thing about personal problems. Janet had strict lines drawn up and wouldn't tell tales out of school."

"So you don't know how angry Tom was, then, when their friendship ended."

"Sorry, no. But why wouldn't he be upset? Janet was a beautiful, caring person, Mr. McLaren."

"I don't know why he wouldn't be upset. That's

what I'm trying to determine."

"Unless it was Tom's idea to break off with Janet. Then he might not be upset."

"Did you know Tom Murray? Would you believe he had made that decision to end the relationship?"

"I knew him, certainly. I saw him around sometimes at photo sessions. A Christmas party, once, I think. But we weren't more than nodding acquaintances. I don't know about Janet, but I wasn't sorry to see him leave."

"Dislike the man?"

"No. Not that. Just that I had begun liking Janet quite a lot. With Tom gone…well, I don't know if it was purely psychological or not, but with him out of Janet's life I didn't have to rein in my feelings for her."

"You'd started caring about her."

"More than I think I realized at the time." He took a sip of coffee and put the cup on the table. Four women passed their table, intent on commenting about their recent bridge game. Myles looked up, eyeing each woman in turn before resuming his conversation. "I guess I'd buried my feelings while Tom was in her life. You know…pretend you don't like something so you're not disappointed when you can't have it. Of course, I didn't know how deeply I did care about her. I hadn't stopped to think about it." He ran the tip of his index finger along the handle of the cup. "Well, you don't, do you? What good would it do? Only bring up frustration and hurt." He took another swallow of coffee and held the cup in his hands.

"So you don't know if Tom Murray held any grudge or anger when he left Janet."

"No. Like I said, we weren't mates and we didn't

socialize. You'll have to ask Tom about that. But I do know someone else who might've harbored ill feelings about her."

"Someone other than the former catering employee?"

"Yes. I've seen him at Janet's many times. He's more or less a permanent fixture around her place."

"What's his name?"

"Oh, sorry. Bruce Parrott. Works at Haddon Hall the last time I heard. He was a guide. Might still be. He does something else when there are no booked groups to lead around. Can't think what it is. Server in the restaurant?" Myles frowned and blinked rapidly. "You'll find him if he's not left, though I suppose he might have done in five years. He used to be a musician with Janet's original trio, when it was just forming. She fired him under unpleasant circumstances, I heard. Sorry, gotta run." He stood up, grabbed his car key, and walked out of the pub.

Chapter Ten

The Sleeping Fox was noisy—perfect for Sean's purpose. Perfect for masking their conversation and not being overheard. From his past experience with Helene, she had to be up to something pawky, if not criminal. Talking to her before she got too riled up gave him the advantage. He was off the mark.

Sean sipped his beer and glanced around the pub's crowded room. A little late for Buxton's after-work crowd and a little early for any person wanting dinner, the pub appeared to cater to a healthy mix of locals and tourists wanting a pick-me-up drink or snack. The chatter and body count would increase around seven o'clock, but the circumstances would still work. All he needed was Helene Brogan.

Speak of the devil. The outside door squeaked open, letting in the fragrance of approaching rain. He had positioned himself rather like a police officer would have—backed up in the corner of the booth and facing the entrance. So he had no need to turn to see if she'd come in. It wasn't Helene, he noted rather irritably. Just another twenty-something joining the group by the dartboard.

His gaze shifted to the darkening landscape outside the pub's window. Even now, three quarters of an hour or so before sunset, the lights from neighboring businesses spilled golden and white across the cobblestone courtyard. Buildings farther down the open area hunched over, darkening shapes against the darkening sky. Some windows glowed with life, like eyes staring into the gloom, while other windows closed their sleepy shades to the world, black rectangles in the black mass. Pinpricks of light popped up along the street, more yellow beckons lighting people along their way. In the gloom between the dark face of the two-storey building across the way and the shadow thrown by the pub, he could just discern a tall, feminine figure picking its way across the uneven quadrangle. A flash of amber beneath the overhead light fixture outside the pub's door revealed the walker's short, curly hair, and seconds later Helene joined him at his table.

"You arrived early, Sean. Couldn't stand the thought of losing one minute with me?" She stood beside the booth, holding a glass of wine and a plate of biscotti, smiling.

Sean muttered something intelligible, got up, and placed the goblet and plate on the table.

She slid into the booth and arranged herself on the seat. "Thank you, darling. There are so few real gentlemen left these days, so it's refreshing when a man comes to a lady's aid, like seating her or opening doors. And no one stands up anymore when a lady enters or leaves the room. When did that all start, do you think? With the women's lib thing?" She bit off a mouthful of the biscotti and flicked the crumbs from her suede skirt. It matched her brown boots and accented the flecks in her otherwise navy-colored tights. Readjusting the plunging neckline of her cotton pullover, she crossed her legs.

Sean's thumb stroked the edge of the pressed paper beer mat. It advertised a local brew. "Okay. You're here. Now, what's so damned important?"

"Darling! Such an attitude. And we've just got together. You're looking quite handsome, I might add. Keeping yourself fit. You do weight lifting?" She gazed at his broad shoulders and tanned face.

Sean snorted and swept an unruly lock of his hair back over his ear. He settled back against the padded leather booth, giving her a look that conveyed "I'm immune".

Helene evidently liked what she saw, for she muttered something low and indistinguishable and stretched her hand across the table. The silver bangle bracelets clattered against the wooden surface. Patting Sean's hand, she said, "You need something stronger than beer. How about a whisky? It'll smooth those ruffled feathers of yours."

He shook off her hand and wiped his fingers on his jeans. "I don't want a scotch. I want to know what's so bloody big deal that I had to meet you. I haven't seen you for years and all of a sudden you ring me up and tell me to high tail it over here." He flicked the beer mat toward the bottles of vinegar, catsup and teriyaki sauce grouped at the end of the table. The mat hit the bottles with a bang, like a bowling ball hitting a group of ninepins. "Never did like this place."

Helene looked around the room. "Why? What's wrong with it? I thought everyone liked The Sleeping Fox."

"Too old timey for my taste, that's all. The food's okay, rather better than most. But all this coaching days décor…" He sniffed and angled himself so he had a better view of the window. "Now, what's so important?"

"All right, darling, I'll put you out of your misery, but I must say I don't remember you being so fussy when you worked for Janet and me."

"That was five years ago, Helene. I was eighteen when Janet died. I should hope I would've matured a bit since then. Anyway, what've my likes and dislikes to do with this cozy little chat? You're not going to offer me my old job, are you?"

"Would you take it if I did?"

He screwed up his mouth and snorted.

"I didn't think you would so I didn't even waste my breath by asking."

"So what—"

"A business proposition of another kind, Sean. You're...what, now? Twenty one or twenty two?"

"Twenty three. Why? You're nearly fifty, I bet, though I have to hand it to you, you don't look it if you are."

"Thank you. We've both weathered rather well after...well, since our catering days together. Though you were so young then. Still are young. I'm sorry I lost track of you. What have you been doing since then?"

"You really interested or is this some play for time?"

"Sean, dear, I was always interested in you."

"More outside the kitchen. You weren't exactly subtle in letting me know what you wanted."

"It never worked though, did it?" She smiled and saluted him with her wine glass.

"You weren't lacking in skills, Helene. I just wasn't interested."

"You and Kathryn still together?"

"We're married." He wiggled the fingers of his left hand and Helene nodded.

"Imagine me overlooking that. I had eyes only for you, darling, when I came through the door. Never occurred to me to look for a wedding ring. Congratulations. I hope you're both deliriously happy." She leaned forward so he had a good view of the swell of her breasts.

"You were never more sincere, Helene. I'll take that as a warm wish for our future." The corner of his mouth skewed upward again and he gazed at her with half-lowered eyelids.

"Oh, Sean, I've always wanted you to do well. That's why Janet and I took you into our employment. We knew how hard it was for you with that burglary charge against you. No one wanting to hire you, no one trusting you. Such a black mark ruining your future. And totally undeserved, we found out, because you did turn out to be such a gifted worker."

"You were all heart, Helene."

"Thank you, dear. I told Janet the first time I saw you that we needed to give you a chance. And see? You're married and…doing what?"

"I'm a chef."

Helene blinked, looking as if she'd not heard him correctly in the clutter of surrounding conversation. "Really—a chef?"

"No need to be surprised. Working for you and Janet all those years gave me an education."

"I'm so glad you are able to continue in the culinary field, Sean. Janet and I knew you had real talent."

"So now you can pat yourself on the back, pleased that you rescued a little tearaway from a life of crime."

"Oh, darling, it wasn't that bad. You just took a wrong turn."

"And you were there to keep me on the tarmac. Very obliging."

"It wasn't so hard. You always had the talent." She took a sip of wine, watching Sean from over the rim of her glass.

It was hard to judge what was coming. It had been a risk, agreeing to talk to her in a public place, but the risk seemed less than meeting in a less frequented spot where they might be seen and remembered. And he didn't want to go to her house or, worse yet, have her come to his. He eyed her, steeling himself, for even though he already felt manipulated, he had a suspicion she was about to drop a bomb.

Putting the glass down on the mat, she said, "All right. You want to know what this is all about. It's simple enough. I'd like to know why you torched Janet's artist studio right after you killed her."

Chapter Eleven

Sean's voice raised an octave in tone as he squeaked, "*I* killed her? Are you crackers? Why would I kill Janet? Besides being a pacifist, I liked the woman. Why do you think I killed her? Who's been talking?"

"No one's been talking, darling."

"Well, you got the idea *somewhere*. People don't generally make up stuff like that."

She dunked the end of the biscotti into the wine, shook off the excess liquid, and bit off a piece. She chewed slowly, looking thoughtful, as though wanting to savor every fragment. Her fingers cradled the bottom of the glass' bowl as she took a sip of wine. "Sean, dear, don't look at me like you think I had anything to do with this accusation. You frighten me."

"So, where did this accusation come from and why bring it up now? I thought the investigation had ended years ago."

"Just a friendly warning."

"Friendly…like Janet was so friendly when she fired me?"

Helene reached out her hand again to take Sean's, but he folded his arms across his chest. Instead, her fingers sought the steam of her wine glass and traced the ridges. "That was unfortunate, yes. I wish it wouldn't have happened."

"You couldn't have talked to her, persuaded her to

keep me on, I guess." He said it bitterly, and was dazed to discover he still hurt.

She shook her head. "It wasn't that easy, darling. When it came down to the final vote, it was her decision."

"I thought you were partners, equally sharing in decisions and profits."

"Yes, we were partners, but not equal. Janet really owned most of the company, so it was her decision in the end."

"How fortunate for you that you didn't have to soil your hands in such an unpleasant decision." He eyed her again, searching her face. Her expression hadn't changed. "Or was it so unpleasant?"

"Dear! What do you mean by that?"

"Maybe you got tired of having an ex-con, however refined and reformed he might have looked, for a worker. Maybe I was affecting your business, coloring your company name."

"Sean, no one knew anything about you. You were completely anonymous to our clients."

"Then why fire me?"

"Honestly, dear, this isn't the time or place to discuss this." She paused as a couple passed their table, glancing at her.

"I'll drop it for now, but I want to talk about this later. You—or Janet—can't pick up a down-and-out kid one minute and then turn around and give him the boot. There's got to be a reason."

"I'm sorry you're still bitter."

"Bitter!" He barked the word in a rush of cynicism and anger. "Let it happen to *you* and then tell me five years later how it's colored *your* life." He grabbed

Helene's wine glass and downed the last of its contents, then shoved the glass toward her. "So, you still haven't told me why you're all sweetness and light and brought up the subject of Janet's death. What's going on?"

"Just thought we could come to a business agreement."

"Business agreement? The last time I was in business with you—"

"All right. Bad word choice. Understanding. You like that word better?"

"I thought I understood you pretty well. Obviously not. So, what sort of understanding? You want me to confess to something I didn't do?"

"Of course not! How ridiculous of you to suggest that."

"Then what—"

Helene's fingers lay across the foot of the wineglass, limp and at ease. She said very slowly, "I've been thinking about that day, the day Janet died. Little things pop into my mind, now. Some of them not too pleasant to recall. Like the way you parted from the company." The pub's front door opened as three people entered, and the votive candle flame on the table bobbed briefly in the stir of air. "But, as you said, we're not here to talk of that right now. My little business proposition is simple, dear. In summary, I will go to the police and tell them that you killed Janet and torched the artist studio…unless you pay me a little something to keep quiet." She didn't smile, but merely looked at him, open eyed and waiting. Thirty seconds ticked by, during which one of the dart teams won, a groan came from the people watching the telly, and a police car's siren wailed down the High Street.

Sean leaned forward and kept his voice low. "Your idea being that I had the perfect motive to kill Janet."

Helene shrugged, her eyes large and bright. "Why, darling, of course. Don't you read about those disgruntled employees going back to their former employers and killing them?"

"Those disgruntled employees don't seem too concerned about who else gets in the way. Haven't you read about innocent people being killed…and some not so innocent?"

"There are always precautions, dear. Letters to lawyers, for example."

"Reading 'In case I die, Sean Fallon is responsible. The cassette tape of our conversation is in my desk drawer.' That about it?"

Helene smiled and picked up the last bit of biscotti. "Sounds plausible, doesn't it?" She took a bite, swallowed, and blotted her lips on the napkin. "Now, what's it to be? Me or the cops?" Her voice had turned cold and the humor had left her eyes. "Do I continue to keep quiet?"

Sean stared at the flickering candle flame.

"I'd think your professional career—not to mention your marriage and your wife's good name—would be worth paying me to keep quiet. What's money when your future is, shall we say, cloudy?"

"And how much is this protection going to cost me?"

"Oh, darling. Not much. Not really, when you think of all you could stand to lose."

"How much, Helene?"

"Let's start out with, say, two hundred pounds a month."

"Start out!"

"Inflation, dear. You know how the price of living keeps going up."

"And how long is this going to continue, assuming I go along with your proposition and assuming I have the money."

"Oh, dear. I hadn't quite thought that out yet. But I'll let you know after a few payments. I know how you hate surprises."

"I repeat, why are you doing this now? You could've gone to the coppers when this happened. You need money for a new car or something?"

"Darling, I'm not so crass as that. I hid the truth from the police and the firefighters during their investigations—didn't say a word about you, believe me. But now I think the truth is worth more to you, isn't it? A wife and a thriving career will do that, won't it?" She brushed the remaining biscotti crumbs from her fingers and smiled. "And, being worth more to you naturally makes it precious to me. I always liked you, Sean. I had an idea we'd…get together one of these days."

"You didn't even know what I was doing until a few minutes ago when I told you. So you can't have come prepared to squeeze me dry. What's the real reason for all this?"

"You're right, darling. But that doesn't negate my business offer. There's a man—"

"What man? One of your and Janet's other employees?"

"No. A man came to see me. He got my name and phone number from Janet's mother."

"Nora? Why would she give that out?"

"She's hired this man to investigate Janet's case. She's always been upset with the verdict of accidental death, so she's asked him to find out the cause of Janet's death."

Sean snorted and grabbed his car key. "Let him investigate. There's nothing to find. The coroner ruled on the case long ago. He won't find a thing."

"I wouldn't be so smug about that, dear. I've heard he usually gets what he's after."

"He a cop, then?"

"He was. Michael McLaren. Now he looks into cold cases. Quite successfully, too."

"You said that."

"So, do I go to the cops or not, Sean?"

"Why not talk to this chap, if he's so keen to dig around in Janet's case. He'll probably listen to you." He stood up, looking down at Helene. "Better yet, he'll probably believe you."

"I'm serious, Sean. I want the first two hundred quid by Monday night. You've got a week, or I'll tell a very convincing story to the police."

"I don't doubt it."

"You'll have to work on your bluff, dear. Even I'm not convinced."

"I don't have to convince you of anything, Helene. You know I'm innocent."

"Do I? Funny thing about the police—they're inclined to believe a convicted burglar's capable of murder. You're going to have a difficult time convincing them otherwise. Is it worth it to you and your wife?"

Sean turned toward the door, his face drained of color.

"I'll call you Sunday and let you know where to deliver my money, shall I?"

Chapter Twelve

Haddon Hall perched like a crown on the hill above the River Wye. It threw back the late afternoon sun, its light gray stone taking on the faintest of a yellowish tint under the light. McLaren paid the parking fee and stopped his car alongside a Ford Galaxy. Could do with a wash, he thought, glancing at the grimy exterior. He shook his head. Some people just didn't know how to take care of things.

His shoes scrunched into the limestone gravel, sending up small plumes of dust that settled on his shoes and on the sparse patches of grass that poked through the hard ground. All right, he mentally corrected his assessment of the Ford's owner as he gazed at his dusty shoes. He walked up to the entrance and paid the admittance fee to the Hall. Slipping his wallet into his trousers back pocket, he gazed at the nail heads studding door in the Hall's gateway. Should've kept some folks out without too much trouble… The stone steps, saucer-shaped from millions of feet over the centuries, led from the gateway up to the lower courtyard. McLaren stepped aside as a group of school children ran down the steps and funneled through the archway. They laughed and jostled each other as they made for the restaurant.

Myles said something about Bruce being there, didn't he? McLaren paused, looking through the archway, toward the upstairs restaurant. Maybe that group of kids had warranted a group tour. If so, maybe Bruce had shepherded them about. McLaren mounted the seven tiers of stone steps and made for the Hall.

The building personified Gothic, with its heraldic crests, leaded glass windows, and masses of rose and clematis vines smothering the exterior stone walls. He glanced to his right, at the stone chimney, and wondered how many there were in the medieval house, then walked inside.

Bruce Parrott had, indeed, given the school children a tour of the house and McLaren found him in the banquet hall, a thirty-five foot by twenty-five foot paneled room with large leaded glass windows and a hammerbeam roof. McLaren introduced himself and asked if Bruce would mind answering some questions.

"That was five years ago," Bruce said in response to the topic. His eyebrows lowered slightly as if he were remembering the situation or assessing McLaren. "If the police were so concerned about my information, why didn't they ask me then? No one even bothered to talk to me."

McLaren eyed the man without replying. Bruce Parrott appeared to be in his mid twenties and wore his red hair close cropped. A haze of a beard covered his jaws and chin, suggesting more than his dark rimmed eyes did that he'd had a long day.

"You did say you're from the police," Bruce added by way of prompting McLaren.

"No. I'm looking into a case that the police haven't solved. Are you working much longer today?" He let a man and woman stroll through the room before saying, "I thought we could talk somewhere private."

"I'm off, actually. I just gave my last tour for the day. Is here all right?"

McLaren glanced around the area. Three massive, carved oak beams ran the width of the room, supporting the wooden fretwork of the ceiling. A minstrel's gallery, tapestry and raised dais composed most of room. "We won't be overheard?"

"Nearly closing time. We won't get many more visitors. But if you'd feel more comfortable somewhere else…"

"Is there somewhere outside?"

"Sure. The upper courtyard is empty at this time. Most people have finished looking at the garden." He moved toward the door and McLaren followed, giving one last look at the overhead beams as he passed. The length of the upper edges was nicked into small squares, resembling the teeth of a zipper. This same design adorned the molding below the rafters. He allowed his fingertips to lightly glide across the surface of a wooden chest, then became aware of his footsteps moving across the stone floor. His hand lingered on the satin-smooth doorframe as he stepped into the passageway.

Haddon Hall was laid out in the form of a squared-off figure eight, with the two courtyards enclosed within the two sections of the form. The banquet hall, pantry and buttery separated the upper courtyard from the lower. McLaren climbed the stone steps and came upon a dense, green lawn. Masses of rose bushes and climbing clematis framed the stone parapet that surrounded the yard.

Bruce perched on the top of the railing, near an enthusiastic rose bush, and loosened his tie. He looked at McLaren, who remained standing. "So what's this about? You said you're looking into Janet's death. But you're not a cop?" He angled his head so he could see McLaren's face without squinting into the sun.

"I'm doing this for Janet's mother. She's not satisfied with the open verdict."

"Yeah. I'd heard she didn't believe the accident account. What do you want to know, then?"

"I understand you used to be a member of Janet's group. Is that right?"

"Sure. I played drums."

"Why did you leave? Did she decide she didn't want drums any longer? Didn't you get on with the other band members?"

Bruce snorted and stared into the distance. The bitterness underlying his words was unmistakable. "I didn't want to leave. I lo—liked Janet. Immensely. I loved performing."

"So what happened to make you decide to quit the group?"

"Janet decided for me. She fired me." His gaze snapped back to fix on McLaren's eyes. "Five years ago this happened and I'm still mad about it."

"Tell me about it."

"Why? Because you suspect me of causing Janet's death?"

"I didn't know anything about your firing until now, so I can't suspect you of anything."

"But you're a cop, you said."

"I *was* a cop. Now I'm merely helping Mrs. Ennis come to the truth."

Bruce's eyebrows lowered again, perhaps considering his situation and McLaren's status. The motor started on the school bus in the car park, bursting the quiet. "Fine. Sorry. But I loved that job. I had big dreams, and they died when she sacked me."

"When was that? Do you know why she let you go?"

"Euphemistically said. Thanks." He took a deep breath, then launched into his narration. "She'd formed the group in February. I was with them for a year and seven months before I was...let go." He paused, and McLaren was aware of the word choice. He nodded and Bruce continued. "Janet had written a few songs and we incorporated those into some standard stuff. It was a nice mix. She played piano and sang, of course. I was on drums, and Dan Wilshaw was also on piano."

"Two pianists? That's unusual. Why not a different instrument?"

"Janet liked the sound of the two pianos. She would play the standard arrangement and Dan, on the second piano, would throw in riffs and harmony. It was something different, made the group stand out. I thought it a good sound. We rehearsed six days a week, anywhere from six to eight hours a day. It was grueling some days because I was working a part time job doing lawn care and gardening. Strictly amateur stuff, you know. Just until the trio made it big. Anyway, I couldn't believe how talented Janet was, what an incredible voice she had. She seemed to be Etta James, Peggy Lee, Mildred Bailey and Ruth Etting in one person. Amazing talent.

"Anyway, I borrowed a rehearsal tape one night after we'd finished. Took, if that better describes my action. This sixteen year-old girl who lived on my street wanted to be a singer in the mold of those ladies. She had some talent, I think, but she was delusional about it, as a lot of teenagers are. I took the tape and played it for her, showing her what real talent was, how hard we worked, the hours we poured into it each day. You know, take after take after take until we got it recording-studio-perfect. Well, it shook her up a bit, hearing Janet's singing and all the rehearsing we did for one song and how we worked to polish the smallest phrase. I didn't do it to crush her dream, Mr. McLaren. I only wanted to lift those rose colored glasses from her eyes so she wouldn't fall for some come-on by a sleazy agent."

McLaren nodded and asked if Janet found out about it.

"Yeah. I'd returned the tape, thinking Janet would never know what I'd done. But in playing it for the girl I stopped the tape in a spot different from where we had the previous day. When Janet turned it on that morning, she couldn't understand why the place on the tape didn't jive with what we'd done. She kept asking us if we'd fooled with the tape. I told her what I'd done, thinking she'd understand."

"Evidently she didn't."

"She was furious. If I knew a stronger word, I'd use it, but she was livid. I apologized, amazed she reacted that way. She always talked about helping people, but when *I* tried to do it..." He shook his head, the corner of his mouth turned upward. "She said the tape wasn't mine to lend, that her songs weren't copyrighted yet, that she didn't want anyone to analyze our sound for fear of copying it and her songs. I was angry that she came down so hard on me but I apologized again. That didn't make much difference.

She said the damage had been done, that the girl had already heard what was on the tape. She fired me before I could say another word."

"You haven't joined another group?"

"I tried when I was first let go. But I didn't have any luck. I gave up auditioning. After a while, the rejections hurt as much as Janet's anger."

"Have you been working here since then?"

Bruce nodded and ran his hand over the top of the parapet. "I give tours to groups and I work in the restaurant."

"You've given up on your music, then?"

"For now. Like I said, I'm still sore about the whole thing."

"When did this happen?"

"Three days before her accident."

"Did you try to contact Janet, maybe when she'd cooled down a bit? I thought she'd take you back, since she hired you in the first place."

"I rang her up the following day, thinking she'd have gotten over it. But she hung up on me, so I didn't get to say anything."

"Was that the only time you tried to talk to her?"

Bruce's eyes narrowed. "Why—you trying to pin her death on me?"

"I'm trying to understand what went on and who might be involved. The more I know, the better I can sort through this mess. Now, did you give up trying to contact her after that phone call?"

"No. I went to her house the morning of her death."

If he is innocent, McLaren thought, he's just made a damning statement... McLaren studied Bruce's face, but the gaze remained steady, no flush came to the cheeks, and no perspiration dotted the man's forehead. McLaren nodded, and pulled out his notebook. "What time?"

"Eleven o'clock. Give or take a few minutes."

"Did you speak to her?"

"A minute, maybe. She stood in the doorway, the front door. She wouldn't let me inside, but blocked the entrance with her body. As if she was afraid I'd ram past her and hurt her."

"You told me you're still mad about what happened. Were you mad when you spoke to her at her house?"

"You're bloody right I was mad! She'd just crushed my dream and taken away my livelihood."

"But you didn't know then that your dream was dead. You might have got another position as drummer with another group."

"I know. But I wanted to be with *her* group. I didn't want to play for anyone else." He leaned down and picked up a rose petal. Rubbing it between his thumb and index finger, he said more calmly, "I loved her."

McLaren nodded and asked in a low voice, "Did she know? Did she feel the same about you? If she did, maybe that's what made her so angry. You can forgive an acquaintance of discretions more readily than if it's someone you love." He wanted to say: you have higher expectations of a loved one.

Bruce laughed and tossed the petal over the side of the railing. "She didn't know I was alive. Besides, I was about fifteen years younger than she was, so I hardly think she looked on me as potential husband material."

"So you didn't do anything about it. You just let

your love die."

"It didn't die. It's still within me." His right fist slapped into his chest. "Hell of a lot of good it does me, right?"

"Were you mad enough or hurting enough to do anything?"

"What's that mean? Mad enough to kill her?"

"Or in so much pain that you wanted to have something of hers to keep."

"You're daft."

"On the contrary. Most people in love keep little things that belong to their beloved. Might not be intrinsically valuable, but that's not the point. It's something their loved one touched or used or wore. You have anything like that, Bruce?"

He opened his mouth, anger still in his eyes, his neck muscles taut. But instead of shouting, he nodded and stood up. His voice was even-toned when he said, "You want to see?"

"Where? At your home?"

"No. In the Hall. In a room." He started walking back the way they'd come, and McLaren hurried to keep up with the man.

They were back in the banquet hall. The place seemed deserted but they had passed several small groups of people in the gardens, and the car park still held several dozen cars. Bruce walked over to a short chest, opened the doors, and reached inside. He took out a small manila envelope and cradled it against his chest.

"You weren't afraid this would be discovered here? Why not keep it at your house?"

"I thought the police would question me about

Janet's murder. I didn't want them finding this if they searched my place. It might've given me a motive for her death. You know, I can't have her so no one else will." Scorn colored his tone.

"The staff or visitors didn't open the furniture, I take it."

"Safe as houses, obviously. It's still here."

"Still, I'd be fearful of its discovery if I hid it here. Too bad there's no sliding panel or priest hole in this room. I would've used that."

"There *is* something rather like that, but it's a bit out of my reach."

"Oh, yes?"

Bruce walked to the far end of the room and stood beneath the rafter nearest the minstrel's gallery. The beam stretched across the room's width. "There," he said, pointing upward.

McLaren tilted his head back, staring. He walked around, viewing the beam from several angles. "You mean on top of the beam?" Provided a person could reach it, the beam could hold some flat object, like a photo or letter or CD.

"No. Inside the beam."

"*Inside?*"

"When the restoration on the banquet hall's roof took place in the mid 1920s, a time capsule of the restoration was hidden there. There's a hollow area in one end of the beam. And the date—if you can't see it—is engraved on it. 1924. I think that's where the box was. Inside that beam."

"Who'd have thought?"

"Anyway, this chest is just as good. It's kept its secret for five years." He handed the envelope to

McLaren.

"May I?"

Bruce nodded, stepping back slightly, as if to distance himself from the fresh assault of pain.

McLaren peered into the envelope, then drew out a photograph and a button. The photo was a publicity shot of Janet, nearly the same pose as the one Nora Ennis had given him. The button, however, was a different type of keepsake. He asked Bruce about it.

"It came off her sweater. A week before she fired me, actually. I-it's a silly thing to keep, I know, but it belonged to her and, as such, is an extension of her. She didn't even know she lost it, I don't think. I saw it fall but she hadn't noticed. I was going to say something but then I thought I'd like to keep it. Have it as a part of her. So when we took a break, I grabbed it before anyone noticed it."

"Did you take anything else?"

"Like what?" Bruce's eyes flashed fire at the suggestion of theft. "I never touched her purse or her check book. And I'm not a collector of women's panties. If anyone's told you differently—"

"I've not heard of anything, no."

"Then why ask the question. To trip me up?"

"I had to know if I'm to have all the facts to work with. So, you've just the photo and the button."

"Yes."

"Fine." He returned the items to the envelope and handed it back to Bruce. "You said you arrived at Janet's house around eleven o'clock that day. How long did you stay?"

"How long did I stay? You want me to say something like 'Just long enough to run inside, stab her, drag her into her studio and set it on fire'?"

"I want to know how long you were at her house. One minute, five, half an hour?"

"Don't be daft. I told you she slammed the phone down on our conversation the previous day so she's hardly likely to keep me chatting at her front door, is she?"

"Was it basically the same face to face? Did she slam the door on you?"

"She was civil enough. She didn't invite me in. Just asked what I wanted, why I was there."

"What did you say?"

"I apologized again and suggested that I impress upon the girl she was not to talk about the group to anyone. Offer her a ringside table at some gig, give her a CD when it came out. You know, make her feel special and that she is a personal friend of the group. Anything like that so she wouldn't tell her mates about Janet's original songs."

"Did Janet accept your offer?"

Bruce snorted. "Does the sun rise in the north?"

"I take it from what you're saying Janet was still angry."

"I don't think she had cooled down one degree in those forty-eight hours, no."

"Did you say anything else?"

"I asked for my job back, told her how much being drummer for her mattered to me. I said I admired her musicianship and thought the trio would make it big some day and that I thought she was incredibly talented. I wasn't flattering her. I spoke the truth, straight from my heart. I-I hoped she would see how sincere I was and forgive me."

"Obviously she didn't."

"She stood there, listening to me pour our my feelings. I could hear Dan in the back room, practicing scales. She must've heard it, too, because after I finished making a fool of myself she said 'See you around sometime, Bruce' and closed the door."

McLaren nodded and gazed again at the package Bruce cradled against his chest. He held it like a baby, like a precious object that was in danger of breaking. And McLaren had the oddest sensation that if anything happened to those items, Bruce would break in two. He stared at the man, feeling his pain. "And all that took…what?"

"Two minutes maybe? I wasn't there five minutes. That's too long for all that."

"When did she replace you with her bassist? Do you know why she got a bassist and not another drummer?"

"I don't know. I wasn't part of the trio anymore. But I do know that around that time she stopped playing and Dan became the only pianist."

"Why, if she liked the sound of the two keyboards?"

"Maybe she wanted to put her energy into singing. There are a lot of pianists around. Makes sense she'd let Dan take over if she wanted to just sing. Dan was more than competent to be the only pianist. Anyway, I rather suspect singing was her first love; she could take or leave the piano."

"Less rehearsal for her, too, I suspect."

Bruce said he guessed so and put the envelope back into the cabinet. Glancing at his watch he asked if there was anything else.

"I'm looking at this from the police point of view, Bruce. You had been fired, you had been insulted in front of Dan Wilshaw, your musical career as well as your hopes of a romantic relationships were over. That's a lot for one person to handle. Why should the police believe you didn't come back later and kill her?"

"Because," he said, "that day I was in the Buxton Hospital from around one o'clock onward and wasn't discharged for two days."

McLaren blinked, clearly surprised. "I hope it was nothing serious."

Bruce shrugged and rolled up his long sleeves. He held his arms out to McLaren, the underneath of his wrists visible. Pale, puckered ridges were still visible in the pale skin. "Depends on your definition of serious, I guess. I attempted suicide when I got back from her house. Like everything else, I failed at that, too."

Chapter Thirteen

McLaren sat in his back room, his calves resting on the edge of the coffee table, his cordless phone in his hand. The tea things were washed and draining in the dish rack, and a cup of tea sat next to him on the side table. He glanced up from the sheets of paper that held his case notes and punched in Dena's phone number. He needed to empty his heart.

He had tried doing that several minutes ago, grabbing his guitar and aimlessly strumming chords. But he couldn't find the song that would bring him comfort. Each choice had been about murderers or unfaithful lovers or parting spouses, and so he had given up that particular song after a few measures. Folk music was like that, so what had he expected? Perhaps he felt too close to Janet, fellow musician and a case that had been tossed aside with no feelings for Nora. Injustice, if his investigation did disclose Janet's death as murder.

And so he was restless, dissatisfied with the music that he loved and to which he usually gravitated for support. He ran his fingers over the steel strings, the silk-wrapped ones brilliantly bright beneath the tableside lamp's glow, the naked steel ones shiny and reflecting the light. Except where his fingers had left sweat and oil from chording or picking. He moved his right hand off the strings and grabbed the metal button on the bottom of the guitar body. His left hand closed around the neck. For a moment, he considered trying again; surely he could find solace in some song he knew. "There Is a Time" usually brought him great peace, but it seemed too melancholy for his mood. He played the first verse and chorus of "Goodnight and Joy," but stopped abruptly in the midst of the second verse. He sat for a moment, his mind wandering through the snatches of songs in his mind, discarding title choices until his fingers began chording the introduction to Pete Seeger's "Sailing Down My Golden River." This, too, he abandoned partway through. His left hand draped listlessly over the guitar neck, his mind still meandering. Finally he realized he was singing "Why Shouldn't We" by Mary Chapin Carpenter. The words poured from him, the melody rising into the quiet. He sang smoothly and powerfully until the tightening of his throat stopped him after the last verse. Tears threatened to spill from his eyes. The lyric was something Dena would have said to him, about believing in things people say can't change; about having heroes once upon a time, yet knowing they will some day come back.

He closed his eyes, his eyelids forcing the last of the tears from his eyes. Could he change Janet Ennis' case? Nora looked at him as some hero, able to find Janet's killer. Dena believed in him, too. Was he able to personify their dreams, bring justice to a dead case?

The guitar's polished body threw the lamplight onto the far wall, spotlighting Dena's photo among the hung certificates and artwork. He laid the guitar on the coffee table and turned off the light.

In the short time he'd sat there, dusk had made

rapid advances across the land, the deep purple shadows melting into the blackness blanketing the land beyond the sunlight's reach. The golden glow splashed across the western horizon slipped into rose, vermillion and indigo hues before it, too, succumbed to the gray and black that veiled the land. A sprinkling of stars poked through the somber eastern portion of the sky, but beyond his window no other light shone. His house, an ancient dwelling backed up to fields and a stretch of wood beyond that. He had no neighbors within eye- or earshot. He revered the sweep of wind-tossed land that surrounded him as much as he cherished his solitude. Which was one reason he had put off marriage.

And the other?

A few months ago he would've put it down to the bitterness over losing his job in the police. A job he had loved and had quit in a blaze of intense anger and feeling of injustice. But he had struggled out of that depression, reconnected with Dena and some friends, and admitted privately that he had missed them all. So why couldn't he make the commitment to Dena? Because he was afraid he couldn't support her, at least to the degree in which she'd been reared? Because he knew the slide back into depression was lurking in the background, that he still felt the anger and hatred for his situation and for Charlie Harvester in particular?

What would happen to Dena if he lost his temper with Harvester, if the need to avenge his wronged friend Nigel Forester overwhelmed his common sense and he assaulted—or accidentally killed—Harvester? Dena would not bless him if he spent the rest of his life in prison. No, it was best if he stayed single in case the near soul-consuming blackness exploded from him and harmed everyone he loved.

Yet, he had decided in July to ask Dena to marry him. It was now September. He had neatly forgot that decision. And if Dena hadn't, she had never asked him about it. So what's the real reason he was scared to marry her?

Without thinking about it, he punched her phone number into the phone. He hadn't time to consider an answer to the marriage questions for Dena's voice sailed into his ear. Instantly the tension of the day melted and he pictured her curled up on her couch, smiling as she heard his voice. He held the mobile phone closer.

"Michael. I'm so glad you called."

Just the way she said his name weakened his resolve.

"How are you? Working on a stone wall?"

Mention of his 'make do' job since leaving the police brought the blood to his cheeks. Not that he was ashamed of his occupation—far from it. Derbyshire had a couple thousand miles of dry stone walls that needed repair. A job that required skill and muscle. Both of which he liked to believe he had. But mentioning the wall work now, with Janet's death so heavy on his mind... McLaren leaned back against the sofa and said, "Working on a case. Don't laugh."

"Why should I laugh? That's your true calling. You're a skilled detective."

"*Was* a detective."

"*Are*. You've had two cold cases recently and solved both of them even though the police couldn't originally. I think 'are' is the right word."

"Well, I won't argue with a lady."

"Especially if it's to your favor." She laughed and the ripple of silver flooded McLaren with warmth. He could picture her brunette hair and flawless skin, the silk or cashmere or linen clothes she usually wore. But more than those familiar things he loved the sound of her voice.

"Did you work today?"

"Yes. Oh, Michael, another tiger's coming next week. A white one. We're getting his compound ready."

"Mixed feelings about it already, then."

"See? You are a detective! Yes, mixed feelings. I'll love spending time with him—a white tiger, I can't believe how beautiful they are! But I'm sorry he has to come to the shelter."

"Knowing you you'll keep him company." McLaren paused, picturing Dena in her jeans and pullover, cleaning the tigers' cages, helping at the gift shop, taking people on tours. She put in a lot of time at the tiger sanctuary, all on a volunteer basis. She could've got a job elsewhere, making a nice salary, but she chose to help the big cats. Coming from old money, Dena didn't have to work; her parents had set up a trust fund for her, and she had made canny investments in her twenties. The money poured into her bank account, seemingly without ever stopping. Due to her wealth, she knew the right people, had spent time at social engagements, and could solicit funds for her charity. She knew poverty, having worked with homeless people for a few years, but had gravitated to the tigers. Perhaps as an offshoot of her time with society's poorer people, Dena had grown level headed about her wealth and how she spent it. She liked to dress well, but her house was not lavish; she fit in with her working class neighbors. McLaren often wondered where she got her common sense.

Dena's voice cut in on his thoughts. "Anything in particular you wanted to talk about, or just chat?"

"It's this case, Dena."

"Is it a bad one?"

"It's a bloody awful mess. I can't make top nor tail of it."

"How long have you been on it?"

"Since this morning, actually."

"Well, Michael, give yourself a break. You think you should have it solved in a few hours when it's been cold for—how long?"

"Five years."

"I rest my case, your honor."

"Maybe I just need to talk to you. The victim was a thirty-five year old woman. Quite talented singer."

"She died in not so pleasant circumstances, I suspect."

"Yeah." He broke off again, anger at the waste of a talented life boiling within him.

"Can you talk about the case?"

"You sure you want to hear? It's not pleasant."

"If you don't mind going through it, yes, I'd like to know what you're going through."

McLaren took a deep breath, then related the case as Nora had presented it to him and added what he had found out.

"You're thinking the police botched the investigation."

"Not on purpose. I know the Derbyshire Force has a good record. But in my opinion the P.M. findings and conclusions point to a suspicious death and foul play—the drought, the trash burning, the wooden artist studio…"

"If so, I'd have thought the postmortem exam finding would have alerted someone on the investigation team to delve more closely into the fire and death."

"Yeah, you'd think so." He stretched and yawned vocally. "Maybe I'm pushing this. Maybe the mother is a nutter, like Harvester says."

"Implying your dislike for Harvester has pushed you into the investigation, whether you think it's justifiable or not, just to prove the man is wrong once again."

"I don't know, Dena. I'm too tired. You think so?"

"It's not what I think that is important, Michael. You need to go with your instinct and what you find out."

"I suppose so, yes."

"Tell me about her."

His voice sounded more alive now, animated with his image of Janet and his inquiry. "She had a magnificent singing voice—I've got a CD of her and her group. She sang torch songs. But there's another side to her. She and another woman were partners in a catering business."

"So she can obviously cook or bake quite well."

"I suppose she must do."

"That's quite a talent."

"She also painted, though I don't know how good she was or what subject matter she concentrated on. But she evidently was serious enough about her art that she had a separate place for her work. And she liked to garden, though that was a hobby, as it is to millions. But I think she would have made a mark in the music world."

"Her singing was that good, then."

"I'm no expert."

"Maybe not with that type of music, but you know folk and classical, Michael. You have a good ear. If you think her voice quality and phrasing and interpretation were of that caliber, I expect they were. I'm sorry she's gone."

"Yeah. Hell of a raw deal." McLaren laid the papers beside him and snuggled back into the sofa cushions. "So, make me feel better."

"I love you, if that helps."

"It does. Have I told you that I love you?"

"Not since lunch time."

"How like a woman. Keeping score."

"Not on many things, Michael. Just on you."

"I know."

****

Charlie Harvester typed in the word 'dementia' in his home computer's search bar, pressed the return key, and waited while the hundreds of choices popped up on the screen. He hadn't the patience to scroll through the pages, so he clicked on the first entry on the first page and read the information. Finished, he typed in the word 'Parkinson's disease' and again chose the first selection that presented itself. He leaned forward in his chair, his attention on the last sentence. 'The disease does not cause death, but memory and thought processes may deteriorate in the later stages.'

He sat back, a smile engulfing his face. He was right! He had pegged Nora Ennis correctly. She had the symptoms of Parkinson's—he had spotted that the first time they had met. And she had admitted that she suffered from dementia. Two strikes against her, as far as he was concerned. How could anyone seriously believe her about her daughter and the fire and the death threat? The woman was ready for a room on the psych ward. He'd be joining her if he even considered opening the case. And wouldn't that get him accolades from the Chief Constable! Wasting time and money and manpower on the ravings of a lunatic.

Harvester ran the mouse cursor over the word in the search bar and typed in *Candidate for a Cold Case*. Immediately the film title showed up on the monitor screen and he opened the article.

He read it quickly, then re-read it more leisurely to be certain he hadn't missed anything important. The synopsis was short—basically a story about a woman knocked unconscious and dragged into her house. She was left in the kitchen, a pot of soup cooking on the stove, and the kitchen set on fire. The investigators from the police and fire service wrote it off as a tragic accident but the father wouldn't accept it. He doggedly crusaded for two years, talking to organizations, individuals and the police, pleading to have his daughter's case re-examined. He finally convinced one maverick cop and...

Harvester uttered a disgusted 'hell' and logged off the computer. Of course it would end that way for the television film. Everyone wanted a happy ending, the father justified in pursuing the case, the ineptness of the investigating teams exposed, the outrage and support of those interested parties validated.

He got up and walked into the kitchen. He poured

water into the electric kettle, flicked on the switch, then got a china teacup out of the cupboard and dropped a teabag into it. As he waited for the water to boil, he looked out into his back garden. The darkness of night obscured the tool shed but the black shape stood silhouetted against the back fence. Not too much unlike Janet Ennis' fancy art studio. Not too different in basic storyline. But miles from the film in fact.

The kettle clicked off, and Harvester poured the hot water into his teacup. He glanced at the wall clock's sweep second hand. Two minutes—that's how long he let his tea steep. Two minutes for a perfect cuppa. That was fact. Unlike Nora Ennis and her fanciful world.

When the tea was ready, he walked into his lounge, turned on the telly, and sat in the leather chair. Poor, deluded woman. If the Parkinson's didn't rob her of her reasoning, the dementia most certainly would. It was already taking hold. She had already confused the television film with her daughter's death. Too bad.

As the film *Snake Pit* started, he took a sip of tea and sat back. It really was too bad she didn't know what was going on.

****

After talking with Dena, McLaren put on Janet's CD. The sky had deepened to black during the phone call and he sprawled on the sofa, looking out the window and imagining walking through that blackness. Every night it happened and every day he couldn't envision what that darkness would feel like. Not smothering, like a mask. Quite the contrary, for the night sky alternately gave him the sensation of wanting to soar among the stars or feeling incredibly small and earthbound. How could there be such a difference in the land, the enchantment of night versus the humdrum of day? Because time is what we make of it, he thought.

But there was more to the illusion of night for McLaren. Night had been the time of his great childhood terror, when the shadows had crept toward him, covered him, overpowered him to cut off his sight and left the sounds of mice. They had surrounded him, gnawing at the wooden walls of the closet he'd been locked in. He heard their claws and teeth on the studs, envisioned the dozens of sharp, chewing teeth, prayed that the walls were thick enough to keep them out. He had banged on the closet door, rattled the unyielding doorknob, screamed until he could barely hear himself sob in his fright. Yet, no one came.

Time had ceased to flow. Trapped in the claustrophobic darkness, he'd set his mind as best he could on other things: music, walking through the wood, baking with his mother. When he had finally been found and rescued, he slept outdoors for weeks, afraid of dark, interior spaces. Mice still frightened him, bringing back the scene and emotions in petrifying reality. Dena was one of the few people who knew his vulnerability.

But right now, with Janet's voice washing over him and the darkness of the land soothingly thick like a blanket, he could concentrate on Janet's case. The curved indentation on her skull drew him with a coaxing finger. If she hadn't been hit on purpose and left in the burning studio, he'd go back to dry stone wall work full time.

He punched up a cushion behind his head, rolled over on his side, and fell asleep with midnight stars in his eyes and Janet's voice in his ear.

Chapter Fourteen

McLaren woke Wednesday morning, blinking in the confusion of where he was. His bedroom had evidently been exchanged for another room, but what it was and how he got there he didn't know. He sat up and looked again around. His guitar sat on the coffee table, sheets of paper sprouting from a manila file folder—dented from where he had lain on it—sprawled at the end of the sofa. Dena's photograph smiled at him from the wall.

Groaning and rubbing his scalp, he got up. It was a hell of a way to start the day, stiff from a night on the sofa. He shuffled over to the stereo cabinet and turned off the amplifier and CD player, grabbed his guitar, put it back in its hard-shell case, then showered and dressed. After a second cup of hot tea he phoned Nora.

Her voice, steady and positive, responded without hesitation. "I don't know what Janet usually kept in her studio, Mr. McLaren." If Nora thought the question odd, she didn't challenge it.

"Because she kept shuffling things about, you mean?"

"No. Because I hardly frequented the place. Not because I wasn't interested in Janet's art, that's not the reason. She'd take me in, show me a work in progress sometimes, but the finished pieces she'd either have leaning against the sofa in the house and I'd see them that way, or she'd tell me to sit down and close my eyes and she'd bring the painting out from her bedroom or some place and hold it while she stood before me. I don't think she really wanted people, even me, to go to her studio. It was the intrusion into her creative world, I think, that bothered her."

"So you can't tell me what might or might not be missing from that building."

"Nothing specific, no. Not like a certain lamp or mug or file of paper."

"She kept files in her studio? What...like correspondence from art galleries?"

"Could have done. I know she kept bills and receipts for art supplies there. She told me once that it was logical to keep the art things all together. You know—bills for art supplies in the art studio. I don't know if she did that with her music bills and correspondence, though. I can't say how much she used the studio for practice sessions."

"Her band rehearsed there?" He tried to keep the surprise from his voice.

"I don't think very often. You'll have to ask her pianist about that. Do you have his name?"

Wanting to confirm Bruce's information, he said, "No. You have it?"

"Dan Wilshaw. Wait a moment. I've his phone number right here."

The thud of the receiver rattled in his ear as Nora laid down the phone. Her murmuring of the man's name grew fainter in her retreat. Seconds passed before he heard her voice again, increasingly louder this time. The receiver slid across the hard surface on which it rested, there was a muttered "Sorry" and Nora's voice rattled off a phone number. "He may not be able to tell you details, but you can ask. I know he'd do anything to help, Mr. McLaren."

"He's worth talking to. Thanks."

"If he doesn't know, perhaps Janet's former boyfriend might. He and a friend built the studio and he helped Janet move her things in there. He could remember. Or her fiancé might, of course."

"And her former boyfriend's name…"

"Tom Murray." She gave McLaren both men's phone numbers. "I never was too keen on Tom."

"Didn't like the way he treated Janet?"

"I suppose he was good enough to her. I never heard anything to his detriment. Not that Janet would divulge that, particularly."

"Private about her life, I expect."

"Being an only child may have had something to do with it. Of course, I had her late in life and already had my own career. Her father did, too. We were busy, but we made as many school plays and music recitals and hockey games as we could. We missed some. Well, that's to be expected, isn't it? But we tried. No one could fault us for that. So I suppose Janet found it simpler to keep things to herself, or confide in her friends."

"Did she have a diary? Many girls do. It would be a natural outlet for her, kind of like talking." To parents who weren't always there, he wanted to add, but didn't.

"I never heard her mention one, and there was never one on her Christmas list. She could have bought a notebook, though."

"Well, maybe she was just a private person."

"A girlfriend or boyfriend usually takes on that

role, I believe."

"Did she have a close girlfriend?"

"In primary school, but we moved around, either for my husband's work or for mine. She never formed another close attachment with a particular girl after that."

"And she has a current fiancé and a former boyfriend."

"Yes. I am quite taken with her fiancé, Myles Tyson. I-I'm sorry he had to go through losing her."

"And the former boyfriend, Tom Murray?"

Nora hesitated, as if carefully choosing her words. "No warm and cuddly feelings for him. I don't know why I never liked him much. Just one of those vague feelings, you know?"

McLaren nodded, all too familiar with unexplained reactions.

"It's not because he was named in her will, either. She named a few friends and organizations in it, including me. There was just something I didn't like."

McLaren was beginning to get that feeling, too. He thanked her and rang off.

****

Tom Murray's first reaction on seeing an ex-cop on his doorstep was surprise. It changed to trepidation, which emanated from being asked if he had been Janet Ennis' boyfriend.

"Why do you want to know?"

McLaren thought the man could have been a construction worker. Or a firefighter. Or a boxer. Any profession requiring shoulder and arm muscles. Not height, particularly, though the man stood nearly as tall as McLaren's six foot-plus frame. But strength. Light on the balls of his feet, with the reflexes of a cat and the darting eyes of a criminal, McLaren noticed. He mentally put Tom in the amateur boxer league.

"I'd like to ask you a few questions about Janet's death." McLaren kept his voice even.

The town of Bakewell stretched and yawned and roused itself from sleep as McLaren waited on Tom's doorstep. Several roads west of Tom's residence cars and trucks threaded their way through Matlock Street and King Street, around the traffic circle, and then onto Rutland Square and over the bridge or else onto Granby Road to the car parks. The town center stirred with pedestrian traffic, too—shoppers making for the supermarket or other retail shops. Or residents calling in at the town hall or library. McLaren knew Bakewell well enough to know that this traffic was just the beginning of the non-ending stream. The town was big on tourists' lists.

A car's motor sounded nearby, followed by the yap of a dog. McLaren's stare never left Tom's face.

Evidently sensing the man before him wasn't going to leave, Tom said, "Why? What questions?" He rolled up the sleeves of his shirt—a light blue pin stripe with button-down collar—and finished tucking in his shirttail. He obviously had just woken, with his damp, dark hair and morning stubble darkening his face. He squinted into the low-lying sunlight already warming the air, then shielded his eyes as he looked at McLaren. "What's going on? All that was five years ago. The cops have already been through it all. It doesn't do any good to dredge it up again. Only brings back hurtful memories and opens old wounds."

"Both of which you have, evidently."

"Well, sure. Yeah. Everyone knows that. Her mum, her friends, her fans. I guess even the manager of the club where she used to sing a lot knows that. I didn't keep in the background."

"I wouldn't expect you to, being her boyfriend. Had you two been engaged?"

"We were talking about it. Did all the preliminary stuff. You know—decide where we would live, how our careers would mesh, philosophy on bringing up kids... All the usual."

"But you never were officially engaged."

"No. What's this in aid of? Why's Nora stirring up everything again?"

Again McLaren got the half-hooded, half-skeptical stare, implying Tom didn't quite believe Nora was behind this.

"You can ring her up if you don't believe I've got her blessing on this," McLaren said. His mobile vibrated in his back pocket but he ignored it. "You need her number?"

"I've still got it, thanks. So why are you asking around about the fire? I thought it was all done with."

"Just a few questions still unanswered. You helped with the construction of her artist's studio, I understand."

Tom nodded, his gaze still on McLaren.

"You helped her move her things in, too."

"What's wrong with that?"

"Nothing. It's commendable. I wonder if you recall what she kept in the studio."

"What she *kept* in it? Like..."

"I don't need a detailed inventory. That'd be impossible. Just a general idea would be helpful. Did she have anything she especially valued? Or a small safe, perhaps?"

"Nothing like that, no. She had a filing cabinet, but that held nothing of real value. Just bills for art supplies, letters from gallery owners. That sort of thing."

"When did you and Janet part ways?"

"Now, what kind of question is that? That's none of your business, McLaren."

"I ask merely to understand the time frame."

Tom wiped the back of his hand across his lips. "June. We broke up in June."

"A few months before the fire, then."

"Yeah. Why?"

"Were you still friendly?"

"Well, we weren't as matey as we had been—who would be after a breakup?—but we didn't send each other hate mail, either."

"Did you still go to hear her sing?"

"Not at first. I was still hurting from being dumped."

"She broke it off, then."

Tom's gaze raked McLaren sideways. "Yes. I didn't believe it at first. Well, it sounded like a joke. She realized she really didn't love me and didn't want to marry me and she'd found someone else. It hurt."

"It would."

"I didn't want to see her again or have anything to do with her. I used to flip the newspaper page fast if I saw her photo in the entertainment section. I didn't want the reminder that we'd been friends. But a month or so later…well, I had accepted it. You have to, don't you, if you want to retain your sanity."

"You go to her singing gigs, then."

"Some. Sure. She was a smashing singer. Even if we weren't headed to the altar I couldn't deny she had a super voice."

McLaren forced a lyric of one of Janet's songs from his mind. He had to concentrate on his job. "Where were you the time Janet died?"

The question caught Tom off guard, as McLaren had intended.

"You don't suspect me of her death, do you? We loved each other. I wouldn't harm her."

"I'm just asking a question."

"Well, it's a hell of a question. I was at a concert. I can't prove it, but I was. With some friends, so you can ring them up if you need confirmation. It was at one of the clubs Janet used to sing at." He gave McLaren the name of the club. "You want names and phone numbers?"

"Maybe later. Were you and Janet friendly enough that she'd ask you over for after concert drinks or dinner or anything?"

"No. She may have done, but I would've felt uncomfortable. You know how it is. That was a part of her life she shared with her good friends. I didn't want to intrude."

"But you two had been good friends."

"Sure, but you have to cut the cord sometime. She couldn't keep on having me over. That'd be like we were still together again."

"You never went to her house, then, after your break up."

Tom shook his head and stuffed his hands into his jeans pockets. "I struggled a lot with that, wanting to be included like I had been when we were going together, but realizing she had someone else in her life. That would have hurt me more than anything, to be at a house party and see this new bloke with his arm around her. It would've killed me."

"Were you aware at the time that you had been named a beneficiary in Janet's will?"

If McLaren thought the statement would evoke shock from Tom, he was mistaken. Tom nodded, said in a rough voice that she had told him about it and that he had tried to talk her into changing it.

It was McLaren's turn to ask why.

"Because," Tom said, his words rushing, "if anything would happen to her, I'd be suspect for having caused it so I could get my portion of the money."

"Why would you think anything might happen to her? Had she some disease, like cancer?"

"No. Nothing that I know of. But there was that death threat—"

"When did she receive that?"

"In June, I believe. Somewhere around then, at any rate."

"In what form did it come? A phone call, or a letter, email..." If it had been a mobile phone, there would be a phone number Jamie could trace for him.

"Letter. Kind of old fashioned, with the message spelled out in words cut out of a magazine or newspaper." His upper teeth pulled at his bottom lip. "I guess the bloke figured out that phone calls and emails can be tracked."

Bloody bad break for our side. "What did the letter say? Do you know how many she got?"

"I saw only the first one. It said 'Pay Up or Die,' or

something like that. There may have been others...I don't know. We broke up a few days later."

And you were conveniently out of the way, McLaren thought, staying in the background because you didn't want to see her with another guy.

"I asked her what it meant," Tom said, "but she just laughed it off and said it was a game a chum and she played."

"Do you think that was true? You knew Janet."

"Yeah, I knew her, but I couldn't tell if she was telling the truth. She didn't seem bothered, at least around me."

"What did the message refer to? Why should she pay someone? Had she done something in her past that was, shall we say, shady or might cause her embarrassment now?"

Tom shrugged. "If there was, I didn't know about it. But I guess she could have paid off the demand without too much trouble. And keep up her lifestyle."

"And without her altering her will, I assume"

"You'll have to ask her lawyer. I've no idea. I just knew I didn't want any part of being a beneficiary. It made me nervous."

"She was fairly wealthy, then," McLaren said, the astonishment evident in his tone.

"Maybe not by film star or sports star status, but she had money."

"What are we talking about, then?"

"From what she said, I reckoned I'd get around ten thousand pounds."

McLaren left, thinking maybe that had been enough to kill for after all.

Sitting in his car, McLaren looked at the caller ID display on his mobile. While he'd been talking to Tom, his friend Jamie Kydd had called. McLaren punched the Missed Call option and seconds later asked Jamie what was up.

"Not the jig, if that's comforting," Jamie said. McLaren could hear the warmth of friendship in it.

"So, why the call? You've learned something, I gather."

"Nothing to win itself a headline in *The Sun*, but something interesting."

"Stop toying with me. It's not your strong suit."

Jamie laughed. "Do you know the names of the beneficiaries in Janet's will?"

"Her mother and father, I assume. Her former boyfriend Tom Murray had been, though I'd think in three months she would have changed it."

"What do you mean?"

"She and Tom parted ways in June and she took up with a new bloke in August. They were engaged. She lived through most of the month of September, so she had those three months after dropping Tom Murray and before her death to change her will. You're not telling me fiancé Myles Tyson isn't named."

"Seems odd any boyfriend or fiancé would be named for just this reason. Who's so certain before a marriage that you're going to stay on terms good enough to warrant inclusion in a will? That's bloody major, Mike. I don't know anyone who names their friends in their will."

"You're in mine."

"I, uh...am I?" Jamie broke off, startled by the information. "Thanks. But that's different. We're just friends, not potential spouses."

"Implying that a person keeps his friends throughout his life but significant others may come and go."

"Could do. Anyway, what I called to tell you is that, besides former love interest Tom Murray, she also included her former catering business helper, Sean Fallon. Interesting?"

"She *was* spreading the wealth around, wasn't she?"

"Wish she would've spread some my way."

"If wishes were horses…"

"Okay, okay. But perhaps the most interesting part is that Sean Fallon is a convicted criminal."

"You're joking."

"Oh, nothing like murder, Mike. Don't get excited."

"Lovely."

"A bit of burglary."

"Not much for him to steal at the catering co but a few copper saucepans, I guess."

"As I said, Mike, interesting, eh?"

"You're sure this is the current will."

"I got it from Nora. The inclusion of Sean should tell you it's legitimate."

"Won't be if there's a later one. Did you check somewhere besides with Nora?"

"It's current, Mike. She said that's how the lawyer read it and that's how Janet's estate was dispersed. Don't worry."

"I'm not worried, Jamie, just puzzled. Why would she add her—you said former helper? 'Former' because she died, you mean?

"'Former' because that's exactly it. She fired him."

McLaren rubbed his forehead. A headache threatened somewhere behind his eyes. It was too early in the day for this. "When did she fire Sean? Do you know why? Got addresses for me?"

"I thought I was going to be lauded for handing you this much info. Instead, you come after me with more questions."

McLaren heard the thud of a heavy ceramic mug being set down and a piece of paper rustling, then an emphatic tap, as though Jamie flicked the paper to keep it upright.

"Right," Jamie said, once again ready to talk. He read off Sean Fallon's address. "A few more you might like…" He gave McLaren several more names and addresses. "That should hold you for the rest of the morning."

"Any idea from Nora why Sean's in the will?"

"Odd, isn't it? Nora doesn't know. She hadn't seen the beneficiaries until the will was read."

"I guess there was no reason for Janet to confide in her mother, no."

"I don't have the 'why' part of your answer, but Janet fired Sean in May of the year she died. Do anything for you?"

"Besides throw more smoke screens at me?" He leaned his head against the car's headrest and tried to untangle the quickly forming web. It threatened to wallow in that gloom.

"You've come through heavier smoke than this, Mike. This is just a small campfire."

"I think I need a Boy Scout, then. Why would she keep her former boyfriend on the list, and why *add* her former employee?"

"That's something else for you to think about over your tea."

****

Catering partner Helene Brogan sat opposite McLaren, stirring coffee as she considered his question. The rectangle of sunlight fell obliquely across her and the kitchen table, bringing out the texture of her silk blouse and the woven linen napkins at their place settings. He would have liked Helene's face to be illuminated also, for she sat with her back to the light and he couldn't read her expressions. But for now, he had no choice. If her story didn't ring true he'd talk to her again…and he'd be looking at her in full light.

Helene laid the teaspoon on the saucer, picked up the coffee cup and took a sip before asking McLaren why he wanted to know about Sean Fallon. "That's ancient history in our business, Mr. McLaren." Her eyes suggested a bit of amusement. "I don't even know where he is."

"The circumstance of his firing is what I'd like to know right now, Ms. Brogan. Did you or Janet Ennis actually dismiss him from his job?"

"Janet did. Although she and I were partners, Janet had ultimate control. She had the lion's share of the stock, had put most of the money into the business, and more or less took me on board when she was already knee-deep in setting up the company. We hadn't opened for business yet, but she'd done the preliminary work of getting financing, the building and equipment. So it was only right that she had the final say in everything."

"Were you consulted about Sean's dismissal?"

"Oh, yes. We talked things over any time there was a business decision, even down to whether or not we should take on a particular catering job, if she thought it borderline."

"Borderline?"

"If we'd have enough time to do it properly due to the number of guests or food required or location. Things like that. Janet wasn't a dictator. We discussed most things."

"Including Sean Fallon's dismissal."

"Yes."

"Were you comfortable with her decision? Or did you want Sean to remain? What type of work did he do for you?"

Helene shrugged, not looking very concerned. "We originally employed him to help with the heavy things—lugging tables, the pots with the cooked food, boxes of decorations. Those types of things."

"But he migrated into other work, I take it."

"He still did most of the heavy lifting and carrying. He was eighteen, I believe, and quite strong. But he showed such an interest in the actual cooking that we eventually let him do prep work."

McLaren glanced around the room. It held the professional grade equipment of a serious cook: heavy-gauge pots and pans, steel utensils, a sturdy mixer, and wicker baskets marked with their contents of parchment paper, biscuit cutters, thermometers, kitchen torch, pastry mats and brushes, tart tampers, sauce syringe... He shifted his position so he avoided the gleam of sunlight on the scale, and look again at Helene. "Prep work...slicing and dicing?"

"Yes. Also things like making sauces and stock.

Anything that's basic for recipes."

"He was content with that?"

"I believe so, though I think he made noises about one day being a chef and opening his own restaurant. I don't know if he did that. We lost touch after he left our company." She took a sip of coffee and wiped her lips on her napkin. "Well, I had no reason to keep up with him. Not that I'm not interested to know if he's in culinary school, but Sean and I weren't exactly mates."

"Just the hired help." McLaren felt like adding something derogatory, but he let it pass.

"Yes, but more talented."

"Some brains to his brawn, then."

"Yes."

"How did Sean apply for the job?"

"Pardon?" Helene blinked, her eyelashes catching the sun and throwing shadows across her blue eyes.

"Did you know him? Was he a friend of a friend? Did you advertise for help, maybe go to an employment agency?"

"Oh. I see." She turned her head slightly as she replaced the cup on its saucer, and kept her focus on it. "I don't quite know how he came to us. Janet just announced one day that she'd found a young man to help in the kitchen."

"You didn't know him, then."

"Why, no! What an odd thing to ask. I'd not met him until his first day of employment."

"So, since Janet did the hiring, you didn't know him or his...background." He wasn't sure if he should bring up Sean's past conviction of burglary, but he could always mention it later.

Helene picked up the spoon and again stirred her

coffee. Her voice was slightly muffled, turned as she was from him. But the words were distinct. "No. She just mentioned that Sean was a young, strong lad, enthusiastic to get into the trade, and that he'd begin work on the following Monday." Turning her face toward McLaren, she added, "He certainly lived up to my expectations. It was nice to have the kitchen help. And he was a pleasant young man."

"So you all worked well together, then."

"Oh, yes. That is, on the whole."

"What was wrong?"

"Nothing major. I just meant, well, you know how it is when you're up against a deadline and working in confined quarters. You sometimes get on each other's nerves and little squabbles ensue. But it was never anything major and it never lasted. We didn't carry over our tiffs to the next day."

"Clean slate each time, eh?"

"Of course. Life's too short—and the company was too small—for ongoing tiffs. It would not have been pleasant working conditions for anyone."

"What were you doing when Janet died?"

She answered the question quickly, evidently remembered from the original investigation. "Home, doing errands, fixing supper for the hubby. The usual things of life. Why? Do you suspect me?"

"I'm just gathering information right now. Did Sean and Janet get on, do you know?"

"Not best mates or mother and son, but well enough. She liked him, thought him bright. There were never any problems as far as I know."

"So what brought on Sean's dismissal?"

"I really can't say."

McLaren exhaled and pushed his empty coffee cup from him, then leaned his forearms on the tabletop. "Try."

"I mean, I don't know."

"Janet didn't tell you why she was letting Sean go?" McLaren snorted, the disbelief evident in the way he pulled in the corner of his mouth. "No offense, Ms. Brogan, but I find that hard to believe. You, as a partner—no matter if you were junior, silent, or equal—should have been told. Or if not, surely your curiosity would have compelled you to ask. Walking into work one day and not finding Sean would have brought on a question, I'd think."

"I did ask, certainly. But all Janet said at that time was that he'd done something inexcusable at our last affair."

"Which event was that?"

"A wedding reception. The bride's mother made a big stink about the mishap, threatened a lawsuit. The usual tirade. Honestly, I think it was just an excuse to get something out of the whole thing, to get back some of the money they'd poured out for the ceremony and reception."

"Money heals any wound, repairs any problem."

"That's about it, isn't it? She finally told me later. Personally, I didn't think it that big of a mishap, but evidently Janet was of a different mind, so she let Sean go."

"And Sean's inexcusable mishap?"

Helene's voice rose, screeching with indignation. "He poured a pot of cream sauce into one of the steam pans."

"One of those two-part pans that has hot water in

the lower, larger one?"

"Yes. The pan of shrimp-and-beef was supposed to be placed over that water bath, so the bottom pan holding just the hot water was sitting on the table. Sean, for some reason, poured the cream sauce directly into the hot water. It was sad, but not the end of the world. Some sauce splashed onto the white tablecloth, but I dabbed at it with a wet cloth and got it out. But of course we didn't have the sauce for the dish it was to go with. I doubt if anyone but the woman was aware of that. The dish was perfectly good without it."

"Was the bride's mother the only person who was vocal about it? I suppose she complained immediately, not later after the reception had finished."

"She let us know her feelings right then, yes. Janet, however, waited until we had returned to the shop before firing Sean. I don't know how she did it—she took him into her office, away from everyone else. I thought that a decent thing to do, not berate him or fire him in front of all of us. Sean came out of the office first, Janet right behind him. He had no expression on his face, just kind of dazed. He walked right past me, didn't say anything or look at me. Didn't say a word to any of the other employees, either. Just pitched his white jacket into the laundry bin and left. That was the last I ever saw him."

"Did you hear any yelling or words coming from the office when he and Janet were in there?"

"No, Mr. McLaren. No argument, no threats, no slamming of the door. When I found out later, I was surprised he had taken his dismissal so well and so quietly. He just walked out like it was any other day and he'd be back tomorrow and we'd see him again."

McLaren wondered if Janet had seen Sean later, only hadn't lived to tell Helene about it.

Chapter Fifteen

"I'll give you one point for finding me." Sean Fallon watched McLaren pull out the chair and sit down before continuing. "Though I'm not hiding, Matlock is still rather large to go knocking on doors to see if I'm behind any one of them. So I suppose all it took was looking me up in the phone directory. Still…" He eyed McLaren again, a smile half formed on his face. "You needed my name and town. That's worth another point."

"That's more than many folks give me." McLaren leaned back in the chrome and leatherette chair, his left hand resting on the round curve of the cold metal. The tubular chair's design matched the style of the lounge— 1960s modern, left over from the Carnaby Street and the Mod movement influence. Hand-me-downs, wondered McLaren, or preference? He angled himself in his chair so that his shadow did not block Sean's face, and asked again how he'd come to be fired.

The story mimicked Helene's version, even including the irate mother of the bride. McLaren commiserated with Sean, adding that he must have been angry with Janet for letting him go.

"Not at first." Sean jiggled his right foot as though he were trying to dislodge it from his ankle.

"But later on?"

"Yeah. That night and the next day it hit me. I was

without a job, had no connections to get me another one, had no other skills—" He broke off, and McLaren expected a comment about the burglary conviction.

But nothing came. McLaren let the silence build, a composition in patience and relaxation. Like a priest waiting for a confession. Or a copper expecting a declaration of guilt. "I'd be madder than hell."

"Yeah, well, I was after I thought about it a bit. When Janet fired me, it didn't really sink in. I think I was stunned, to tell you the truth. It came so quick, you know. But when I got home that night and realized I had no job to go to on Monday, well, I blew up. Well, who wouldn't, as you said? It's damn near impossible to get a job at eighteen when you've no…work experience." He swallowed, gazing at McLaren from the corner of his eye. The man remained impassive so Sean went on. "I thought my future was set, you know. I'd been working for the company for five months, since January. I got a nice place—nothing fancy, just a bed-sitter. Still, it was mine, you know?"

McLaren nodded. Those one-room flats that made do as your bedroom, living room and kitchen were symbols of poorer days—the student, the struggling artist, the transient. A hot plate was usually provided, along with a lumpy upholstered chair, small table and a reading lamp. Better than sleeping rough on the street, but only just.

Sean continued. "I had a few quid saved up but that wasn't gonna last me long. Not with inflation and the general cost of living. I panicked at first. I remember slamming things around in my place. Well, I was angrier than hell and I had a right to be. I needed that job."

"Where were you living then?"

"What?"

"At the time of your employment with Janet, where were you living?"

"Here in Matlock, but in a different section of town. Farther north." He named the area, then asked, "Why?"

"You think Janet was over the top with her decision?"

"I don't know. That night and the next day I thought so. I mean, it was a damned cock-up. She's so perfect she never made a mistake?" His voice had taken on the rough edge that comes from anger and feeling picked upon.

"I don't think that was the issue right then."

"So I misunderstood. So I'm an idiot. You'd think the world was coming to an end. And that damned woman…" His lips flattened against his teeth as he breathed heavily through his nose.

"Weddings and receptions are usually nerve wracking. You can understand the bride's mother wanting things perfect, can't you?"

"It was one stupid batch of white sauce, for God's sake! Who's gonna miss sauce on their chicken?"

"If the sauce went with the chicken, they might. What was it?"

"Chicken cordon bleu. It was to have had a nice cream sauce accompanying it. It's made with white wine and cheddar."

"Sounds good."

"Those people got on very well without the sauce. It was a damned mistake!"

"But Janet reacted out of proportion, you're

saying."

"Like she'd never made a mistake in her life. Like that bride's mother was gonna kill her. If I knew where the berk lived I'd have put her out of her misery."

"You didn't go back a few months later and take care of Janet, did you?"

As though coordinated, Sean's mouth and eyes flew open, giving him the look of a marionette. He uttered half detectable sounds, coughed, then snapped, "I never did anything to Janet Ennis. Never! If I'd have wanted to do something, I would've punched her out that day in her office."

"You told me you weren't that angry right then, that it took you until that night and the following day to realize your anger."

"Well, yeah, sure. I mean, when I thought about it and it dawned on me that I had no income." He shut his mouth, causing a 'pop.'

"So, did you think about it that night? Stew about it, get angrier by the minute, and then decide to do something to her?"

Sean slammed his palm down on the table top, causing the small battery operated clock to jump. "I didn't touch that damned woman. I didn't want to get into trouble. I've had enough trouble in my life. I knew where it would lead and I didn't touch a hair on her head. Not that I didn't want to, but I didn't do a thing. Anyway, I was let go in May. She died in September. You think I'm gonna wait four months to top her if I hated her? I wouldn't have gone that long to deprive myself of the pleasure of feeling her neck between my hands."

****

As long as I'm talking to business associates, McLaren thought, glancing at the addresses he'd written down on his query sheet, I may as well deal with the pianist of her vocal group. Get all the tears and grief over with this morning.

He turned the key in the ignition, glanced again at Sean Fallon's residence, and eased the car away from the curb. Sean had moved up in the world since his bed-sitter days, residing now in a two up/two down dwelling in a nicer section of Matlock. Nice for him and his wife, McLaren thought. Lounge and kitchen downstairs, two bedrooms upstairs—a bit of privacy and still giving them a bit of space. He realized Sean's current residence was a fifteen-minute drive from Janet's former house, but the bed-sitter address was closer by a handful of minutes. Maybe not significant for some things, but if you needed to get home quickly from a murder… McLaren shelved that idea for the moment and headed toward Buxton.

The A6 was crowded with Wednesday morning drivers, cars, lorries, and farm vehicles making up the procession crawling north. Sunlight, ochre-hued and warm, lit up the landscape beneath a blue sky. A fringe of white and gray clouds draped themselves along the western horizon. The hint of rain did not affect McLaren's mood, and he rolled down the window and took in deep breaths of the warm, grass-scented air. He punched the 'play' button of his CD player and immediately the lyrics to "When Morning is Breaking" filled his car. He threw back his head and sang along.

When morning is breaking
O'er mountain and dale,
And sunlight illumines

Our home in the vale
Fresh, soft balmy breezes,
The lark's thrilling lay,
Are heralds foretelling
The gladness of day.

He passed a tractor as he came up to the turn off for the B5055 and took the smaller road wanting to avoid the traffic in Bakewell. The September sunlight glinted off the hood of his car and threw reflections onto the yellowing grass nodding at the road's edge. The second verse of the song started and McLaren's mood shifted with the lyrics.

When ev'ning is closing
On mountain and dale,
And darkness o'ershadows
Our home in the vale.
The field flowers drooping,
As fast fades the light,
Give warning foreboding
The sadness of night.

****

The ancient village Monyash, with its fine stone pub bathed in the lemon-hued sunlight, sprang up on his right. The area for the most part sprawled open and sun drenched over the rolling land of the High Peak District, Derbyshire's vast acreage of mountains, caves, streams, dales and forests. The sinkholes and pitch-black caverns belonged to another part of the Peak and always filled him with uneasiness. As the song's second verse suggested, he felt that foreboding at dusk, when inky shadows emerged from their retreats and smothered the land in their claustrophobic embrace. Not that he didn't like the night—he did when he was in an open expanse or with someone. But he understood the lyrics. Night held him in its spell and whispered of something out there, gave him the sense of soaring among the stars but being lost and alone. If out after sunset he constantly had to assure himself that he'd be fine.

Traffic on the A515 into Buxton was heavier but he made good time and soon turned onto Dan Wilshaw's street. The man lived on Hardwick Square South, a residential area of ancestral tree-bracketed streets, tall houses and mossy stone walls. On the eastern side of the High Street, McLaren realized as he slowed his car in front of Dan's house. On the other side of town from Charlie Harvester's place. The memory of that June night when he had broken into Harvester's house flashed upon his mind, filling him with the mixture of anger and resentment that cropped up when he thought of the man. But McLaren had accomplished what he had had to do, and Harvester, evidently, had been none the wiser to McLaren's burglary.

Don't know why he would be, McLaren thought as he turned off the car's motor and checked the house address. Thinking was not the man's strong suit. The berk had struggled through police training, getting by on his father's famous name and tacit strong-arm threats from that exalted rank. A smile flashed across McLaren's face as he remembered his satisfaction from the rose bush incident, then he was out of his car and ringing Dan's doorbell.

Dan Wilshaw—blond, blue-eyed and over average height—sat McLaren in the front room, disappeared into the kitchen, and minutes later emerged with a pot of hot coffee, chocolate biscuits, and a ready recital of the items usually located in Janet's artist's studio.

"It's not such a strange question," Dan reassured McLaren, handing him a mug of coffee and then sitting back in his chair. Although in his early forties, Dan's face held the worry lines and cracked skin of someone older. Or someone who spent much of his time outdoors. Which McLaren knew Dan didn't, being a pianist and recording engineer. Still, there were always hobbies that would take him outside. McLaren put Dan's late-fifties appearance down to smoking and the hard life of a musician, and got out his pen and notebook.

"I know you might not recall her artist's studio," McLaren said. "Five years is a long time for something like this, but any recollection would be helpful."

"So you are convinced it's arson, then." He flicked his cigarette ash onto a convenience ashtray and studied McLaren as he glanced around the room.

The ceilings were tall, as befitted the older style of the building, with ornate, white plasterwork visually joining the ceiling to the walls. Potted plants capped white painted radiators, bringing a bit of dimension to the floral wallpaper. The furniture, McLaren noted, was as ornate as the plasterwork. Museum quality. Surely family heirlooms and not auction purchases.

"I'm not convinced of anything, arson or otherwise," McLaren said, answering Dan's implied question, "except that I think Janet's case needs to be reevaluated."

"But you think there's a strong possibility of it."

"It's what the police think that's more important…if they'll do anything about it. Do you recall where you were that day?"

"Engraved on my memory, as the saying goes. I was out with my wife. We dined at a restaurant because I had the night off. A rare treat when most nights are filled with gigs. I didn't hear about Janet until the next day."

"How? Who told you?"

"I heard it from Myles. He told me he'd arrived at her house to find the police and fire service there. I was sick about the news. Myles could hardly string three words together into a coherent sentence, but he finally told me what had happened. I don't know how he kept his sanity through it all."

"Do you remember anything she had in her studio?"

"Besides the usual artist's supplies—you know, canvases, wedged stretchers, easels, paints and brushes. Well, that was about it. She had some bits of furniture. A sofa, desk, filing cabinet and a chair. A hot plate and a small fridge so she could make tea or something light to eat when she was there for an all-day session. Photographs, of course." He took a puff of his cigarette, swallowed the smoke and then exhaled into the air above them. "I think that's it. Nothing out of the ordinary, I shouldn't think."

"The photographs…what were those?"

"Oh, scenery, mostly. She'd drive around the Peak and snap scenes she wanted to paint. Then, back in the studio, she'd either do a watercolor or a pen and ink drawing of them. That was her specialty, watercolor."

"Did she use that as a place to rehearse her music?"

"If she did, it wasn't with me. I can't speak for the other group member, but I wasn't included. We'd rehearse in her house. We had more space there. She kept the sound equipment in her house, in a back room that we used for rehearsals. It was out of the way and we could keep our music there, too. The art studio wouldn't have held all that. It was too small."

"She have a piano, then?"

"Certainly. She was a singer and she practiced on her own so that when we'd have rehearsals she'd be up on her material. She enjoyed accompanying herself. She also liked the two piano sound. Like Ferrante and Tischer or someone. She had a drummer, which made a solid foundation for the pianos. But a bit later she admitted to me that she realized quite quickly that she couldn't rehearse her singing and write songs *and* keep her keyboard up to excellence. So she opted to let me be the pianist of the group when Bruce left us. I must say, I thought it a wise move. That was a lot she was trying to do and eventually one thing would suffer. She was a professional in every sense of the word, never kept us waiting on her. She knew her music down to the smallest rest or breath mark, knew the workings of her piano, and had a superb ear and intuition for original arrangements."

"You didn't do those? As her pianist, I would've thought that would fall into your job."

"Oh, I suggested things, but Janet had the final say."

"How was she about that—demanding?"

Dan waved away a cloud of smoke, his gaze still on McLaren. "Not at all. She may have been our focus and reason for being, but she didn't think of the group as 'hers.' We were all equal. She needed me as a pianist and she needed Ian's bass."

"And he joined after she let Bruce go."

"Yes. He had one month with us before Janet died and we disbanded. Ian hadn't had any previous professional experience, but he wowed her during his audition. So, she took him on."

"Anyone else?"

"Just we three. Cozy little group."

"Tom Murray wasn't part of it, then."

Dan laughed, his head tilted back, his cigarette dangling between his fingers. When he looked again at McLaren, he said, "The only part of the group he was interested in was Janet. He had no ear for music, wouldn't know a Sousa march from a Brahms lullaby."

"I understood Tom went to the venues the group played, was a common fixture and supporter."

"He was a fixture, if you want to call it that. More like a leech. He clung to Janet as though she were his meal ticket. Maybe she was—I shouldn't assume. Just seemed to me he would've tried harder to learn the history of our music and such if he truly loved her."

"And he didn't."

"Naw. They were going together for over a year, as far as I know, and the clot still couldn't name any of the greats of the field. Didn't know the titles of any of Janet's songs, either. Now, you tell me. Does that sound like a man who's really in love with his girlfriend?"

McLaren agreed that it did present a conflicting façade.

"But—" Dan sniffed, crushing his cigarette in the ashtray "—I shouldn't judge others' relationships. Maybe she didn't mind, or she didn't want him that close. Several big name performers keep their entertainment and private lives separate. Gives them a slice of normality in their lives, I expect."

"You mentioned your impression that Janet might be handing money to Tom to live on. Do you have anything concrete to base that on?"

"Sorry, no. Just that several times she'd hand him a fistful of money. I saw fifty- and twenty-pound notes in the wad and he'd come back later with a new mobile phone or a pair of shoes or a watch. Things like that."

"Nice items."

"Nice, yes, and not cheap."

"Perhaps he repaid her. You know, later, when they were alone."

Dan shrugged and reached for his cigarette packet. He tore a match from the matchbook and lit it. "Could do, I expect, but I just wondered why he never had the money with him. Not even putting it on his credit card. You never know about people, do you?"

"Was she generous to others in her life?"

"I don't know to what extent, but she was. She'd always be there to help, whether financially or emotionally. That was the super thing about Janet—she might not have been religious, but she was spiritual and she believed in God. She worshipped in her own way and yet still believed in helping where she could. If you were down on your luck, she'd try to turn your luck around."

"Perhaps Tom was one of those. Down on his luck, I mean."

"I wouldn't know. I'd have thought if he had been, she'd be giving him something more basic than a mobile phone."

"Like dossing down at Janet's," McLaren suggested. He took a sip of coffee, waiting to see how the suggestion set with Dan.

"I never went into her bedroom area, so I can't say. But I have the impression he didn't sleep there. Or eat regularly there, either. I don't have any basis for this. It's just a feeling."

"Still, you were over there for rehearsals. You would've seen Tom's shoes in the front room, or a book of his, or maybe his toothbrush in the bathroom. Most people don't live that pristinely that they wouldn't have a few personal items scattered about, even if they were just there for a short duration."

"All I know is that I never saw anything like that."

"Was Tom there for rehearsals?"

"Never. I think it was some sort of rule or understanding he and Janet had. Janet didn't like any outsiders around while we rehearsed. My wife never sat in, and neither did Ian's girlfriend. Bruce never talked about anyone in the year and a half he was with us, so I don't know about anyone near and dear to him. She allowed no relatives in, either. Just a work session, which was fine with me. Outsiders would have wasted our time. And Janet was a stickler for punctual arrival so we could get on with our work and then leave."

McLaren closed his notebook, stood and pocketed the book and pen. "Sounds like a fairly normal life, whatever 'normal' is." He walked to the front door, Dan following. "If you think of anything odd or out of place in her studio, I'd appreciate it if you'd—"

"Dan?" The voice was feminine and came from the kitchen. A door thudded shut, several metal keys clattered onto a hard surface, the squeak of rubber on linoleum grew louder, a softer clunk like a fabric purse being placed on a worktop, and the conversation started up again, louder now that the speaker was nearing the front room. "Honestly, Dan, if that woman doesn't keep her dog fenced up—Oh!" Her sentence broke off as she saw McLaren at the front door. Her gaze shifted from him to Dan, silently asking for an explanation. Coming forward, she smiled. "I'm sorry. I didn't mean to interrupt. Are you coming or going? Would you like tea or something?"

"This is Michael McLaren," Dan said. "We've just had coffee, but thanks for the offer. My wife, Ruth, Mr. McLaren."

"I'm just leaving," McLaren said as she wrapped her hands around Dan's upper arm. "I was asking your husband about Janet Ennis."

"Janet? Why—haven't the police finished with that case?"

"They have, yes, but Nora Ennis has asked me to look into one or two discrepancies. She's not satisfied with the verdict."

"The verdict! Are you serious?" Ruth's voice echoed the astonishment obviously in her mind. "That was…what? Four years ago?"

"Five, and yes, she's serious."

Ruth sagged against her husband, looking like she needed his support. "Why did she wait all this time to start an inquiry? Or are we just hearing about it?"

"Did you know Janet, Mrs. Wilshaw?"

"Only superficially. She owned a catering company and I did a review of it once."

McLaren was clearly surprised. He had expected to hear about the musical trio. "Really? You write, then."

Ruth released her grip on Dan's arm and plunged her hands into the pockets of her jogging shorts. She mimicked Dan's height but was in better shape, her muscles toned from the jogging or other exercise. Her red hair glistened with perspiration at the scalp line, yet the curl still held. The slight, faint lines on the sides of her face suggested she wore sunglasses and ran a lot in the summer.

"My wife." Dan smiled at Ruth "My wife is a food critic. She writes a weekly column that appears in the newspaper."

"Oh, right." McLaren snapped his fingers. "Ruth Wilshaw. Sorry. You threw me for a minute. I didn't connect the names, nor did I expect to actually meet you."

"Especially when you're investigating a death." Dan pulled Ruth's hand from her pocket and clasping it.

"Everyone has to live somewhere, but you don't imagine you're going to meet someone famous."

Ruth laughed. "I'd hardly classify myself as famous, Mr. McLaren."

"Maybe not, but a lot of people follow your column regularly. Myself included. That should count for something."

"Well, it's nice of you to say, but I'm just a writer." She bent over and pushed the used ashtray to the other end of the coffee table. "Honestly, Dan, if you must smoke, and I wish you didn't, I'd appreciate if you'd empty the tray afterward. It's bad enough you inhale that stuff. But I don't care to."

"It's my fault," McLaren cut in. "We'd just concluded our talk and I was on my way out."

"I hope Dan was some help to you. It must be hard on Mrs. Ennis to be still feeling so bad after her daughter's death. Have you made any headway in your inquiry?"

"Actually, I've just started. Were you ever a visitor at Janet's house?"

"Once, I think. No...twice." She turned to Dan, the question in her eyes. "Twice, wasn't it, darling?"

Dan blinked, looking confused. "I'm afraid I don't—"

"Yes, it was twice. Those Christmas parties she had."

"Right. I'd forgot them." He addressed McLaren, his voice louder in his explanation. "Janet had the trio and their significant others over for Christmas Day...twice, as my wife said. Nothing elaborate like a sit down meal. More for drinks and appetizers and gift giving around the tree. It was nice, wasn't it?"

"Was Tom Murray there?" McLaren asked.

"Why, uh, yes. But just the Christmas before she died, that previous December."

McLaren nodded, aware of the September date of her death.

"They weren't together long enough to warrant the previous get-together."

"And Myles came along that summer."

"Yes. She...she wasn't around for that Christmas." Dan screwed up his face, the topic evidently distasteful.

Ruth chimed in, relieving the tense atmosphere. "Janet really did those parties very well. I thought she had a real gift for that. Her taste carried over into her catering business, you know, with exquisite table decorations and place settings. She did very well with her company."

"How did she find time to do both?" McLaren asked. The question, so casually uttered, elicited surprised looks from Ruth and Dan.

Dan stammered that he had no idea, and Ruth shrugged and said that was why she had her business partner, Helene.

"Were most of their catering jobs of a smaller nature so that Janet could leave the food preparation and other details to Helene?"

"I don't know much about her business," Ruth said. "But that's possible. I should think most of the events she catered were weekend affairs, such as wedding receptions and anniversary parties. She didn't need to be present at the actual event. After all, that was what she had servers for. She was involved with just the office part of it all, leaving the baking and cooking to her chefs. She worked a lot from home. Well, a good portion of her business came from online reservations. She could take a minute or two off from rehearsing to answer a computer inquiry, couldn't she, and still rehearse at home. And Helene would oversee the party. That always seemed such a brilliant way to combine both occupations." Ruth dusted her hands, freeing them of any clinging cigarette ash. "Anyway, I believe Janet did her music gigs at nights and weekends. So even though she was occupied, I doubt if the two overlapped. Still, she was busy, wasn't she?"

What's that phrase about the one-armed wallpaper hanger? McLaren thanked them and left.

Chapter Sixteen

"Darling, don't tell me you've come up with the money already." Helene's warm tones cooed into Sean's ear. "I *am* impressed. What's it been...a day? You *are* fast."

Sean wiped the back of his hand across his mouth. He'd just finished a beer, yet his throat still felt as dry as parchment. He needed another one, not only to relieve his thirst but also to steady his quaking hands. How could he cook if he couldn't grasp a knife? He tried clearing his throat and was aware of the raspy noise. He forced a swallow. "No. I don't have the money. I—you need to know something."

"If you've another idea about payment, I'm listening, dear."

Even with his heart thudding against his Adam's apple and eardrums, he curled his lips at her insinuation. He'd go to the cops before he'd wind up in her arms. "No. I—a man came here this morning."

"Is this something unique in your life?"

He heard the derision in her voice, the attempt to belittle him. The old anger simmered within him and he felt a tingling in his blood. Would it be better to tell the cops of her extortion attempt, or lull her along and deal with her afterward? He struggled again to swallow, this time hampered more by the anger constricting his muscles than from his thirst. His words came out clipped and short. "He's a cop. Actually, an ex-cop. He's asking questions about Janet's death."

The momentary pause on the other end of the phone told him that the information startled Helene. He walked into the kitchen and grabbed another beer from the fridge. The chink in her armor called for a celebration. "Did you hear me, Helene?" He couldn't resist twisting the knife in the wound.

"Uh, yes, dear. I, uh, just had to let the cat in."

"Didn't know you had a cat. When did you get him?"

"You don't know a lot of things, darling, but that doesn't prevent them from being." Her tone had returned to its smooth, unflappable quality. A clink of ice cubes against glass, an audible swallow in his ear, and she said, "Was his name McLaren?"

"Yeah. No. I don't remember. Yeah, it was. Shock it was for me. Why? You know him?"

"He came here, too, dear."

"Why? To ask you about Janet, too?"

"Yes. Janet's mother hired him to look into her death. At least, that's what he said. I suppose he could've lied, could've been from the insurance company or someplace. I didn't think Mrs. Ennis would stir things up again and get someone to nose around. It didn't sound authentic, so I had my misgivings about her and this McLaren."

"Surprise, Helene. I know she bloody well *did* hire him." Sean's usual caution had returned and he was ready to release his anxiety on anyone handy. "That's what he said when he was here. You think he knows anything?"

"About…"

"Knows anything about me. Us. Why's Janet's mum so worked up all of a sudden? Did this bloke go to her with some barmy story just to get some money out of her?"

"I think it was the other way 'round, dear. She came to him and employed him."

"Well, what's he know about us?"

"Nothing, if you keep your mouth shut."

****

"So, my wife mentioned me, did she?" Stuart Ennis leaned against the handle of his garden rake and glared at McLaren. "*Ex*-wife, I should've said. First thing she's probably got right in years. And how is the old idiot? Living in Bedlam yet?"

McLaren felt his jaw muscle tightening as he looked at the man. Bald, mustached and wearing wire-rim glasses, Stuart Ennis stood by the pile of leaves he had raked together. Other small mounds of leaves dotted his front lawn and a large bin liner sat by the garage door. McLaren could smell the scent of burning leaves coming from the back of the house, a residence in one of Buxton's older neighborhoods. Golden leaves littered the garden and the pavement beyond the stone wall marking the front of his property. The seventy-three year old looked to have his entire day mapped out for him if the side yards were as carpeted in leaves, McLaren thought. He watched a squirrel gather a mouthful of leaves and run up a tree trunk. "I got your name and address from Nora, yes. I want to ask you about your daughter's death."

If McLaren thought the subject would soften Stuart's demeanor, he'd have been wrong. Stuart picked up a fallen tree branch and threw it onto the leaf pile at his feet. "Why?"

"I'm looking into Janet's case and I thought you might be able to tell me something about that day."

"'That day' being your euphemism for the day she died, I take it." He spoke in unhurried beats, yet with a tinge of sarcasm in his voice. His reddish eyebrows were tinged with gray, and lowered as he glared at McLaren.

"I'm trying not to distress you, Mr. Ennis. The death of a loved one is usually hard to discuss, never mind it being the person's child."

"I've had five years to get over it, McLaren. If I'm not over it now, I never will be. Anyway, I don't know anything about it. You're wasting my time. Now, leave." He turned his back toward McLaren and drew another rakeful of leaves toward the pile.

"I would've thought you'd want to clear up the questions concerning your daughter's death, that you'd like to help me settle the circumstances once and for all."

"You'd think that, eh? Well, you'd be dead wrong. Now, out of here before I get my dog."

McLaren walked around to face Stuart. "You were Janet's father. You have no feelings for her? You don't care about how she died, whether it was an accident or murder?"

Stuart's voice was muffled from his bent over position. "The bloody hell I do not. I'd finished with her long before 'that day,' as you put it. I don't give a damn what happened. She died and it makes no difference to me how it came about. I'm just glad she's out of my life."

McLaren kicked the mound, sending the leaves

flying in all directions. He stepped toward Stuart and grabbed the man's nylon jacket, holding the fabric taut in his right hand while his left hand squeezed Stuart's upper arm. "Overflowing with parental love, aren't you?"

Stuart released his rake, letting it fall to the ground, and placed his hands on top of McLaren's. He twisted his lips into a sneer. "Yeah. Show me the rulebook that says I have to feel different."

"You know, Ennis, you're giving me an idea."

"Glad to hear you're not as dotty as Nora."

McLaren felt Stuart's fingers tighten and dig into his hands. The muscles contracted in slow yet steady increments, as though Stuart were trying to prove his strength. McLaren twisted his hand and brought Stuart's arm behind his back. He pinned Stuart against his own body, the sides of their heads touching, and whispered into the man's ear. "My idea is that you had something to do with the fire."

"What did I say about associating with Nora? You're daft, man."

"You just admitted you had no feelings for Janet, that you had brushed her out of your life before she died."

"So?"

"So, perhaps Janet wasn't far enough out of your life. Perhaps you made it a permanent departure. Huh? What about it?"

"You're insane. No one will believe you. I wasn't anywhere near her house."

"Convince me."

"I don't have to. The police have investigated the case. They've closed it. They're satisfied."

"I'm not." He tightened his hold on Stuart's jacket. "Tell me."

"You're not a cop, McLaren. I don't have to talk to you."

"No, you don't, but I thought a little chat would be nice. Clear any misconceptions I might have of your…sterling qualities."

"Won't the newspapers be over the moon to get my story, of how I was harassed and threatened by a much younger man? It'll make you a laughing stock and end your dabbling."

McLaren spun Stuart around so they were standing face to face. "I don't give a damn about the newspapers or your threat. I'm trying to get to the truth about your daughter's death. If it takes me walking over a few bruised bodies to get to it, or if I have to sit in the nick for assault, it means nothing to me. And there's always *my* side of the story, Stu. Can you imagine the headlines? 'Heartless husband hampers murder investigation'. Maybe 'Unfeeling father turns his back on daughter's death'. Or if you like this one better… 'Father unmoved by daughter's murder; Refuses to help find killer.' I rather like that, but I wonder which one will bring the most public outcry?" He let Stuart think about the implication for a moment before adding, "I believe it's worth your cooperation, don't you? As a concerned father, you will most likely agree with me." He released his grip on the jacket, dusted off the shoulder, and smiled.

"I wasn't at Janet's house that day, McLaren. I don't know what happened."

"How do I know you weren't at her house? I'm an awfully suspicious man, Ennis. As I said, convince me."

"All right, all right."

McLaren released his hold on Stuart's hand, and he rotated his arm, as though he were trying to waken his nerves.

"Talk to my daughter. She'll tell you."

"Your daughter." McLaren eyed Stuart, wondering if the man were suggesting attending a séance or mind reader.

"Don't know everything, do you, smart guy? Connie. Constance Long. My daughter by a..." He shrugged, his eyebrow raised. "Let's say Nora wasn't Connie's mother. She doesn't know about Connie, either. I prefer to keep it that way."

"You can remember so exactly that you were talking with Connie? Five years seems a long time to remember a conversation with someone on 28 September."

"I was talking to her. Believe me or don't."

"And where do I find your daughter?"

"In Temple Normanton. Off Church Lane, near the junction with Birkin Lane."

"How about a specific address."

"You can't miss it, McLaren. Biggest place in the village. Now, I've told you what you want to know, so bugger off." He turned his back, picked up his rake, and walked into the back garden.

****

The village of Temple Normanton sat on a hill to the south and slightly east of Chesterfield. There wasn't much to the place—a cemetery, a primary school, and an odd, fiberglass-constructed church. Perhaps the village was better known for what it lacked: shops.

McLaren turned off the B6038 and onto Birkin Lane. He passed the southern edge of the Grassmoor Country Park and minutes later turned left onto Church Lane.

The church of St. James the Apostle—a pale yellow thing that looked more like a can of beer split lengthwise than it did a church—and its cemetery took up the largest area on the lane, McLaren soon found out. He stopped his car at a nearby house, knocked on the door, and asked the resident if he knew Connie Long.

"Sorry," the man said, moving his pipe to the side of his mouth, "never heard of her."

"I don't suppose she's a new resident," McLaren suggested.

"Could be, but I don't know of anyone recently moved in. Best try the church. The vicar might know." He shut the door on McLaren's "Thanks."

McLaren found the vicar outside, near the low stonewall that enclosed the graveyard. Rather like a paper blowout, the man unbent from his weeding, wheezed slightly, and straightened up with the speed of a moving snail. Even standing upright, the vicar still had a hint of the curled-up party favor, as though not enough air had been blown into the paper tube to straighten it out and show the feather at the end. So he stooped slightly, a short, thin man with browned, wrinkled skin, looking like the sun and wind had dried him into a human raisin. He removed his work gloves, knocked them against his faded, brown trousers, and brushed a lank lock of hair back over the top of his head. As he tilted his head to look at McLaren, the sun glanced off the lenses of his glasses and, for an instant, obliterated his eyes. In that brief moment, McLaren thought the man looked more like a caricature than a person.

"May I help you?" The vicar swept his hand again over his hair. It was snow white and thick, like swan's down tossed by the breeze.

"Yes, thanks. At least, I hope so." After he explained that he was looking for Constance Long, the vicar pointed to the area behind the wall.

"Sorry?" McLaren shifted his gaze to the weathered tombstones. Was she squatting, weeding a plot?

"Connie Long. You want to see her grave, you said. She's in that section by that nearby pine. Do you need help to locate her?"

McLaren shook his head. "Sorry. I'm a bit confused. Connie Long...Constance. The daughter of Stuart Ennis who lives in Buxton." He paused, aware that he was rambling, aware that he sounded insane or mad. Glancing again at the row of lichen-dusted arches, he said, "I...perhaps I made a mistake. I thought Mr. Ennis visited his daughter here in the village."

"We have many visitors to the graveyard, Mr. McLaren. Some people bring flowers, others bring a small birthday cake. Some just come to talk. I don't discourage anyone from visiting their loved one."

"But Mr. Ennis led me to believe—"

"He comes here regularly to visit Connie. He's been coming since her death six years ago. Pity, that. Connie died so young. She was nineteen, I believe. Such a nice person, she was."

"She lived here in Temple Normanton?"

"Until her death. For one year. Not very long. Since she was eighteen or so. I don't know where she lived before that. Perhaps in Buxton, with Stuart and his wife. She moved here, and a year or so later Stuart arrived. He lived here for a while, even stayed on after Connie died. I always thought he remained because he had associations with Connie here, but he liked the village and the area, so I expect that's the reason he chose this as her resting place."

"How often does he come? Any particular dates?"

"Nearly each holiday. Christmas, in particular. Many times a year."

"Has he been here in September? I know it's a lot to ask of you, to remember something like that when you have so many folks coming."

"It's a small village and a small cemetery, Mr. McLaren. I've been here for longer than some of the cemetery residents." He smiled, and the sunlight again masked his eyes. He seemed to be masking the knowledge of God behind the lenses. "I know Mr. Ennis and I know he normally comes at Easter and Christmas and for Connie's birthday."

"When is that, if I may ask?"

"End of September. I don't know the exact date. Around the twenty-eighth or twenty-ninth, I believe. Around Michaelmas. Shall I look it up for you in the church registry?" He made a move toward the church but McLaren shook his head.

"No. That's fine. I doubt if anyone as caring and warm as Mr. Ennis would be mistaken about this. I must have misunderstood." He thanked the vicar and strolled back to his car. Stuart Ennis might be laughing at the moment, McLaren thought, but *he* would have that famous last, best one.

Late afternoon flowed into the open window of McLaren's car as he drove home. His house was in Somerley, hardly more than a speck on the map, nestled in the Hope Valley region north of the village of Castleton. He liked the area, picturesque and renowned for its caverns and mountains and wild streams. Lead mining, while giving employment to thousands of miners for centuries, had at last dwindled out and the mines were closed. He empathized with the miners, who had lost their livelihood, but he disliked the aftermath of mining and the unhealthy outcome of men and land.

He hunched his shoulders, trying to bring some relief to his sore muscles. Hunched over periodicals in the Chesterfield public library was not his idea of a fun hour, but he needed the background information of Janet's case. Now, with the details in his notebook, he was headed home to a cold beer and a hot dinner.

His watch showed just on to six o'clock and though it wasn't particularly late, he'd put in a full day. The beer and pork chop called to him and he realized how hungry he was when he drove past The Split Oak, the pub in Somerley. The aroma of fried fish and cider-baked potatoes settled on his tongue and he nearly parked in front of the pub's door. But he wanted to kick off his shoes, lie on the sofa and digest the day's information; he'd talked to five of Janet's acquaintances since yesterday—seven people if he counted the firefighter and her father. That got top priority besides figuring out whom he'd speak to tomorrow.

He turned off the main village road and soon was headed toward his house. The narrow lane, barely more than a black ribbon through the tans, yellows and crimsons of the autumnal landscape, threw back the day's heat and sunlight. Like a glossy black snake, he thought, staring at the road. Sleek and lazy in the warmth of the day.

His driveway came upon him before he realized it and he trod down on the brake pedal. The car's tires gripped the road, threw up a shower of dust, then slanted through the opening in the dry stone wall running along the length of his property. The sunlight, low on the western horizon, angled into his eyes and he held up his hand to shield his vision. When the shadow of a tree bough obliterated the light, he withdrew his hand.

In that instant he jerked the steering wheel hard to the left and braked his car on the grass alongside his driveway. For a second he thought the sun lay on the ground or at least reflected off something on his house. He stared out of his window, trying to understand what he saw. His driveway was on fire.

Chapter Seventeen

The improbability of the situation didn't hit him at once. But as the blackening mound cracked from a sudden eruption of flame, McLaren leapt from his car. He ran around to the front of his house, grabbed the nozzle of the garden hose, turned on the water spigot and raced back to the driveway.

Flames at least three feet tall blazed in the thickening dusk, casting gigantic shadows across the hard-packed gravel drive. The flames bobbed like a boxer, coming back stronger and stretching for the sky, as though wishing to join the dark gray sky with the quickly blackening debris at its base. The flames glared yellow and white, blinding in their brightness and the backdrop of the darkening land.

McLaren flooded the burning mound with water, aiming first at the fire's base and then spraying the top of the heap. The flames quivered and snapped at the deluge, as though screaming in their death throes. A finger of fire reached for McLaren as he redirected the water to that section. He stepped back, bending to avoid the flame, and soaked the mound until the water seeped from the rubble and pooled around his feet. He grabbed a stone, lay it near the smoldering remains and set the nozzle on the stone so that the jet of water pelted the heap. Then he ran to the tool shed in the back garden.

The doors banged and vibrated against the wooden

structure as he threw them open. McLaren yanked a rake from the tool rack on the wall and ran back to the dying fire. As he raked the burnt debris, tendrils of steam and smoke spiraled up from the still-hot remains. He pulled the charred residue away from the fire's center, spreading the ashes and chunks of debris in a wide arc on the drive. Then he tossed the rake onto the grass, picked up the hose, and wet down the smoky remains. It sizzled and hissed as the water hit hot spots, and the steam shone light gray in the light from the car's headlights.

McLaren spent several minutes alternately raking and watering the mound. When he was satisfied he'd extinguished the fire, he turned off the headlights and looked at the mess of ashes and water. No red spark winked at him. An occasional sigh as the fire breathed its last seeped into the stillness, but other than that, it lay black and dying at his feet.

McLaren turned off the water and recoiled the hose, laying it near the house foundation. After locking his car, he opened the kitchen door of his house and walked inside. As he laid the keys on the table, he glanced at his feet.

His shoes and lower portion of his trousers were sodden and splattered with ashes. Water oozed down his legs, into his socks, and seeped from his shoes. The floor was fast becoming a small pond.

He pulled off his shoes, socks, and trousers, wadded them into a bundle, and deposited them on the top of the washer. Then he picked out a change of clothes, went into the bathroom, showered and redressed. As he was toweling his hair dry, it hit him. For the fire to be burning as he drove into the driveway, the arsonist must have started it a minute or so before McLaren arrived home. The man must have been in the area, perhaps watching McLaren battle the blaze. Cursing himself for a fool, McLaren snatched a torch from the kitchen and dashed outside.

He walked around the house, playing the beam of the torchlight behind the bushes and clumps of flowers near the house foundation. Not that he expected the berk to be lurking there—if he ever had—but he needed the assurance that he had checked. He jogged over to the stone wall paralleling the road and searched along its base on both sides for several hundred yards. The other section of wall that ran perpendicular to the road harbored no one, nor did the far side of the tool shed. He snapped off the torch and stood in the twilight.

Had he just obliterated any footprints or clues at the arson scene, not only while he extinguished the fire but also while he searched the area? And the fire itself...he knew that the color of the flames and the smoke denoted the substance burning, whether accelerant had been used or if the fire was natural. Did that signify anything? He walked back to the house, poured out a beer, made himself a roast beef and cheese sandwich, and rang up Jamie.

"You've ruffled someone's feathers," Jamie said, his voice sounding more concerned than amused.

"Great. I called you up to hear what I already know."

"I'm just saying I don't want a repeat of this past June's case, that's all. Have you such a short memory?"

McLaren swallowed a bite of sandwich and muttered, "No. It's all too vivid." He glanced in the direction of the kitchen, half-expecting to see himself unconscious on the floor, where he had managed to drag himself after the beating.

"Then take it easy, for God's sake. Someone's upset with your investigation. I don't want to visit you in hospital." The other obvious visitation place he left unstated. "You have any suspicion who could have started the fire? Did it do any damage?"

"That's the odd thing, Jamie. Whoever set the fire chose the driveway where it would burn more or less harmlessly. If he was serious about this thing, why didn't he torch the tool shed or my house? That would've made a lovely blaze." He took a quick sip of beer. "Because he wanted to make a statement. The fire served to warn me, not physically threaten me."

"Very slight difference between a warning and a threat, Mike. But I agree that it would've been at a nastier location if this person seriously thought to harm you. I repeat—who have you talked to who might be threatened by your questions?"

McLaren stretched, suddenly overcome with fatigue. "Well, maybe five people, not counting Nora, the mother."

"Why not count the mother?"

Silence greeted Jamie's question as scenes of June's case flashed in his mind's eye. Why, indeed, not count Nora? If it had happened once... McLaren finished his beer and slumped into the sofa cushions. Besides, if the woman had bouts of confusion, if reality and fantasy were so mixed in her mind that she acted out her delusions or the past, it could very well have happened. McLaren sighed heavily, not liking where the case was heading. He said, "I don't want to think she's responsible, that's why. She's had a hard few years. She's trying to get to the truth about her daughter's death. Someone that determined, that devoted…well, I just can't consider her as my arsonist."

"That's the stupidest thing I've ever heard you say." Jamie's frustration and anxiety exploded into McLaren's ear. "That's first year probationer talking. No. It isn't. I'm mistaken. A first year cop wouldn't be that dumb. That's Dim-witted and Head-in-the-Sand talking. Thick as two planks and one sandwich short of a picnic talking. If it was anyone else—Dena or your sister or me—you'd be foaming at the mouth, telling us to open our eyes and see that Billy Hughes or Doctor Crippen or Fred West weren't the innocents they looked like. You'd be screaming at us that killers don't usually look like monsters." He took a breath and his exasperation seeped over the phone. "Was there time for anyone you talked to today to get to your house and set the fire? When did you finish up for the day?"

"A bit after teatime, I guess, though I didn't note the exact time. I interviewed those people, as I said, then had a late lunch and did some research in the Chesterfield library for a bit. Maybe an hour."

"Why Chesterfield? A bit out of your way, isn't it?"

"Janet's dad, uh, steered me to Temple Normanton, to confirm his alibi. Since I was there…"

"That library's as good as any, sure."

"After that I drove home."

"Could anyone have followed you? How would someone know where you live?"

"Well, I didn't hand out a card with my address on it," McLaren barked. "Give me credit for *some* intelligence."

"Not such a big concession. Even a moron has some intelligence." Silence wedged between them, and Jamie apologized, saying he hoped he hadn't strained their friendship, and added that his wife could supply McLaren with a long list of his other faults.

There was no response. After several more seconds, Jamie apologized again. "It's admirable to help people, Mike, but you need to think before leaping into the raging river. Your tunnel vision frequently obscures any thoughts for your own safety. And if you think that isn't bloody hard on us who are concerned for you—"

McLaren broke in. "I know. I'm an idiot at times."

Jamie snorted. "I don't know about being an idiot, Mike, but you're enthusiastic."

"Nice way of saying I'm a nit."

"I appreciate that you feel so strongly, that you're trying to right the original wrong, but you won't solve the case or endear yourself to your friends if you're severely hurt. Think about that before you throw yourself in front of a speeding bus."

"Why do Charlie Harvester any favors, right? He couldn't get rid of me while we worked together, so why should I delight him now with a lengthy hospital stay?"

"Shelving Harvester for the moment, do you think anyone could have followed you home, Mike?"

"I don't know. I suppose so." He started to reach for the beer mug, realized it was empty, then sank back into the sofa again. "Looking back, I didn't realize I was always so damned careful when I was in the job. You know, Jamie. That's drummed into us until it becomes second nature. But I was so damned—I don't know…happy, confident, optimistic—and submerged in singing along to the CD in my car."

"You weren't checking your rear view mirror as frequently as you normally do."

McLaren grunted and swung his legs onto the couch. "You do have a way with words, Jamie. I would've said I did a complete cock-up and deserved what I got."

"But it still doesn't explain how whoever it was knows where you live, Mike. Following you home implies the fire would be started when you were already snuggled inside your house, eating dinner, or sleeping. But that didn't happen. It was *already* burning when you drove up. Which means to have it blazing for your arrival, your friend already knew where you live." He let McLaren consider the implications before adding, "Who would know that? And don't say Nora Ennis. I assume she knows, at least."

"Yes, she does. But I can't imagine her giving anyone my address. Why would she? There's no need for her to do that."

"I'd be rich if I knew a lot of things. Well, it's something to keep you awake tonight. What else?"

"The color of the flames and the smoke."

"What about them—were they odd?"

"The fire burned primarily yellow and white. The smoke was thick and black."

"I assume you don't know what your lovely conflagration consisted of, what the arsonist burnt."

"I'll have a look in the morning. Poking about now, in the dark, won't get any answers. But no, I don't know, although yellow and white flames usually denotes a petroleum base, doesn't it?"

"Yeah. And black smoke."

"I guess he soaked whatever he used for the core of the fire with petrol or something similar."

"You might detect an odor, Mike. All of the petrol might not have burned off."

"Don't know what that will tell me, but you're right."

"When you poke about tomorrow, you might find some sort of timer device. That might tell you something more."

"What, like some rigged up gadget? A timer? God, I hope this berk isn't that sophisticated."

"Doesn't have to be that elaborate. I was thinking of a candle. He could have put it inside something, like a cardboard box to protect it from the wind, and set the thing in the middle of the combustible material. He then lit the candle and left, and when the candle burnt down far enough the cardboard ignited and that set off the fire. You don't need an Einstein for that."

McLaren didn't reply for a moment, his mind trying to recall something he'd heard. As the conversation became clearer, he sat up, swinging his legs to the floor, and leaned forward. His voice was low and tense. "He wouldn't have had to get here before me today, Jamie. He could have been here, waiting for me, and ignited the fire when he was sure that I drove into Somerley."

"But that doesn't make sense. You said the fire was burning when you drove into your driveway."

"It was. And the bloke could've been sitting safely in his car, laughing like a hyena as he watched me run around."

"Then how—"

"Maybe my arsonist wasn't someone I talked to today. Maybe it was from the group I talked to yesterday."

"Then someone could've followed you home yesterday."

"Yeah. And now knows where I live and fixed this warm reception for my return home today."

Chapter Eighteen

Jamie stuttered, "Uh, yeah. Sure. Makes sense. You were trailed to your house yesterday." He broke off briefly. "Th-the idea of some sinister, dark clad person tracking you isn't exactly spirit-lifting."

"I'm not saying that was how it was done," McLaren returned. "Just that it would explain it."

"Did you see anyone running away when you drove up?"

"Well, no." McLaren yawned and stretched again. "He could've been along the hedgerow by that time. Besides, it's amazing how an inferno attracts your attention."

"I believe it. Did you look around for tire tracks or trampled vegetation?"

"That wasn't exactly on my mind, Jamie. After putting out the fire, it was too dark to explore. I'll tackle that tomorrow. Besides, those are enough knotty problems for tonight. I need to relax my brain."

"I just hope you relax your slap-dash method. Call if you need anything. And that doesn't include a stretcher." Jamie rang off before McLaren could fire off his comeback.

McLaren finished his sandwich, took the dish and mug into the kitchen and put them into the dishwasher. He double-checked the back door was locked, kicked off his shoes and turned off the light.

But he wandered into the back room and put on Janet Ennis' CD. As the first song wove through the room, McLaren lay on the sofa and closed his eyes. Darkness permeated the house and filled it with the mixture of nighttime magic and his apprehension of things associated with the night. He could've moved into his bedroom, turned on the light and read a bit to hold the monsters at bay. But he remained in the dark room, letting Janet's voice wash over him.

Nora seemed emphatic about the circumstances of Janet's death. The firefighter he had talked to yesterday underscored those circumstances, thereby lending credibility to Nora. But did Nora talk to McLaren during one of her lucid periods? Did she swing between rationality and fiction? And if so, during one of those fantasy moments did she confuse him with someone else, did she see his house as Janet's and act out the fire episode by setting a fire on his driveway?

Those were hard questions to answer, and as Janet sang about the falling autumn leaves McLaren got up and padded into his office.

He flicked on the desk lamp, woke up his computer, and typed *Candidate for a Cold Case* in the computer's search bar. Seconds later he scanned the film credits. He nearly shouted and rang up Jamie as he read the film's release date: November 2008. Two years *after* Janet had died.

McLaren sat back in his chair, his gaze alternately on the computer screen and his phone. Jamie helped him keep his thinking straight, but what did he need to talk over with his friend? The facts were not arguable. Charlie Harvester was wrong when he suggested to Nora that she wove the film into Janet's accident. The movie wasn't around when Janet died; Nora had nothing to confuse.

McLaren returned to the search bar and scrolled through the offerings. He opened a newspaper article and took notes as he read it. When he finished, he smiled. Tomorrow, after he sifted through the fire debris, he would contact the writer of the article. He put the computer to sleep, turned off the desk lamp, brewed a cup of coffee and returned to the back room.

Janet was in the middle of "Love Me or Leave Me". McLaren stood by the large window and looked out into the night-wrapped world. It was easy to imagine another era, to place Janet in that time of velvet-voiced singers lamenting their unrequited love. He could picture her on stage, the audience in darkness and a spotlight picking her out of the gloom. Her seamless sound would entrap the listeners, bring them to her world to show them her broken heart.

Like a vocal version of Eddy Duchin, McLaren thought, amazed he had dragged the 1930s pianist's name from the recesses of his mind. Lyrical and silky, swan's down floating on unruffled water—that was Duchin's style. Satin smooth in a sea of boisterous jazz and swing. A caress in the turmoil of the day.

McLaren took a sip of coffee, letting the warmth of the liquid and Janet's voice transport him back in time. His dad had talked about the torch singers who performed during World War II, the women who braved the rough conditions of the front line or who toured the military canteens to bring a bit of Home to the troops. The subjects of the songs didn't vary much: women who loved and were left broken hearted, lost love, a love for someone who knew nothing about her, a romance that shaped a relationship. They carried a torch for their loves and sang about it in a bluesy, melancholy style. Though a few male singers were known in the field, women dominated. It was as though their hearts broke more easily or they could convey their grief more convincingly. The songs spoke to a generation who were forced apart by war and who knew the agony of separation and losing a love.

"She'd like you to have it," Nora had told McLaren when she gave him the CD. "You'll know my daughter better by listening to her. She *is* her voice, Mr. McLaren. That's Janet. There's nothing phony or stage-face about her. She's the same person wherever she is, and that's the person you hear in her voice."

A nice person, McLaren thought as Janet wove "At Last" around him. A caring person. A person who didn't deserve to die by arson.

He finished his coffee, laid on the sofa, and let the caress lull him to sleep.

McLaren woke Thursday morning with a stiff back and a head crowded with Janet's voice and Eddy Duchin's piano music. He eased to a standing position, padded to the CD player and turned it off. Becoming a habit, he thought as he picked up the coffee mug and wandered into the kitchen. But was it a habit he wanted to break? While wrapped in Janet's world he felt no desire to move on or rid himself of her company. Was it a harmless habit or a step into insanity?

He showered, and as he dressed in tan trousers and a short-sleeved green shirt, he wondered if Nora suffered more from that than from the dementia that claimed her. The potential was there, he admitted. He already knew that from his short personal experience.

How much worse would it be for a grieving mother who submersed herself in convincing Authority to open Janet's case, who kept Janet alive through this crusade? McLaren shook his head. Cold cases notoriously fell into a kind of black hole. Unless a detective sifted through the case notes occasionally, or the victim's relative or friend impressed that detective enough so he'd look into the event. McLaren knew the odds of the success rate. Nora Ennis might be delusional but she was persistent.

But she wasn't delusional, McLaren realized, and hurried into his office. The notes he'd taken at the library whispered to him. He had looked up Connie Long's obituary in the newspaper file. She had died on 29 September, six years ago, aged nineteen. Which made Stuart Ennis fifty-three or fifty-four when he'd fathered Connie. A married man to Nora. Had Nora suspected the affair? Did she know about Connie, then or now? She hadn't said anything to McLaren. He scanned the article, learning nothing of great interest except the time of the wake and burial in Temple Normanton's churchyard.

If Connie died one year before Janet, it was possible the two women knew each other. Had Janet been marking Connie's death that September day, been distracted with the rubbish burning, and got caught in the fire? Was it really a mistake after all?

He sighed, giving it up as a dead end. What motive would Stuart have, anyway, to kill Janet or torch her studio? Just a bitter old man whose love had run out for Nora and Janet. Give it up, Mike, he told himself as he punched in the phone number of the film studio. Not every angry person is going to be a suspect.

He picked up a pen and doodled on his notepad as his call was passed from person to person. Today was starting out gloriously.

After introducing himself to the screenwriter, McLaren asked where she got the idea for the film. "I realize it's been a while since you wrote it but I thought that perhaps you'd remember your source or inspiration." He tapped the tip of the pen on the notepad "Would you mind telling me?"

The writer seemed to mull over his request, for she didn't answer immediately. While she considered her reply, he heard the background conversations, phones ringing, and a computer printer or fax machine spitting out its pages. He wanted to emphasize how important the information was, that a woman's emotional and perhaps mental state hung precariously on her answer. But he knew better than to prod like that. It would produce only animosity and a brick wall.

"Who are you again?" The writer's voice broke into McLaren's thoughts of Janet.

"Michael McLaren. I need the information for an investigation I'm working."

"What type of investigation—criminal?"

"I don't know for certain. It's early days yet."

"But you suspect something criminal happened, right?"

"I could speculate all day about anything, but I don't know right now."

"And the information about my article will help."

"Yes."

"Help you or the other side? I assume there is another side."

"There always is."

"Good guys against bad guys."

"Of course."

"And which are you, Mr. McLaren?"

"I guess it depends on the outcome of the case as to how my client refers to me."

Wrong answer, he thought as the silence grew between them. Smart-mouth response. I've just dug my grave on this one.

The clock's sweep second hand counted off fifteen seconds before the writer said, "You sound like a police officer. But you wouldn't be talking about a client if you were. What are you?"

"Former police officer. I'm looking into an old case for a woman."

The silence wasn't as lengthy this time. Maybe his words nudged her to a decision. He heard the sound of a metal desk drawer closing before she replied, "All right. You want to know what sparked me to write that screenplay. Nothing earth shaking there. In fact, it was like most other articles or stories or screenplays written. I got it from a newspaper article. And I used a lot of the actual event in my screenplay. I've got it here…wait a minute…yes. It happened five years ago in Derbyshire, in a village north of Matlock. There was a fire and a woman's body was discovered in the debris. I recall there was a question at the time of whether her death was accidental or murder, that the postmortem examination revealed the rounded depression to her head. Add to that the evening meal cooking in her house and the assumption of the rubbish burning leading to the artist studio fire. Well…" She inhaled as though she'd just finished writing the script. "All those elements brought up the suspicion of murder at that time, though of course it was officially clad in 'Accidental Death' nomenclature. I always thought there was more to it, that it should have been investigated further. Which is why the storyline intrigued me. So, plain and simple, I used that as the basis for the film plot. Is that what you wanted to know?"

"This was the fire and death reported on 28 September."

"God, I hope there wasn't another one!" Her tone conveyed astonishment.

"Not that I know of. Just being thorough, that's all."

"This is what you need? Will this help you?"

"I believe so, thanks."

"Let me know the outcome. Maybe there's another screenplay in this."

McLaren doubted it but thanked her and rang off.

That nails it. The movie hit the screen *after* Janet's death. Nora is right; she couldn't be making it up. It underscores the case for her sanity. He grinned as he walked outside and grabbed the garden rake.

Minutes spent combing through the ashes and partially burnt pieces from last night's fire produced nothing interesting or conclusive. Nothing, that is, until the rake's teeth hit something substantial. McLaren scraped the teeth along the hard-packed gravel of his driveway and pulled the object toward him. He squatted and cleared it of the ashes.

The item was a button. A metal button like the kind that adorned jeans or denim jackets. The company name was a bit grungy but he could read the word plainly enough. His fingers closed slowly over the button, his mind racing. The castoff button put his enquiry into the Threat category. It came from a brand of jeans he didn't wear. An apropos brand, unfortunately. Firetrap.

****

Of course there was no way to trace his arsonist, McLaren realized later while driving to talk to Eva Lister, Janet's disgruntled catering customer. He hadn't seen the person leave, nor did he have any telltale evidence to point to anyone. Unless he noticed someone without a button on his or her pair of jeans. He was no farther in learning who had set the fire than last night. He was up the creek like any other stymied copper, McLaren glanced contemptuously at the jeans he wore.

He made good time getting to Hathersage, a village linked with author Charlotte Bronte and folk hero Little John. He reduced his speed to a crawl, and glanced at the Hanoverian Hotel and the chemist shop as he passed. The buildings' façades held no hint of the odd occurrences he'd been part of in June. But what was he expecting—a banner?

As the A625 meandered out of Hathersage, McLaren gazed at the car's speedometer. He wasn't going to get caught again by a motorcycle cop. He eased up on the accelerator pedal, making certain he was traveling within the legal speed limit, and changed the CD for Ian and Sylvia's greatest hits. The big, powerful notes of the guitar filled the car and he sang along to "Short Grass." He always thought Sylvia should've played autoharp on the song. Maybe they had tried it during rehearsals and didn't like the sound. But he'd heard a folk group use the autoharp with it and he thought it a super addition. Well, each group had their own song interpretations.

The autumnal foliage blazed in brilliant reds, oranges and yellows across the hills. Spent leaves, mostly dull browns and robbed of their vibrant hues, cascaded from tree branches, swirling or spiraling down to the cast-offs on the ground. Stalks of tufted hair-grass blazed white in the sunlight, the feathery inflorescences waving plume-like in the cars' passing breezes. Dried ferns, their fronds not yet withered by frost, held on to the last days of warmth with a show of gold and dandelion yellow. Patches of heather accented the hills in brilliant lavenders, and from somewhere up wind came the scent of damp moss. He lowered his window and breathed in the rich scent of the changing world.

Chesterfield never seemed to be devoid of traffic. McLaren waited through two cycles of the traffic light. Business, evidently, showed no appreciable slowdown, for shoppers jammed the pavement, some stopping when a window display attracted them, some entering shops. Cars, buses, motor cycles and light cross-country lorries crowded the road like ants on a piece of bread. It's a wonder anyone ever gets anyplace, he thought, then turned his car down the street where Eva lived.

The house sprawled over its acreage at the bottom of the cul-de-sac, an upscale section that spoke wealth by the landscaping and house size. McLaren parked in front of the stone edifice and walked up to the front door. An emphatic barking within the depths of the house announced more than his presence. It told any would-be burglars they might want to rethink their target.

Two locks clicked on the other side of the door and

a voice told the dog to hush as the door slowly cracked open. A face appeared in the opening between the door's edge and the doorjamb and enquired who he was and what he wanted.

"I'm Michael McLaren. I'm here to talk to Eva Lister."

"When did you phone her?"

McLaren glanced at his watch. "About an hour ago. I want to ask her about the wedding reception that Janet Ennis' company catered."

Evidently he'd said the magic word or given enough information. A chain slid noisily from its catch, the dog barked and was reprimanded, and the door inched open.

The face that appeared before him looked to be in its fifties. Dark hair framed an oval of flawless skin that had only a touch of rouge and lipstick applied to it. Dark eyes took in his frame, as if to confirm his identity, and his clothing, as if to confirm that tan trousers and a green shirt were good enough to enter her house. When the door opened to admit him into the entryway, he could see the woman was tall, attractive in a 1940s film star way, and obviously worked out. The white halter-top she wore showed off her tanned, muscular biceps quite well. She extended her hand, and confirmed she was Eva Lister.

McLaren restated his name, feeling the face-to-face meeting warranted a more formal introduction.

"I hope you'll forgive the seemingly exuberant precautions." Eva walked into the front room. She moved with a fluidity that suggested floating. "We had a burglary a month ago and I'm still not over the shock."

Her voice was lower in pitch than McLaren would have guessed if he'd just seen her, standing in a room, perhaps. He said the precautions were understandable and didn't have to be excused.

"Better late than never?" She seated herself in an upholstered chair of cream and gold fabric. He noted that the gold tone complemented the streaks in her hair. It also contrasted nicely with her turquoise slacks. The dog, a brown boxer, lay at her feet.

"Were the police successful in locating your stolen items?"

She grabbed a cigarette from an enamel box on the side table, lit it and took a puff before saying, "Not yet. They keep telling us the things could turn up sometime, but I don't hold much hope. Don't those people usually move the stuff on pretty promptly?"

"I believe so, though it depends on the burglar. I don't have much experience in that."

"But you were a police officer," she countered, gazing at him through the bluish smoke that hung in the air between them.

"Yes. But I didn't know that many burglars."

Eva's eyebrow lifted. "Not my idea of good company, either." She flicked the ash from her cigarette. "Now, what did you want to talk about? I can give you fifteen minutes."

"Janet Ennis' company catered for your daughter's wedding reception, I understand."

"Yes. One of the worst affairs I've ever struggled through."

"Why was that?"

"One of her servers, I believe his name was Sean, dumped the white sauce for the chicken cordon bleu into a pan filled with water. Besides having no sauce for the chicken, the sauce and hot water splattered onto the white tablecloth. It was terribly soiled, and when he attempted to remove the cloth from the table, it caught on a wrought iron statue nearby. The statue fell onto the table. *That* collapsed and the china and food slid off and crashed with it. Half the food was ruined. Thank God we had the cake, fruit, salads and hors d'oeuvres on another table. Though the main course and the vegetables were on the floor. Stacks of plates broke and the mess was horrendous." She glanced at the portrait of a young couple in wedding attire. "I was *livid*. It ruined the day." She spoke so loudly that the dog raised its head, looked at Eva, and growled. Eva patted the dog and it calmed down.

"Did Janet Ennis make amends?"

Eva's laugh was bitter and snarled into the air. "That woman...what a joke. I hired her due to someone's personal recommendation. Obviously she didn't suffer the same mishaps as I did."

"But Janet Ennis didn't offer you some sort of compensation?"

"She offered me a refund on part of the buffet bill. Generous, of course, but it didn't erase the fact that the reception was ruined." She sighed deeply and scrunched up her mouth as she shoved the album of wedding photos toward McLaren. "You can see for yourself the before and after views. I had the photographer snap the mess in case there would be any problem settling it all."

McLaren flipped through the pages, noted the fiasco, and closed the book. "Not a nice reminder of your daughter's big day."

"No, it's not. I should remove them. It's been long enough. Actually, I think about doing it at odd times, but it's always on the way to doing something else." She accepted the album from him and put it back on the coffee table. "I don't think of it daily. I'm not bitter. Nor do I seek revenge. It's over and done with. I'm just deeply sorry for my daughter. Though I think I took it harder than she did. They can at least laugh about it now."

"It's nice that they can take that attitude."

"Yes. It was unfortunate but it wasn't something that ruined their lives."

"Do you know if the server is still with the company?"

"I have no idea. I wasn't out for revenge. I just wanted an apology and some sort of compensation."

"Which you got, I assume."

"Janet Ennis wouldn't have been a very savvy businesswoman if she hadn't. I did appreciate her offer of refunding part of the fee, but aside from that..." She shrugged and took another puff on her cigarette. "I don't know if the boy was inept, nervous, or wanted to wreck Janet's company, like he had something personal against her. But he couldn't have created a bigger mess if he had tried."

The phone on the side table jangled into the conversational lull. The boxer barked, stood up, and wagged its stumpy tail. Eva glanced at the Caller ID display, excused herself, and picked up the receiver.

"Oh, hello, dear. No, I have a minute. What's up?...You're joking!...You're not serious." She leaned forward, as though curling up for an intimate talk. The smoke from her cigarette twisted upward, losing itself in the overhead chandelier. The caller seemed to be imparting interesting information, for Eva remained huddled up for nearly a minute, during which time her only responses were faint murmurs and rapid blinking of her eyes. When she eventually straightened up, she glanced at her watch. "Thanks. I'd no idea, obviously. Yes, I'm on my way. No, at the—Yes, there. I'm just leaving." She signed off, recradled the receiver, and stood up.

McLaren got to his feet, wondering what had happened.

Eva's voice had a hardness underlining her words and the open look had faded from her eyes, leaving coldness and a distinct suggestion the interview had ended. "I'm afraid we'll have to end this now. An emergency. I have to go."

McLaren nodded and followed her out of the room.

She did not speak, but hurried to the door, the soles of her leather moccasins tapping out her eagerness to be rid of him and accentuating the sudden strain that lay between them. At the door, she turned the knob, stepped aside and flung the door open. She stood there waiting for him to leave, her lips bloodless and pressed together. The boxer stood by her side, staring at McLaren and giving threatening, low-pitched growls.

McLaren hovered on the threshold, clearly astonished by Eva's change. "If you think of anything else that might help me with this investigation—" He got no further. Eva pushed him outside as she closed the door. The dog barked loudly, then broke off, evidently directed to be quiet.

McLaren got into his car and drove onto the main road. He found a spot a few dozen yards from the junction and parked on the verge. Eva would have to go this way, for she lived on a cul-de-sac. While he waited, he wondered who her caller could have been. Obviously she had learned something about him or the case, for her demeanor had changed as abruptly as a criminal seeing evidence against him. But who did she know who was connected to Janet's case? And who had he scared enough into contacting Eva, whatever her association was to this?

A silvery Mercedes-Benz shot out of the lane and onto the main thoroughfare. Eva sat behind the steering wheel, a determined, attentive look on her face. She passed McLaren, her eyes fixed on the road, her left hand holding a mobile phone to her ear.

McLaren straightened from his slouch, tugged at the bill of his baseball cap to set it lower over his forehead, and eased his Peugeot onto the road. He was two cars behind Eva but could still see her car, shiny and bright in the sunlight.

Traffic was moderate on the A632. Nearly sparse at times. McLaren found himself wishing for more vehicles as one of the cars ahead of him turned off, leaving a single car between his and Eva's. As they passed Kelstedge he wondered if they were making for Darleycote, the village where Janet had lived. His hands tightened on the steering wheel as he thought of the people he'd spoken to and any reasons why Eva needed to consult with one of them. But as they passed Matlock, still traveling south, he abandoned the idea of Eva talking to Janet's neighbor Ian O'Connor. She appeared to be heading for a rendezvous.

They had turned onto the B5035, a smaller road connecting Wirksworth and Ashbourne. Miles of open fields flanking both sides of the tarmac did little to ease McLaren's concern that Eva would spot him, but as she turned into the Carsington Water nature preserve he smiled. No one would turn in here to elude anyone, he reasoned. She was meeting someone here.

He parked his car one lane west of Eva's and fell in behind a group of chattering school children and teachers walking to the main building. Eva continued along the path to the left, heading toward the lake, and McLaren briefly felt exposed as his talkative camouflage deserted him. He stopped at a large sign recording the birds seen that day and waited for several seconds, pretending to read the list. When a family group passed him, he followed them.

The path ran alongside the lake, weaving through clumps of trees and open fields. At times McLaren didn't know why Eva didn't see him, but she marched resolutely ahead, her focus on her destination.

As he rounded the northwest tip of the lake the family stopped to consult a bird book. McLaren sent up a prayer, hoping Eva wouldn't turn at that moment and notice him. He took several steps, then bent over, pretending to tie his shoe. As he straightened up, Eva glanced his way.

She recognized him. That was obvious from her startled look. But she also thought quickly. She ran across the small footbridge and dashed toward a thicket of trees where the path branched farther up ahead.

McLaren dashed after her, his shoes pounding on the sandy, packed soil, his lungs pulling in air scented with dry leaves and moist earth. The path dipped and rose, sometimes rutted, sometimes smooth. He raced along, conscious of the thud of his feet hitting the hard earth, the nettles grabbing and snagging on his trousers, the cry of the birds startled from their feeding.

Ahead, the path divided, one branch lower and merging into a copse, the other branch on elevated ground thick with tall grass and shrubs. Eva dashed up the slope and disappeared around a bend. McLaren, several hundred feet behind her, tore over the level ground, trying to ignore the rocks that poked through the earth like whales breaching in an ocean.

His shoe slid off the polished surface of a rock and he lurched sideways. The ankle muscle tightened and for a moment, he felt a sharp pain shoot through his lower leg. He fell onto the rocky soil, his knee hitting a smooth stone and the palms of his hands pushing furrows into the loam. Wincing against the pain and cursing his clumsiness, he remained on his hands and knees for several seconds, sucking in the air in deep gulps. He got to his feet, uncertain if his ankle hurt from the trip or if he was merely out of breath. But he charged ahead, and as he regained flatter ground, the pain subsided. He rushed around a stand of trees. Eva had vanished.

It seemed impossible, yet it appeared to be true. The path stretched before him, a tan, straight line aiming toward the south and the sun, with not a human being on the sandy strip.

McLaren jogged down the path, scanning the land on his right and left sides. To his right, the land sloped slightly downward to the lake. Ducks and other water birds dotted its light blue surface and tall brown reeds poked through the unruffled water that threw back the color of the sky. Clumps of cattails snuggled up to the shoreline, the fuzzy heads nodding in the breeze. He squelched the impulse to wade through the shallow water to see if Eva were hiding among the thickets. No woman dressed as expensively as Eva dressed would muddy up her clothes like that.

He ran several hundreds yards farther south, glancing into the forest of pines and hardwoods lining the path on his left. Eva could be crouched behind a large boulder or tree trunk, but the search for her would be laughable in such an extensive area. Was she behind him or before him? How far into the forest had she run? Perhaps she had hid just around the bend and was even now doubling back the way they had come. It would be a useless search.

He dusted off his sandy trousers and started back the way he'd come.

A man and woman walked toward McLaren. He had a pair of binoculars around his neck and she held a bird book and a piece of paper. They chatted and looked toward the lake, alternately pointing to something and consulting their book. As they came within a few yards of McLaren, he walked up to them.

"Excuse me." McLaren smiled and stopped alongside the path. What was he going to say? "Have you seen a smartly dressed woman running and looking over her shoulder..." He glanced at the glasses. "Would you mind if I used your binoculars for a moment?"

The man's head jerked back and he frowned. "Where? I'm sorry but I don't lend them to anyone."

"I don't mean I'd run off with them. I just want to look into the wood for a minute. I won't go anywhere. I'll stay right here."

"Into the *wood*?" Clearly he hadn't expected this. "Now? Here?" He glanced at the thick stand of trees crowning the ridge. They sat black and solid, a shield against the sunlight, a harbor of night and fears of the darkness.

"Yes. Just for a second. I saw a…" He paused, near panic. What bird could he name? He pulled up a word from deep within his memory. "I think it was a goshawk." When McLaren's choice wasn't challenged, he added, "I'm not sure. Could be a female sparrowhawk, but I'd like to find it, if I can." He waited for what seemed hours for the man to remove the binoculars from around his neck and hand them to McLaren.

"Goshawks are rather rare," the man said as McLaren put the glasses to his eyes and scanned the woods. Where the hell was Eva?

"I know. That's why I didn't want it to escape me if I could see it."

"The goshawk is bigger and heavier in the chest than the sparrowhawk. Could you tell anything as it flew?"

"No, worse luck. I just caught a glimpse of it."

"Well, both species need woodlands to nest in and like open land for hunting. Though, if you saw one here, it most likely is a sparrowhawk. They like marshlands." He watched McLaren do a second, slower sweep of the wood. "See anything?"

"Just trees, squirrels and sparrows," he added hurriedly, hoping the bird visited the wood. He handed the binoculars back to the birder. "Thanks. Hope I haven't kept you too long."

"That's all right. We're just walking the route. Well." He slipped the glasses strap back over his neck "Good luck on finding your bird."

"I hope I find her, too. Thanks." He strode past them, wondering if Eva were watching the comedy from her perch high in a tree.

Chapter Nineteen

Who Eva had spoken to on the phone and why that conversation evidently demanded immediate reaction niggled McLaren the rest of the day. The short talk nearly sounded like code, with Eva conveying the meeting place without stating it. And the astonishment from her exclaimed "You're joking" implied something rather crucial between Eva and her caller.

McLaren turned off the CD in his car, not wanting the distraction of music as he considered the identity of Eva's caller. Someone she knew, obviously, and who was a good friend. You wouldn't greet an acquaintance or business associate with "Hello, dear; what's up?" So, who fit that description?

Too many people, McLaren decided, as he eased his car out of the nature reserve's car park. But as to why she'd run from him, that was clear. She was protecting the person she was meeting. Protecting his or her identity, reputation and future. He cursed as the question he'd just asked himself reverberated in his mind: who fit that description?

Someone Eva cared about very deeply. Her husband? A lover? Did she have a lover? He doubted she was shielding the daughter. She'd married and had moved out; five years ago was too long to come to light now.

He shoved the CD into the car's player. He needed

the distraction of the music to drown out the unceasing questions thundering in his ears. Eva Lister had given him more than a good run around the lake; she had probably handed him a sleepless night as well.

****

Ian O'Connor had been the bass player with Janet's group. He'd been her neighbor, and he also surprised McLaren when he opened his door.

Janet would have been forty if she were still living; Dan Wilshaw, her pianist, was forty. McLaren had assumed the third member of the trio would be of similar age. That's why he feigned a cough to regain his dignity when Ian identified himself. He was twenty-five.

The two men looked at each other, each, perhaps, expecting someone different from what stood before him. Ian had the coloring of the Scots native to the Highlands—red hair, blue eyes and a sprinkling of freckles across his cheeks and nose. Of medium height and a wiry build, Ian seemed only marginally taller than the upright bass he played. But McLaren thought the man had a strength that belied his thin frame. That strength showed itself in his eyes and his confrontational tone.

"I told everything to the cops." Ian crossed his arms over his chest. He remained in the open doorway, legs apart, breathing heavy, for all the world looking like a good bouncer. He also wore jeans.

McLaren eyed them, looking for a missing button. "I appreciate that," he said, his neck muscles tightening at the tacit confrontation. "But that was five years ago. I'm doing an independent investigation of Janet's death and I'm hoping you can give me information on it."

"Her studio went up in flames and she was trapped inside. She died. What's more to learn?"

"You don't seem very sorry about her death."

"Sure I'm sorry, but that doesn't alter the fact of what happened." His eyes swept over McLaren, one corner of his mouth twisting in disdain. "I already sent a card to her mum and went to the funeral."

"How magnanimous of you."

"Yeah. Now, hop it before I call the real coppers."

McLaren thrust his foot over the threshold, blocking Ian's attempt to close the door.

"Good way to get your foot broken, mate."

"Good way to continue our nice, friendly chat. Now." McLaren put his hand on the edge of the door. "I'd like some information about the day Janet died." He smiled but his eyes stared into Ian's, underlining his determination not to leave. "Had you been to her house that day?"

Ian shrugged. "That was five years ago. You remember what you were doing on a particular day five years ago?"

"If it were linked to a big event I would. You don't call Janet's death a big event?"

He shrugged again. "Sure. Yeah. I lost my job."

McLaren grabbed a handful of Ian's t-shirt and pulled the man forward until only inches separated them. Towering above the man, McLaren said slowly, "Tender-hearted, aren't you? A woman dies in a fire and all you can say is that you lost your job." He twisted the shirt until it tightened around Ian's body. Bringing his fist level with his chin forced Ian onto his tiptoes. His tone didn't conceal his contempt, rushing out in a sneer contradicting his words. "You want to reconsider your demeanor?"

"Bugger off."

McLaren's right knee jammed into Ian's crotch and a groan escaped Ian's lips. He would have bent over if McLaren hadn't held him upright by his shirt. He leaned forward so his lips were near Ian's ear. "Now, shall we converse like gentlemen, or shall I take a few minutes of boxing practice here instead of at the gym?" He smiled, waiting for Ian's decision.

Ian stared at McLaren, his eyes never wavering. Although McLaren's fist was wedged beneath his chin, Ian managed to make his words understandable. "I could have you up for assault, McLaren."

"Me?" McLaren's eyebrows raised in surprise. "Why? I'm just helping with your wardrobe. Getting a few wrinkles out of your clothes." He swept his free hand over Ian's back, as though brushing lint from the shirt, then slammed his open palm against Ian's cheek. "How's that? Better?"

Ian blinked, his eyes tearing from the sting.

"You're awfully quiet, Ian. Haven't decided yet to help me?" His palm found Ian's cheek again and the smack echoed against the wooden doorjamb.

Nodding as best he could, Ian mumbled that he just thought of something he'd like to tell McLaren.

"I'm *sure* it will be interesting and helpful. Won't it?" McLaren made sure his expression mirrored the threat in his words. "You know, I have only so much patience. And I've had a bad day. Know what I mean?"

Ian nodded slightly, too nervous to move.

"And trying to get justice, after all these years, for a beautiful lady who died in a fire...well..." He lowered his fist, allowing Ian back to his normal stance, but he held on to the shirt. Just in case. "Now," McLaren said, his voice lazy and warm, "what did you want to tell me?"

Ian swallowed several times and cleared his throat. He avoided McLaren's gaze and talked instead to the tree near the street until McLaren reminded him that wasn't polite. Ian murmured his apology before adding that he thought there was more to Janet's head wound than the police acknowledged.

"And why is that?" McLaren said, relaxing his grip.

"Just that the firefighters found the remains of a mic in the fire debris."

"I know about that."

"But you probably don't know that we never rehearsed in her studio. It was too small."

"What's that mean?"

"It means that someone had to have carried that mic into her studio. Maybe on the day she died. It sounded to me like the curved indentation in his skull could accommodate the round end of a mic quite well. Think about that."

"Since you're her neighbor, did you hear anything that night? A call for help, a car back firing…anything?"

"Nope. She lives kind of far back, at the end of the cul-de-sac. Well, you can look outside and see it."

McLaren turned and stared across the lane.

"More like half buried in the woods, her house is. Not like mine. She's kind of remote. No, I didn't hear a thing that night. Or see a thing, either, until I took a walk. Then I saw the smoke and the flames."

"What time was that?"

"Around half past six. I'd rung her up an hour earlier to ask if she'd like some extra eggs the next day. I keep a few chickens—not enough to cause problems, just for some fresh eggs. She said she'd be happy to get them, so I set aside a half dozen for her. That was it. A brief conversation. Then I went for a walk around half past six, as I said. I saw the flames shooting from her studio."

"You knew it was her studio and not her house."

"Yes. Absolutely. The back of her property slopes upward. Her house is on flat ground, but the hill starts in her back garden and goes up fairly steeply. That's where her studio was, on the higher elevation. You can see the roof from the lane. They threw a kind of light on to her house's roof. I dashed around the house, thinking she might be in the studio and might not be able to get out. The fire had a good start by then, a good section on fire, including the door, but I ran to the windows on the side that still was in pretty good shape. I thought I could break in and get her out if she was inside. I couldn't see into the room, though. The flames were like a curtain at the windows, obstructing my view, so I grabbed a stout branch from the woodpile and broke out one of the windows. I yelled as loudly as I could, thinking she might hear me over the fire's roar." He paused, running the tip of his tongue over his lips. "There was no response. I called again but I got no answer. So I thought maybe she wasn't in the studio. I ran back to her house, to the kitchen door since it was the nearest to the studio. I rang the doorbell and pounded on the door but again got no response. I prayed that she'd left on an errand or something and wasn't home. By then I guess I'd been there five minutes or so. I didn't want to waste any more time so I ran home and rang up the fire service in Matlock. They got there about fifteen minutes later."

"You went outside again, I presume, and watched the proceedings."

"Yes. I had mixed feelings about that. I didn't want to look like one of those thrill-seekers, watching a fire so I could talk about it the next day. But I thought maybe the firefighters or police might have questions as to time I first saw the fire...that sort of thing." Ian shook his head. "I was also hoping to see Janet coming out of a neighbor's house, perhaps, when she saw the commotion. No such luck."

"You said you didn't see anyone around the time you saw the fire..."

Ian paused, as though replaying the scene in his mind. He stared at the window that looked onto the lane and Janet's house. He lowered his gaze and mumbled, "No one. No stranger or anyone I knew."

"Did you smell anything odd while the fire was burning?"

"What do you mean odd?"

"A strong odor that normally you don't smell."

"Like petrol?"

"Something like that, yes."

"I thought I smelled some sort of petroleum product, but I assumed it was her artist paints and paint thinner and such. You know, the studio was filled with those things."

"So, you didn't see, smell, or hear anything odd prior to discovering the fire."

"No. I'm sorry. But the fire was as much a surprise to me as to anyone. I'm just glad I saw it before it spread."

McLaren raised his palm and Ian shrank back a step, but McLaren barely touched Ian's cheek. "So much nicer when we're friendly, isn't it? Thanks." He walked to his car, his mind thinking about what Ian had just suggested.

He also wondered why Ian had been so obstructive and uncaring about Janet. Was he telling the truth about his part in the fire? If he were angry about his dismissal, would he have even tried to put out the fire? Either way—helpful amateur firefighter or unconcerned onlooker, the reaction was odd for a person who had been supported at one time through Janet's employment. McLaren grabbed his handheld tape recorder and made a note to himself about checking out the history of the two people. There might be some old wound that still rubbed Ian raw.

****

Nora woke suddenly, and found herself in a strange room. She blinked several times. When did she get that new television in the corner? It *was* a telly, wasn't it? But it looked odd, nothing more than a thin, flat screen. The turntable was the same, as was Janet's photo on the table. But a book on the couch didn't look familiar. She picked it up and read the title and author's name. Had Janet dropped it by while Nora slept? You'd think there'd be a note if she had.

Nora got up, stiff from the position in which she'd fallen asleep. Late morning sunlight fell across the sofa and the nearest section of the area rug. The oak tree outside the window blazed in autumnal red and orange hues. Her hand went to her forehead, pressing against it, as though the presence of her fingertips affirmed the reality of the scene. Hadn't it been April just moments ago? Hadn't Janet been urging her to come outside to see the spring crocus and tulips? Hadn't she been singing, teasing in that funny way of hers? Nora glanced around the room. Had Janet been playing a trick? Did she and some friend—Dan, perhaps, or Tom—carry me into the front room? Shouldn't Janet be here?

Nora walked into the kitchen and surveyed the room. Everything looked familiar. Nothing had altered or morphed into an odd, futuristic object. The curtains were the same yellow print, the walls were still painted light blue, and the table and chairs were the same white wooden set she remembered. Even down to the gouge on the table edge when Janet had tipped over her father's heavy, metal camera tripod. Nora placed her fingertip into the indentation, wanting a connection with the past. But nothing changed in the room: Janet didn't appear; Nora's husband wasn't standing at the door; the chipped teapot wasn't pristine. Sighing, Nora filled the electric kettle with water, flipped on the switch, and dropped a teabag into the mug, a souvenir she'd bought from Marks & Spencer, to commemorate Charles and Diana's wedding.

When was Janet's and Tom's anniversary? Was it coming up, or had she missed it, overlooked it in the rush of their first CD release party? Nora walked to the phone. She'd ring up Janet to ask, never mind the embarrassment of forgetting the date.

But as she reached for the receiver a voice whispered in her head. Janet hadn't married Tom; she hadn't married anyone. She had a new boyfriend—her photographer, Myles. That's how they had met. Janet had died five years ago. And the police were still working on the case, searching for her killer.

Nora's hand dropped from the phone. How could she be so confused? Was her hope that the police would call any day that strong that the borders between reality and fantasy blurred? Or was the dementia progressing more rapidly than she had thought?

She sat at the kitchen table, her hand gripping the mug handle. It had been a long time since a police detective had phoned. Maybe they were busy on another case. Maybe they had run out of leads. Nora took a sip of tea. Tom, the castoff boyfriend, might have been angry enough to kill Janet. And there was Sean, Janet's former employee. Nora stared ahead, seeing nothing but her daughter's face. It happened all the time, angry employees seeking to avenge themselves on former employers. Maybe Sean had been that angry employee. Or perhaps Janet's catering client from that fiasco of a wedding reception. But that had happened in May, hadn't it? And Janet had died in September. Why would an irate client wait that long to retaliate? And there was Bruce, the former drummer with the trio. He'd been fired. That might've turned into a spite revenge. And Janet's bass player, Ian. While he hadn't been fired, there'd been bad blood between the two of them. Did bad blood ever become violent?

Nora walked over to the phone and punched in Charlie Harvester's number. Funny how she could remember that and get so muddled on other things. Perhaps because he was the last person she'd spoken to, had such faith in the police, wished so desperately to have the case solved before she was committed.

Harvester's voice crackled in Nora's ear, rousing

her from her thoughts.

"Detective-Inspector Harvester," she said, her voice quivering slightly from expectation. "This is Nora Ennis. I hope you remember me from my visiting with you last year at your office. I'm calling to ask if there are any developments in my daughter's case."

"Mrs. Ennis."

Was she mistaken, or did a heavy sigh escape from Harvester's lips?

Harvester paused, as though thinking of a suitable response. "There's nothing new. The case is closed. I thought you understood that."

"You've found Janet's killer?"

The sigh seeped out, louder this time. "There is no killer, Mrs. Ennis. Unless you classify the fire as the killer. We've been over this matter many dozen times, either with me or with other detectives. Her death was an accident. I spoke with you a few days ago about all this."

Nora opened her mouth. There were so many things she didn't understand—about Janet's death, about police work, about the people she termed 'suspects.' Why didn't Charlie Harvester understand this?

In the pause, Harvester added, "I'm sorry about this, Mrs. Ennis, but there is nothing more I can help you with. Any other detective here, as well as our Superintendent, is in the same position as I am. No one can do anything more with your case. I'm sorry because I know what it means to you. I appreciate your concern, but it only frustrates you to keep calling here. If there is ever a change in the case, I'll let you know. But right now, it's officially closed. Now, I must get on with my other work." He rang off in a hurry, the click of the closed connection loud in Nora's ear.

****

Charlie Harvester exhaled loudly and stared at the phone on his desk. Last year, she had said. It had been a few days. Couldn't she keep track of time? Really, the woman should be committed right now. She kept harassing him, getting in his way, wasting his time. He had other cases that needed his attention. What did she think he could do with a five-year-old cold case? He hadn't been the SIO, hadn't even been part of the investigation. He was no magician or soothsayer. He couldn't pull the guilty party from a silk top hat.

He picked up his pen, ready to get back to the report he was reading, but set it down. The conversation had left him unsettled. It was more than annoyance at her constant calling; it angered him that she didn't have a keeper who could prevent her from disrupting his day.

On the other side of his closed office door he could hear two of his colleagues talking as they walked down the corridor. They were working on a case of theft—some paintings, a wallet and a mobile phone left in an unlocked car. Honestly! Some people deserved to be ripped off. Where had common sense gone? Didn't they know they were asking for a car break-in and theft of their articles if left like that? Didn't they listen to the televised publicity on crime prevention? Bunch of berks.

His gaze traveled to the photo on his desk. His fiancée, Linnet Isherwood. He'd go see her this weekend, take her something to read, some flowers. Were flowers allowed in prison? He didn't know. All his years as a cop and he had no idea about prison regulations. He'd find out.

Damn McLaren, anyway. If it weren't for him, Linnet wouldn't be in the nick. It hadn't turned out how they had planned. They were so confident McLaren would muck up the case.

Harvester averted his eyes from the photo. It was easier to pretend it hadn't happened. The whole damn thing, beginning with the dust-up last year when they were both still in the Staffordshire Constabulary. Harvester leaned back in his chair, conscious of the squeak of the frame and the lumpy padding. There'd been bad blood between them since their first day at police training school. McLaren so popular and him ignored. He'd had to struggle for everything he got, although his daddy's name helped ease him through a few doors and courses. But McLaren'd been the blue-eyed boy, the star on which everyone set their sights.

Even the instructors liked McLaren, a fact they had tried to hide but it had been obvious. Harvester's lip curled as he recalled the honor bestowed upon McLaren for his top grades. The man had accepted the award so humbly; Harvester could have puked. What a bunch of codswallop.

The animosity and silent competition hadn't ended at school. If anything, it magnified on the job, both of them members of the Staffordshire Constabulary. And it came to a violent head that night in June when McLaren intervened in Harvester's criminal investigation. Damn McLaren for interfering, for ridiculing Harvester in front of his men, for starting the office gossip. Harvester picked up a pencil and snapped it in half. Damn the man for tossing him into the rose bushes.

Harvester subconsciously rubbed his arm. He swore that some days he could still feel the thorns embedded in his skin. Damn McLaren.

But despite the bitter recollections, Harvester smiled and looked again at Linnet's photo. Even if Nora went to McLaren with her daft story, and even if McLaren took on the investigation, Harvester was one step ahead of his old nemesis. He knew about the marijuana found in Janet's house, and McLaren didn't.

Chapter Twenty

Morning and early afternoon slid by in a rush of chatting up people associated with Janet's case, however remotely. McLaren had exhausted his initial list and returned to talk to Dan Wilshaw, the pianist in Janet's group.

They'd been talking for several minutes, seated in Dan's front room. The afternoon sunlight had moved westward, leaving the room in the gray light that proceeds dusk. McLaren found himself looking at Janet's photo instead of at Dan, and he made an effort to ignore the mesmerizing brown eyes.

Dan settled back in his chair. "The only thing I know is that Ian thought he was better than any bassist around and that he deserved a higher salary than Janet paid him."

"Did he tell her that?" McLaren asked.

"Constantly. At least once a week."

"Even in front of you?"

"Yeah. What can I say? The bloke was totally uncouth."

"And Janet didn't relent and give him a raise, I assume."

"Hardly. We'd not been together that long. One or two months, I think, when Ian began whining. I believe she was going to increase Ian's and my salaries that Christmas—she was going to wrap up the notice and the extra pay as a present and give it to us at the annual Christmas party."

"She told you?"

"No. But I got the impression from Myles. He didn't say anything in so many words, but you know how one gets a feeling about things."

McLaren nodded. He glanced again at the photo, then asked if the ill feeling manifested in any other way.

"Like what? Air let out of her car tires? Crank phone calls?" Dan fished around in his jeans pocket for his lighter, pulled it out and lit a cigarette.

"That surely wouldn't have garnered him a raise or a job, would it?"

"No. It was just a bad joke." Dan grimaced, looking uncomfortable.

"So there was nothing else Ian did but grumble to Janet."

"I suppose there could have been, but I never heard anything. Janet wasn't one to gossip, especially when the harmony of the group was at stake. And Ian and I weren't particularly drinking buddies. Nor were Bruce and I."

"Didn't get on too well with them?"

"Oh, it's not that. Bruce kept to himself. Ian, though more outgoing, wasn't my cup of tea. No blowups or fights. Just didn't socialize outside the group."

"Only at the Christmas party."

"Right. No hard feelings or anything. He was a nice enough bloke to work with. But he never said anything to me about him and Janet. That wouldn't be professional."

"Was there a reason why Ian wanted more money?"

"Besides his swelled head, you mean?" Dan chewed on his lower lip as he thought. A dog in the neighbor's yard yapped at a squirrel, and Dan shifted his position in his chair. "He hadn't any huge bills that I know of. He roomed with his girlfriend in a flat in Matlock Bath and his car was paid for. I know that because we were talking about cars one day when I was looking to buy something newer. He'd not gone to university so there was no student loan to pay back. No, I don't know why he was so insistent on the pay increase."

"No medical bills, then, either for himself or his girlfriend."

"If there were, he kept it a secret from me."

"How about his parents? Sometimes a child feels the need to help out in a medical crisis. Anything like that going on with him?"

"I never heard, though he could have done, I expect."

McLaren leaned forward, the exasperation evident on his face. "So Ian O'Connor was in excellent health, owed nothing on his car, had no house payment or university tuition to pay back, and had no outstanding debts. What about drugs?"

"Pardon?"

"Pot. Dope. Cocaine. Was he a user then?"

Dan shrugged and pressed his lips together. Glancing at Janet's photo, he said, "No. I don't think so. I would have known. Janet would have known. The group was too small for him to conceal his habit."

"Do you think Janet did know and that's why the

ill feeling was there?"

"I think I would've heard," Dan said, his voice hardening. "That was five years ago. I was thirty-five. Not exactly a child, and Janet's trio wasn't the first musical group I'd played with. I started in the music business when I was nineteen and I saw a lot of back stage shenanigans. Enough questionable activities to last me the rest of my life. I don't do drugs, McLaren. I don't tolerate it and I don't like hanging around those who do use. Janet was clean and she expected her band members to be clean. We knew that from the beginning. She made it clear before she signed us up. If Ian got involved with drugs Janet might have warned him to get sober, might have given him a deadline to clean up his act. She was like that, one to give you a chance. She'd stick by her morals, too, even if it meant tossing out a family member."

"Which family member? Don't tell me her mother—"

"No, no. But it looked as though Ian might have ended up in Janet's family. He was dating her sister, Connie."

"Do you think it was a love match and not marrying for money?"

"I can't say, of course, but I think they were in love."

"I assume Janet had some money. With the recordings and catering and performances, she had to have something in her bank account."

"She probably did. I wouldn't know."

"But she dressed nicely. I've seen a few photos."

"She liked to look good. Not just for her publicity shots, but all the time."

"Even to her casual wear, like at home? Including her jeans and t-shirts?" McLaren sent up a prayer.

"Sure."

"Expensive jeans, were they? Top brand?"

Dan shrugged, looking exasperated. "I don't know. I'm not a bleeding couturier. What the hell difference does it make, anyway?"

"Just helps me get a picture of Janet and her life. Firetrap jeans, for example, gives me a different image of her than if she wore, oh, say, Marks and Spencer, however nice they are."

"Yeah, well, I have no idea. Ask Helene. She might know. Women are keener about that stuff than men are. Is that it?"

"Yes. Sorry if it sounded like an inquisition. Just my curiosity taking hold."

"No harm."

McLaren thanked Dan for his time and as he walked back to his car wondered if Ian's deadline had come and gone, and he had killed Janet rather than kill his habit.

****

Haddon Hall lacked an hour before it closed for the day, so McLaren drove to the stately home. He parked and wandered into the Hall, then inquired for Bruce. Bruce was in the restaurant, the guide told McLaren. Could he be of any help?

"Thanks anyway. I need to talk to Mr. Parrott." He turned, feeling rather than seeing the man's stare following him as he retraced his steps through the stone archway.

The Hall's restaurant showed the signs of end-of-the-business-day. Only two tables were occupied, no one waited to be seated, and no line angled away from the counter. A low murmur of conversations mixed in the air but they did not compete with vocalizing babies or the hurried clatter of dirty dishes. McLaren stood near the doorway and glanced around. Wooden beams ran the width of the room and contrasted nicely with the light gray walls. Small square tables, seating four, dotted the main section of the room, with the self-serve counter at the farther end. The cook was singing to herself and Bruce was clearing a table near the drinks cabinet.

"Afternoon, Bruce." McLaren extended his hand as Bruce turned around.

"McLaren. Didn't think I'd see you again." He wiped his hand on his towel before shaking hands.

"Just wanted to ask you something else, if you don't mind. Is this a bad time?"

The couple at the table nearest the cash register got up and left. The cook exited through a Staff Only door. The room took on the tone of late afternoon when energies were spent and the air seemed thicker and warmer with approaching sunset.

Bruce glanced at the room; the remaining customers seemed content to linger over their tea and biscuits. "Sure. Five minutes or so should be all right. What do you need?" He sat and looked at McLaren as he took the chair opposite him.

McLaren flashed a half smile and wondered if he were about to make a mistake. But as Bruce sat, unsure of what to expect, the shadows outside the tearoom window deepened to indigo. "You told me were part of Janet's trio for more than a year."

Bruce's right eyebrow rose as he wrapped both his

hands around the bowl of sugar cubes. His words were barely audible, even in the stillness of the room. "Yes. A lot of people know that, including Dan Wilshaw and Janet's mother. Why?"

"And during those seventeen or so months you were at her house rehearsing."

"You already know that. Dan probably told you, too. I repeat, why are you asking me?"

"So you saw Janet dressed casually as well as formally, as for your performances."

"What the hell are you on about? Of course I saw her in a lot of different clothing. I never said I didn't, even if you asked me before." He frowned, as though he tried to recollect their previous conversation. "The way she dressed, what she had on that day of the fire, has nothing to do with anything. You want me to tell you what she was wearing when she turned me away from her front door? Well, I can't. Lock me up, but I don't remember. That was five ruddy years ago. I didn't even remember what she wore every day."

"I'm not trying to pin anything on you, Bruce. Or trick you. I merely want to know about any particular style or brand that she preferred."

"Well, I can't help you. I'm sorry, but that's life. Ask her mum. Or Helene. Someone she spent more time with."

McLaren nodded and chewed his bottom lip, considering Bruce's suggestion. Of course Bruce hadn't killed Janet; his hospital stay eliminated him as a suspect. But he could've heard about McLaren's investigation from Dan or another involved person, and have his own reason for setting the fire on his drive in the hope of scaring McLaren off the case. Bruce might have another item of Janet's, like the Firetrap button from her jeans. Maybe he kept the jeans button with him in his own jeans pocket, as a good luck token. Maybe he was never parted from it and had it with him all the time, as a link to Janet. There were a lot of people who carried around things like that. McLaren glanced at Bruce, who was curling and uncurling the edge of his apron. It wasn't so far fetched. The man had admitted that he had loved Janet. And an unrequited love, especially where the person had died tragically, could be a very strong reason for carrying around an item that had belonged to Janet.

Bruce's fingertips pulled at the ends of his apron ties, the heavy cotton twill fabric stiff from repeated starch applications. His gaze flitted around the room, from McLaren's face to the cash register to the display of postal cards and booklets to the door. He cleared his throat.

"Yes?' McLaren leaned back in his chair.

"Just wondered. You know…if we're finished."

"Oh, sorry. Just another question, if that's all right."

Bruce nodded. His smile had vanished during the lull in their conversation and now he stared at McLaren almost sullenly.

"Did Janet spend a lot of money on her clothes?"

The apron ties fell to Bruce's lap as he gripped the edge of the table. "What is this about her damned clothes? Yeah, she did. Her stage clothes, sure. She had to project a certain image, and that included looking sleek and smart. She liked certain things to wear and didn't let the price get in the way of how she looked. It was part of the business, part of what she had to do."

"Was she as particular about her every day clothes? Nice looking, name brands…that sort of thing?"

"I guess. I don't really know. She didn't walk around in a frumpy t-shirt or worn out slippers, if that's what you mean. But like I said, I don't know women's brands. She always looked good, dressed to the nines."

"Evidently she had the bank account to support this, then."

"Sure. Why not? She made good money from the music and the performances. From her catering company, too. She wasn't hurting for anything that I know of. She wouldn't have planned on giving us raises at the end of the year if she couldn't afford it."

"Sounds like a generous lady."

"She was that. Gave her mum a nice coat and a new telly. She could buy damned near anything she wanted, within reason."

"No yacht or private jet."

"No. Maybe in a few years." His voice trailed off and his face blanched, as if his unvoiced "had she lived" reverberated off the tearoom walls.

"Did she have enough money to buy drugs?"

"What, like cocaine?"

"Or pot. Maybe she wasn't a user but she could have bought it anyway."

"And given it away because she was so *generous*, you mean?" Bruce snorted, throwing back McLaren's word. "Janet and drugs didn't mix. She didn't use and she didn't buy. Simple as that. Black and white. No muted hue between. That was her opinion on the subject. She had her rules for the trio. We knew them and knew what it meant if we violated those rules. She lived by those rules, too. I suppose she had enough money to buy anything like that, but she didn't."

"So no one in the trio used. How about other associates or friends? If someone used pot, for instance, did her rules pertain to them?"

The back of Bruce's hand ran across his mouth and he nodded. "Yeah. Funny, but I haven't thought of that in five years. Guess I shut it away." He tapped his knuckles against his lips, his gaze on McLaren's face. "Our first set was over one night and I thought about nipping outside for a breath of air. Some of those clubs get kind of stuffy, you know. I'd just turned the corner from where our room was when I saw Janet and Myles by the back door. They were arguing so I stopped."

"Myles Tyson, her fiancé. Could you make out what they were discussing?"

"Was hard not to. I hadn't intended to eavesdrop, but the subject and Janet's anger drew my attention."

"She was mad, then."

"Explosive, more like. She caught Myles backstage selling pot to a club janitor. She was furious but he said it was no big deal. He tried to laugh it off but Janet saw nothing funny about it. She told him she wouldn't tolerate any drugs around her, and it made no difference if he was a dealer who didn't use or if he was an addict, she wouldn't have it."

"When was this?"

Bruce screwed up his face, thinking. "Oh, a month or two before the accident."

"Not later, then? Say, a week before she died?"

"No. It was at The Soul's Dance, a jazz club in Manchester. I remember the date because that was our second appearance there. We'd played it six months prior and the management wanted us back. Janet was jubilant, said we were about to hit the big time if a club like The Soul's Dance asked for a return engagement. She pointed out again the necessity for us to be professional, well mannered and prompt. Said a good impression was worth as much as a thousand quid spent elsewhere on marketing. Reminded us that one bad performance or bad attitude or rudeness shown by us could have vast repercussions." Bruce sagged forward in his chair, looking tired and old. "The music world is small. Word travels fast among club owners and concert bookers. If an act is difficult to deal with, if members are impolite or trash the dressing room, for example, the act's out of a job. Janet didn't want that. Well, none of us wanted that. We'd all worked our bums off getting to where we were. Which is why she was over the top with Myles. All that yelling for a bit of weed."

"Had you ever seen him smoke pot?"

"Never. That's why this was such a shock, hearing him admit he sold the stuff. He never gave any indication around me that he did that. I never smelled it on him, either, so I assume he was clean."

"What was his reaction to Janet's tirade?"

"Cool as a cucumber. I could see he wasn't perturbed by her concern. He tried to tell her it was no big deal, that he hadn't sold that much. He said he'd never get caught with anything on him, that he knew how to keep his stuff from being found, so there wasn't a question of him getting nabbed by the police for intent to sell. The amount was under the limit for prosecution."

"What did you think that meant? Have you any idea where Myles would have hidden the drug prior to selling it, if that's what he implied?"

"I suppose somewhere in his house. Maybe he had a wall safe behind a picture or kept it in a canister marked Flour in the kitchen. I've not been to his house so I don't know where he could hide something like that. And it wouldn't make sense to keep it at a friend's place. Every time he wanted to sell some, he'd have to go to the friend's house. Too inconvenient."

"How long did the argument last?"

Bruce shook his head. "I didn't time it, if that's what you mean. I came in on them when it was already going on. But I stood there listening for maybe a minute. When they stopped I still had most of my break left."

"What happened, what was the outcome?"

"I never found out 'cause they walked off. Myles opened the street door and followed Janet outside."

"Taking their altercation somewhere more private."

"Don't know about that, but the alley's good enough for that sort of thing. I felt embarrassed at having listened, but I was curious about Myles. He always professed to be such an upright bloke, supportive of Janet and the group. I don't know. People always amaze me."

Which, McLaren thought as he rose to leave, was as good a way to say it was another instance of someone letting someone else down.

****

McLaren exchanged CDs in his car's player and sang along to "Time Is Winding Up" as he drove to the pub. He wasn't bragging when he acknowledged he had a good singing voice. Many people had told him that. So it always astonished him when he sat with his sister

Gwen in church and heard the cacophony that she called singing. She sang hymns out of tune with a gusto that belied her search for the correct note. God would surely give her high marks for trying.

The Split Oak doubled as McLaren's office away from home and his favorite drinking spot. He had no set day to meet Jamie there, usually whenever they had a case to talk over or Jamie's wife was out of town or McLaren needed his friend. Which, considering the array of choices, made their meetings there fairly constant.

The pub's interior of polished oak paneled walls, old porcelain pitchers, jugs and plates, and age-yellowed maps never failed to cheer him, no matter how grueling his day had been. The welcoming embrace he felt on entering the main room was nearly as soothing as Dena's. It took him back to his childhood, where great aunts and uncles and grandparents welcomed him to their Victorian-style homes. Clutter was not his thing, but he couldn't deny that within the paneled interior and old plates ringing the walls he sensed a coziness and embrace. Maybe the personal objects of past lives stretched to him, linking him with those others. He never had those warm and fuzzy feelings when he walked into a modern décor building.

Jamie signaled to McLaren as he entered the pub, and after getting his pint at the bar, McLaren joined Jamie at the table.

"You look fine," Jamie said as McLaren took a sip of beer.

"Why shouldn't I?" McLaren set the glass mug on the beer mat.

"Just checking your health before I hit you with the bombshell, that's all."

Jamie's jokes were nothing new to McLaren, but this approach made him wary. His hand wrapped around the mug and he cautiously said, "Why? What do you know, or am I suppose to buy you a round before you let me in on the secret?"

"I'll have another bitter. Make it John Smith's, ta."

McLaren glared at Jamie but got up to get the drink. When he returned to the table, he said, "This better be worth more than the two quid I just paid out."

"You'll think it a bargain and praise my sleuthing ability, on top of that."

"Yeah, well, I'll let ya know. Spill it."

"I assume you refer to my golden titbit and not the beer." He grinned, the light catching the hints of red in his otherwise light brown hair. The hair color suited him. A soft hue to go with Jamie's light laughter. A darker shade would have visually shortened him. Which would come as a greater surprise to those unfortunate enough to discover the hardened, toned muscles in the man's slight physique.

"It *will* be the beer—and in your lap, too—if you don't cut the clowning and tell me."

Jamie nodded, said something about impatience and people having no time for humor. "You may find it interesting to know that a quantity of marijuana was found in Janet Ennis' house." He eyed McLaren, waiting for the reaction.

It wasn't slow in coming.

"What?" McLaren looked around the immediate vicinity. No one seemed to have heard him or paid him any attention. He lowered his voice and said, "Are you daft? *Pot*—in *Janet's* house? Where'd you hear this?"

"I'm sure. And I didn't hear it any place. I read it in the police report."

"Who was the SIO?"

"Like, you'll believe it if it's some bloke you like?"

"Trust is a more accurate word, but yes."

They didn't have to voice Harvester's name. The inference was there. Jamie mentioned the senior investigating officer's name, then added, "He doesn't lie, Mike. You know him. Straight as an arrow. Never been a suspicion of anything underhanded or not quite illegal under his command."

"Yeah, I know. I just can't imagine Janet Ennis with pot in her house. Where'd he find it? How much was there? If you tell me she was cultivating it in the basement, I'll move to Fiji and become a hermit."

The hermit comment very nearly hit the mark. McLaren had been dangerously close to embodying that trait months following his resignation from the police.

"The team discovered a large quantity of marijuana," Jamie said, watching McLaren. "Fifteen ounces. Evidently she, or whoever it belonged to, didn't want it found, for it had been placed beneath the sofa."

"A bit of a nod to secrecy, I agree, but it *is* a Class B drug."

"Five years plus a fine," Jamie said. "If they don't get a caution instead."

"Bit of an odd place for her to keep her pot if she's a regular user. Why not the coffee table or kitchen cupboard?"

"There you've got me. I'm not a user."

"Fifteen ounces." McLaren mulled over the

implication. "That's enough to traffic. You don't know if she did, I assume."

"This is the first occurrence of any drugs in her possession—first we know about, at least. Doesn't look good for her, does it?"

McLaren murmured that cannabis and Janet Ennis didn't add up. Not that musicians were all saints. Back stage culture was well known... "But I can't conceive Janet's personality with smoking pot. Or selling it."

Jamie said, "You ready for another non sequitur?"

"Sure. Might as well get it all over with at once."

"The plastic bag that the pot was in..." He paused, readying himself for McLaren's reaction. "The bag was devoid of fingerprints."

Chapter Twenty-One

No yelp came from McLaren this time. He muttered a barely audible "Bloody hell" and stared at the tabletop.

"If you or I had been on the case," Jamie said when the silence grew too thick between them, "we would've been so skeptical that we wouldn't have been able to sleep."

"Cynicism does that, yes." McLaren grunted. "Who wipes fingerprints from anything he touches in his house?" He mumbled, "Bloody hell" again and took a long drink of his beer.

"Have you talked to anyone who has a motive?"

"For killing Janet or for planting the pot?"

"Both. Either. It might be the same person."

McLaren recounted the people he'd spoken to and his impression of their motives. "As to alibis…" He shrugged, as though it had no bearing on his investigation. "Everyone has one. No one has one. They were all together or everyone was alone. I don't know right now who's lying. I need to think." He downed the last of his drink. The glass mug thudded onto the beer mat. "It's like trying to see a shadow in the smoke, Jamie. I think I've got a sharp image of something, then things shift and the smoke obscures my idea. I'm losing what thoughts I had."

"You're not losing a thing, Mike. You're sharper

231

than most coppers I know. But I think *you're* the shadow in the smoke. Even if the suspects don't encounter you, your presence is there. You're hunting through the smoke thrown up on this case and you're making sense of it all. Slowly, perhaps, but if you think about it all, it'll come clear."

"Like my own fire-starter."

"That reminds me. You think any more about who could've set that fire at your house?"

"A frightened suspect."

"And that is…"

McLaren's right eyebrow shot upward and he snorted. "You want a name already? You're joking."

"You must have an idea. You've worked on this long enough to get impressions of personalities and fears and secrets."

"I repeat my earlier statement—everyone. No one."

"Can't be. Think, Mike. Who did you tick off or anger? No one commits arson without motive. Even those lunatics who set fires because they like to see them burn have a reason." He looked at McLaren as thought a flicker of suspicion would consume his face. "When was the fire again?"

"Yesterday."

"Wednesday. Okay. Who'd you talk to Tuesday?"

McLaren leaned forward, his forearms on the tabletop. "Nora. But I can't see her setting a fire. Why would she ask me to take on the case and then turn around and sabotage it?"

"You're forgetting this past June."

"No, I'm not. I'll never forget June. I just don't think Nora would do that. She's not in the same class as Linnet Usherwood."

"Fine. Wear your blinkers. Who else?"

McLaren ticked off the names on his fingertips. "Helene Brogan, Janet's partner in the catering company."

"How'd she seem? Angry Janet had died and left her managing the business by herself?"

"Not at all. Very helpful and concerned."

"May be a front, may not be. Who else?"

"Dan Wilshaw. He was Janet's pianist."

"How'd he come across?"

"Quite believable. Sorry for Janet's death. Seemed like a true friend."

"I can't see him killing her and doing himself out of a job."

"Unless there's some personal problem that got out of hand."

"Is there?"

"I've not discovered anything yet. Ian O'Connor, Janet's bassist, is a real piece of work, though. About as low on the scale of Humanity as anyone can get."

"No empathy for her death, I take it."

"Oh, he's got heart, but it's all for himself. He was mad as hell that Janet didn't pay him more. One of their discussions about his salary could've got out of hand."

"Wonder how you could find out."

"But I didn't talk to him until today."

"Cancel Mr. Warmth's humanitarian award for the year."

"Janet's father is also in the running for the award."

"Terrific group of guys she surrounded herself with, Mike. Next."

"I could've talked to her other neighbors, but they

weren't involved in the fire, as Ian was."

"Being a neighbor does have its drawbacks. Any previous neighborly problems where the police were involved?"

McLaren mumbled that he'd not heard of any.

"So the barking dog or late night noise angle is out. Still, I suppose any of these people could've a motive that's not obvious yet."

McLaren nodded and slowly rotated his empty beer mug. The crowd at the far end of the room loudly encouraged a new player to try his hand at Ringing the Bull, a game in which the objective is to throw a metal ring onto a metal hook on the wall, with the ring connected to a rope and the rope suspended from the ceiling. The ring is then swung in such a fashion that it settles on the hook. The player held back, seeming to want to be coaxed. McLaren turned back to Jamie. "I can't rule out any of them following me home. I hate to admit it, but I wasn't particularly diligent watching my back side."

"So anyone could've followed you and learned where you live, then set the fire yesterday."

"Yeah."

"Or even phoned someone later."

"Meaning…what?"

"Someone you rattled or angered could've rung up a muscle-bound lad, who came over once your angry suspect learned where you live."

"Super."

An ear-splitting cheer rose from the game players as the newcomer's ring throw made two complete circles before landing squarely on the hook.

McLaren said, rather as an afterthought, "I also

talked to Corey Chappell. He's one of the firefighters who attended Janet's fire."

Jamie looked enviously at McLaren. As a working police officer, Jamie wouldn't have been able to pursue that route, but McLaren had no such restriction.

"Corey was belligerent at first," McLaren confessed, "and didn't want to talk."

"But you persuaded him."

"Good word choice. I can't see him starting my fire, though."

"You ever hear of the lust for power, when arson is committed by firefighters?"

****

Sean Fallon waited outside at The Sleeping Fox, slumped against the corner of the pub. The shadows of early evening reached with ever lengthening fingers toward the eastern horizon, wrapping buildings, objects and land in its darkening gloom. Sean gazed across the town square, a brick-paved rectangle that hosted vendors' booths on market days. Lights from storefronts and streetlamps glowed yellow in the gray dusk, pinpricks of sanity in the black whirlpool engulfing him. He'd never been inside the bookshop at the other end of the square, but the illuminated window with its colorful posters and stacks of books looked cheery. Friendly. A piece of normality in his nightmare. Same with the other establishments ringing the area. Commonplace. Safe. Where proprietors welcomed you without threats or looked at you as a golden egg-laying goose.

A sharp footfall on the bricks near him diverted his attention from the blinking pelican crossing light. He stood up, expecting Helene. A stranger approached, glanced at him, then entered the pub. Sean sagged against the wall. Where the hell was she?

Across the square a group of teenagers laughed their way toward him, the girls clinging to the boys and they, in turn, draping their arms over their companions' shoulders. The homogeneous group flowed down the street, past him, and entered the fish and chip shop. The aromas of the fried foods hit him in the stomach. He hadn't realized he was hungry until now.

He glanced at his watch again. The air had turned darker in the five minutes he'd been looking at the lights. Not that he had to work tonight. He'd changed with another chef so he could meet Helene. But the wait angered him. Not only because it wasted his time but it also illustrated Helene's opinion of him: not worth the effort of arriving on time.

Two cars turned off the High Street and into the market square, used as a car park on non-market days. He watched the cars park and the people emerge. Obviously a party too large to come in one car, Sean thought as the group walked toward the pub. They passed him without glancing at him, intent on their upcoming fun. The pub door opened, letting out a wave of music and laughter, then shut to leave him alone in the chilling air.

Sean stood up and stretched. To hell with the woman. He'd spent enough time on her. He had other things to do, a life to live. He'd deal with her some other day.

He'd taken a few steps toward the car park when he heard his name being called. Turning, he saw Helene hurrying up to him. Her figure was a faint silhouette against the indigo sky, but he recognized her. He glanced at the smear of dark gray clouds creeping in from the west and waited until she was within several feet of him before saying, "I thought maybe you weren't coming."

A rumble of thunder underscored Helene's light laugh. "Wishful thinking, dear? Or potentially disappointed? Now, don't tell me. I couldn't bear to hear the wrong answer. I'd be devastated." She grabbed Sean's hand and steered him to a bench on the western edge of the square, away from the main flow of pedestrian traffic and out of the majority of the store lighting glare, a dark pocket that suited Helene's furtiveness.

Sean glanced up at the blackened façade of the town hall, rising phantom-like behind them, a nebulous bulk against the murky skyline. He clasped his hands and wondered what he'd say to her. Wondered what she'd say when his response wasn't to her liking. Had she picked this gloomy spot so she wouldn't be seen when she knifed him? Did she have a muscular friend in the shadows, ready to kidnap him? People were sometimes kidnapped and held for ransom. But whom would Helene extort if Sean didn't hand over the money? His wife and he had nothing in the bank, had nothing of value to pawn. And he had no family. Sean shifted his gaze to Helene, now a vague profile beside him, and tried to swallow. His throat tightened as she shifted and put her hand into her jacket pocket. He felt his muscles tightening, ready for fight or flight.

"I've wasted enough time." Helene's voice came to him from the darkness, startling him in its closeness. She'd dropped her friendly, concerned tone of their meeting; frost now coated the words. "You bring the money?"

His throat went dry as he searched for her face. He choked on his words as he tried to speak. "Uh, no. I didn't."

"What do you mean? You rang me up, said you wanted to get this money deal over with. I assumed—" She stopped, perhaps her sixth sense suggesting she was wrong.

She leaned toward him and Sean could feel her upper arm against his, feel the heat, the flesh, the implied warning. He leaned away from her; she was too close.

"Well?" The one word broke into the silence like a gunshot.

"I don't have the money, no." He could sense that she was looking around the square—not because he could see her movement but because he couldn't feel her breath on his face.

"You have a cash card?" she said when she spoke again. "I think there's a bank on the High Street."

Sean shook his head, afraid to trust his voice.

"I'd make you show me your wallet contents but you could've left the card at home."

"Honest, Helene, I don't have one. Never did."

"Liar."

Strangely, the insult stung. Like a slap across his face. She needn't demean his character... Sean sat up straighter, more determined than he had ever been with her. "I don't have a card, but that's not the point. I'm not giving you any money, Helene. Not now, not tomorrow, not ever. I didn't kill Janet and you can't blackmail me for your silence."

"Can you prove you didn't?" Her voice dropped to

a chilling whisper that cut through Sean's blood. "Just because the police overlooked you five years ago doesn't mean you're home free. I believe there's no statute of limitation on murder."

"You're all words, Helene. The cops never considered me a suspect because they never considered Janet's death as murder. And even if the investigation went that way, I had an alibi."

"Sleeping with your girlfriend is hardly a worthy alibi, dear."

"I wasn't sleeping with her. Or anyone. And I don't have to defend myself to you. I didn't kill Janet, I'm not giving you any money, and you can't fabricate my guilt." He stood up, his heart racing. Looking down at her, he felt more powerful. Like a puppeteer controlling a marionette. Like a cat toying with a mouse.

Helene smiled, and he saw the glint of light from a streetlamp on her white teeth. She tilted her head up. He sensed that she looked at him with contempt, for the tone of her voice was sharp and low-pitched. "You little bastard. Don't play high and mighty with me. I've got position in this community. Who do you think the cops will believe when I tell them about your quarrel with Janet? Me, or you—a convicted criminal whom Janet fired? I heard your argument; I know what you said. You had everything to lose if you lost your job, so that's motive enough for the police. Try to convince them nothing came of your anger." She sat still, the quiet creeping between them, the shift of power inching into Helene's hands.

Sean took a step forward, his fists clenched, his jaw set. A veil seemed to drop before his eyes, for he barely saw Helene. "You on something? Must be. Or you're sloshed. Or barmy. 'Cause there's no truth to anything you're saying and you bloody well know it. Now, bugger off before I make you sorry you didn't."

"Darling, what a tone! So angry! I know you're just talking, putting up a brave front to convince yourself you're fine. But I'm serious, Sean. And your pathetic threat doesn't mean a damned thing." She stood up and stared at him, her breath once more in his face, her hand on his sleeve. "I mean everything I say. I want that money, and if you don't come through with it…" She shrugged and again stuck her hand into her jacket pocket. "I can't predict the future, of course, but in this instance I believe you *will* be sorry you didn't come up with the cash." She patted his arm and leaned into him. "Understand?"

"I understand you're trying to laugh this off. But I want *you* to understand that you can't intimidate me. If you don't leave me alone *you'll* see how fast something can develop. Accidents happen all the time, you know."

Helen's laugh cut through his warning. Her hand slid onto his cheek and she held it there while she said, "Darling, I'm not just a gorgeous figure and pretty face. I *do* have some brains, and I wish you'd credit me with using them. You can rabbit on all you like, but it doesn't change a thing between us. Your words are very brave, but you forgot something."

In spite of his resolve, he asked what she meant.

"Curiosity is a good sign, dear. It shows you're using your own cerebral facilities, limited though they are. What you forgot, sweets, is that there are such things as letters, lawyers and safe deposit boxes. Need I say more?"

Her hand remained on his cheek, warm and

familiar. Sean jerked his head to the left and her arm dropped to her side. She squeezed his arm and turned toward the pub. Calling to him over her shoulder, she added, "Try to remember that if anything happens to me, my lawyer will be the first one to talk to the cops. I'll expect the money, then. Have a nice evening, dear."

She opened the pub door, and a ripple of laughter, conversation, and music slipped outside. Components of ordinary lives in Sean's surreal existence. The door closed as she slipped inside and Sean wandered back to his car, panic and fear formulating the plan that would free him from Helene's trap. The first pelting of rain hit him as he unlocked his car door.

Chapter Twenty-Two

McLaren would have laughed at Jamie's comment if the subject hadn't been so serious. He shoved the empty beer glass away from him and said, "I know some firefighters go the arsonist route. It's a power trip for them: the media coverage, the call out of the service and personnel to combat the fire he set, the police, the crowd of onlookers. Even his 'name' in the newspaper and on television reports…if he's satisfied with a vague reference to himself and his deed. But I don't believe Corey Chappell is my driveway arsonist. He didn't seem the type."

Jamie set down his pint and slid his fingers to the edge of the beer mat, where they traced the rounded corner. "There you go again, Mike. Need I remind you that most criminals don't seem the type? What is the type, anyway? A tattoo declaring 'I'm an arsonist' on their forehead? An ever-present can of paraffin with them? Come on, Mike, think logically."

"I am. You know how you get impressions about people if you're in the job long enough. Anyway, I didn't get physical with Corey. I just got a bit vocal. And there's no reason for him to torch my drive. I didn't imply he was a suspect in Janet's murder. Or arson."

"Sometimes it doesn't take that much to scare folks into acting. Just having a cop—okay, okay, even an ex-cop—sniffing around sets them off. They get spooked and they act." He drained the last of his beer before admitting, "You might be right, Mike. Aren't most fires set by men?"

"Yes. Something about a lack of a father-figure at home, and the mother was domineering and abusive." He looked over at the Ring-the-Bull players. The excitement had died down and they were all at the bar, ordering drinks. "I don't know if he found out where I live, but he couldn't have followed me home. I talked to Myles Tyson after I spoke to Corey, and that was in a pub. I'd phoned him and asked him to meet me there. So even in my befuddled dotage I bet you that I would have noticed Corey's car following me from his house to the pub and then on to my house."

"Does kind of open oneself to more risk than usual for being spotted, yes."

McLaren stood up. Dusk had fallen in the short time he and Jamie had been talking, and he wanted to get home to phone Dena. "Thanks for the tip on the pot, but I'll take it with a grain of salt."

He had turned and took the car key from his pocket when Jamie said, "Hardly anyone's a saint, Mike. Take off your rose-tinted glasses. You're falling in love with her."

McLaren walked toward the door without another word.

****

Sean sat in the front room of his flat and stared out at the night. Darkness had nearly claimed the land but fingerholds of pale sunlight, almost without color, clung to the higher elevations. The light gilded a crest of trees toward the east, crowning the tallest section of yellow leaves with a pat from Midas. The rain had not caught up with him, but it would come. He could feel it. The aroma came downwind, announcing the storm, even if the swirl of dry, cast off leaves didn't.

He fumbled for his beer in the half-light. He hadn't bothered to turn on any lamps; he felt less vulnerable in the gloom, as if Helene wouldn't find him or he could bury himself away from everyone forever. A jolt of lightning crackled through the ebony clouds and the room flashed into stark relief momentarily before dying back to black. He returned the beer to the table and turned back toward the window as the cloud broke overhead.

Where the hell was he supposed to get the money Helene demanded? Even if he sold his car, that wouldn't bring more than half her price. And if he ignored her? He jumped as the rain drummed on the lid of a metal rubbish bin. Could he call her bluff? Did she really have something for the police? Even if she didn't, would they investigate anyway, and would they find out about the bribe?

A car drove slowly down the street. As it braked, its taillights mirrored red in the small puddles. Like blood, he thought, mesmerized by the brilliance of the color. Fresh blood, flowing blood. Or fire. Fire destroyed a lot of things, including people.

The rattle of a key in the kitchen door pulled Sean from his thoughts. A gust of rain-chilled air rushed into the room and the door eased shut. Keys clattered onto the top of the table, a chair scraped, shoes thudded onto the floor, and seconds later his wife padded into the room.

"Didn't you pay the electric?" she asked as she

reached for the light switch. "It's pitchy in here."

"Leave it alone," Sean muttered. "I like it this way."

"Fine. Feed your darker side." Kathryn walked over to the sofa and sat down. She scooted around on the cushion until she was facing him. "What's the matter? You don't usually sit in the dark."

"I feel like it now, okay?"

"Sure." She grabbed his hand and kissed it. "Tell me about it. I'm a good listener."

In spite of his feeling, he smiled. "You forgot to say you're beautiful, too."

"You already knew that."

Sean didn't need the lamp turned on to see her. He could picture her in his mind—a pixie with long, dark hair. Sighing, he squeezed her hand, yet didn't turn to her. The rainy night called to him.

Slowly, almost painfully, he related his talks with Helene. Toward the end of his speech he turned and looked at her. She was a dark shape against the blackness.

"What are you going to do?" she said as she slumped against his chest.

"What do you think I should do?"

"Ignore her. You didn't do anything to Janet, not even plead with her to take you back. Helene's got no foundation for her threat."

"But she'll go to the police. I know her. She'll tell them her story and they'll pull me in for an interview. I can't afford that kind of publicity, Kathryn! You know what that would do? I'd be fired."

"Might not do. You're innocent. Why fire an innocent person and a smashing chef?"

245

"You don't know Helene, or you wouldn't say that. She's got a way about her."

"The police aren't dumb, Sean. They'll want more than Helene's say-so, surely."

"I know there are such things as incompetent or uncaring cops, bribes, influenced juries."

Kathryn bent her head back and kissed his jaw. "I know you're worried, honey, but I really don't believe Helene's got any chance at all with this. We'll give her the elbow and you'll see how fast you're shut of her. Now, you hungry? What do you want?"

"Another beer."

"No, you don't. You want food. Everything looks less dire when you're not so peckish." She got up and turned on the lamp. "It's better already. More cheery. What do you say to lamb chops, leftover bubble and squeak, and a salad? Stay there, it's my night to cook."

He didn't tell Kathryn, but he had no intention of moving. Looking back outside, he stared into the rain and wondered how he could get rid of Helene.

****

The rain hadn't yet moved into the Hope Valley. Leaving Jamie in the pub, McLaren drove the few miles to his house, the stone farmhouse in which he'd grown up. Funny he'd never thought of it before, but now that he considered the house and the land, he'd been surrounded by his new career all his life, even as a child. Maybe his work as a repairer of dry stone walls had been inevitable, ordained from his birth. Maybe he'd gravitated to it when he resigned from the police last year, grabbing onto something that offered familiarity and comfort like an old friend, something that didn't talk back or sabotage your future.

He slowed his car as he made the turn by the cliff face. The wood was denser here and the road slightly narrower. As he passed the rocky outcrop he glanced in the rearview mirror, then leaned forward to peer around the bend. The road was deserted; there'd be no repeat of June's incident.

The car's headlights swept across the spent long grass and wildflowers bordering the road. Leaves tinged with red, yellow and orange lay thick between the wizened stems, filling the air with the pungent aroma of dead vegetation. Several dried leaves by the roadside rose in a spiral and chased his car for a few yards before falling again to earth.

McLaren settled back in the car seat and selected "Green Fields" by the Brothers Four on the CD. The slow tempo suited his mood; he had a lot to think about. He had even more a minute later, for as he turned the car into his drive he saw his garden shed on fire.

****

He jammed the car to a stop, set the hand brake, and leaped out of the car. The roof and the side of the shed facing him were a wall of flames, reaching with greedy fingers to the lowest tree branches just feet above. McLaren ran to the front of the house, grabbed the garden hose, turned on the tap full force, and dashed back to the shed. He soaked the tree branches nearest the fire then directed the water onto the structure. The wood snapped and sizzled when the water hit the hot surface. McLaren swept the stream of water back and forth then dashed around to the other side of the shed.

The fire hadn't taken hold here as strongly, although flames lapped at the overhanging eaves. He sent a blast of water along the eave line, then soaked the three sides of the shed before returning to the main section of fire.

The flames were more intense here; a blanket of heat pushed McLaren back several feet. He angled his head to divert the full brunt of the temperature from his face, and squinted against the glare. The white paint crackled and snapped along the burn line and threw back the intense light of the flames. He shaded his eyes with his left hand, took a step closer to the fire, and felt the hair on the back of his hand curl and singe. But he retreated quickly as several asphalt shingles slid down the roof and landed where he had been standing. The grass turned black around the burning mass and he doused it with water until the pile sighed and smoke ceased to rise.

He had just soaked the foundation, fearful that more dry grass and brush would catch fire and spread, when there was a movement near the far corner of his house. He turned, staring for a precious moment. A dark figure rose from the bushes near his bedroom. He yelled and the figure bolted across the lawn.

McLaren dropped the hose and charged after the person. The light from the fire lit his way for several yards, jerking and stretching his shadow before him as he ran into the night. Even beyond the reach of the firelight he could make out the runner, distinct against an indistinct backdrop. McLaren could track him easily enough. The crunch of dry leaves and the snap of old tree branches marked the runner's route as clearly as if he'd yelled out his directions.

They crashed through the bushes separating his front garden from the road, the brittle branches cracking under the assault. Rubber squeaked against stone as the assailant scrambled over the low stone wall. A thud, as if the shoe hit a log, was followed by an exclamation, then the crunch of more dead leaves until the rubber soles found the tarmac.

McLaren was just seconds behind. Knowing the landscape better than his assailant, McLaren avoided many of the downed tree boughs and tangle of thistles that clawed at the other person. Yet he had got a later start in the chase and his eyes had had to adjust from the brightness of the fire to the black night. As he vaulted over the stone wall, he calculated he would catch up with the man on the road. And on a flat, unencumbered surface he rarely lost a race.

Once he felt the road beneath his feet, McLaren stopped. Should he search up or down from here, or go back for a torch and look through the underbrush lining the lane? He'd waste value minutes if he returned for the light and the man would get away. He stood in the dark, listening, his breath ragged in his throat. No leaves or branches cracked, no footsteps slapped the tarmac. There was no scatter of gravel along the verge. The runner seemed to have vanished.

McLaren jogged up the road in the direction of his house. He had jumped his wall farther south, several dozen yards down from the large willow that sat near the edge of his front garden. If the runner had gone this way, moving along the road, his bulk would have blended in with the mass of the wood. He would be making for his car, no doubt parked farther up, beyond McLaren's house. There was no other place he could logically be headed to; McLaren had passed no car on this road.

As he sprinted across the foot of his drive, he

glanced to his left. The shed had collapsed and was now a burning pile of lumber and garden tools. The nearby trees and grass had not ignited. He dashed ahead, barely aware of the scent of charred wood hanging in the air.

Several hundred yards north of his property line, he admitted he was wasting his energy. He had come upon no one or no car, he had heard nothing but his own labored breathing and the thud of his shoes on the hard-packed road. No movement caught his attention, no shape suggesting a person stood out in the landscape. Begrudgingly, he ran back.

He found the same thing south of his property—or didn't discern anything. The road and the wood bordering it seemed to hold nothing more sinister than nocturnal creatures and clumps of thistle. He turned and walked back, keeping to one side of the road, peering into the blackness. Only the call of an owl answered his unspoken question.

The fire had died to nothing more than a campfire by the time he got back. Yellow flames mirrored in the puddles of water threw back the color and light but it was nothing extraordinary. McLaren picked up the hose and sprayed several areas until the flames died. He stuck the nozzle into the top of the smoldering mass and found a branch on the ground near his drive. As he picked up the hose and redirected the stream of water, he stirred the debris and checked for live embers. Curls of smoke escaped into the air but nothing snapped or winked at him. He spread the burnt remains as thinly as he could over the grass, then soaked the area again until puddles collected and seeped together. He would have remained there longer but the sky cracked with sound and the rain pelted the earth.

He felt nothing—no cold, no wetness. Only exhaustion and anger. He slowly returned to the tap, turned off the water, and coiled up the hose. It was a strange object, part of it cold and stiff, part of it warm and flexible. He wiped his hands on the wet grass, got the key from his car, and, after fumbling with the kitchen door lock and doorknob, entered his house. He peeled off his wet shoes and clothes at the door, left them on the floor, and took a shower.

When he'd brewed himself a cup of coffee and warmed a plate of leftover roast beef and carrots, he wandered into the back room. He wasn't in the mood to fool with a proper place setting; the comfort of the sofa appealed more to him. He sat down, ate his supper in silence, and thought through his day.

The acrid smell of the spent fire had crept into the house but he kept the windows closed. Opening them would bring in more of the stench; he didn't want it in the furnishings and his clothes as a lingering reminder of his enemy.

Of course the obvious question was the man's identity. Was his arsonist the same one who had torched Janet's studio? Had he frightened someone with his questions, frightened someone so much he had to silence McLaren? Get rid of him?

But silence worked both ways. What might have been burnt on purpose, at his place or Janet's, could cover up something missing from the burn site or destroy something planted at the site. And if he focused on the deliberation of arson, he need look no further than his garden shed tonight. The side facing the road had been torched first and more aggressively than the other three sides. Therefore, the arsonist had wanted

McLaren to see the fire as he drove up. But what was the message he was supposed to get? Of course he had angered someone, but was the burning of his shed and the fire on his drive to underscore that anger? Or was it something more?

He rubbed his head. His whole body ached with the sudden, deep fatigue that hits after a tense event. He set his empty plate on the side table and stretched his legs out in front of him. What had he and Jamie said in the pub about arsonists?

Grabbing his coffee mug, he stared at Dena's photograph. He'd planned on phoning her tonight, but he needed to think—about his fire and Janet's death. He leaned back and considered the possibilities.

Most arsonists were male. That was a statistic no one could refute. That arson was the crime of a coward also had numbers to prove the claim. Fire was easy to set and the instigator didn't have to confront his victim. The comfort of distance, time and domination empowered these people and gave them a sense of worth they didn't ordinarily feel. Consequently, their victims tended to be easily controlled, either by being smaller and weaker than the arsonist, or by being made defenseless.

McLaren took a sip of coffee. Did anyone he'd spoken with fit these criteria? Helene didn't match the definition of a coward, nor did anyone in Janet's group of friends and acquaintances. Who felt disrespected or powerless in his or her life?

He wrapped his hands around the mug. There was more to the arsonist profile, though. Victims, if they ended up in the fire and weren't merely inconvenienced with property loss as he had been tonight, were often made defenseless. Whether that happened through unconsciousness or other means, the object was to dehumanize the victim.

He paused again, his gaze wandering to Dena's face. She'd been attacked and abducted recently. Thank God she hadn't been the victim of an arsonist. But had Janet suffered that fate? Cheryl Kerrigan, the Home Office pathologist, mentioned the depression in Janet's skull; a microphone was in the debris of her studio and Ian had mentioned they never rehearsed there. Yet Cheryl couldn't conclusively match the same brand and model of microphone to the skull injury during the post mortem examination. But the incongruity of the mike being in the studio suggested foul play, at least to McLaren.

However, even if this were true, the method of murder was less personal, less confrontational than a gun or knife demanded. Could it have been a revenge arson after all? Janet not being an intended victim?

"What do you think, darling?" he asked Dena, draining the last of his coffee. "Am I completely round the twist on this one? When we're married, you're going to be subjected to a lot of my doubts. Will it be worth it?" He got to his feet and turned out the light. Women committed most of the spite arsons for that reason; it eliminated the closeness needed in using a gun or knife.

But when he finally got into bed an hour later, the questions still whirled in his mind. There were other motives prompting revenge arsons. One of which was labor disputes. He closed his eyes, thinking of Sean and Ian, and breathing in the stench of wet ashes.

Chapter Twenty-Three

McLaren poked through the ashes the next morning hoping to find some clue as to the arsonist's identity. But other than the certain odor of petrol, which could have come from the can he stored in the garden shed, nothing presented itself as suspicious. He tossed the stick over the stone wall, returned to the kitchen, poured himself another cup of coffee, and sat at the table. The button he'd found yesterday seemed to wink at him from the tabletop.

He picked it up, unconcerned about compromising the owner's fingerprints. There would be none. The fire would have obliterated them. He admitted he wasn't up on fashion, but he did know that the Firetrap brand was expensive. He could probably get several pairs of his jeans for the price of one Firetrap pair.

Which suggested the jeans owner was well to do. In Dena's league, though he had never seen her in that brand of jeans. Still, there were others connected with Janet's case who were wealthy.

His mind racing, McLaren grabbed the phone and called his sister. Gwen was the perfect person for his scheme. He told her so when she answered.

"Because you look the part," he said, trying to quell her skepticism.

"The part. What part? This is illegal, Mike. You're saying I look like a burglar or con man?"

"I'll be doing the burglary," he said, irritated she hadn't shown any enthusiasm. "You're just going to engage the person in conversation."

"Super. What am I supposed to talk about? I don't even know this…what—suspect? Killer?"

"Don't overdramatize. You always overdramatize things. Just talk to her for a few minutes until I give you the high sign."

"Something subtle, I'm sure. Like an owl hoot or a meow."

"I'll type up a list of questions you can ask. You'll be taking a survey. Simple enough, even for you."

"I thought you said I was perfect for this and now you're belittling my help."

"Sorry. I'm just anxious to get this going." He waited for his sister to think it through. Gwen was older than he, fifty to his thirty-seven. She had the creative streak in the family, a fine artist who enjoyed a local reputation and earned a nice living through her painting. Looking about as average as anyone, McLaren conceded, mentally picturing Gwen's gray-streaked brunette hair and five and a half foot frame. Add her ready smile and the dog. He cleared his throat, getting impatient. "Well? Will you help me?"

****

"Did I ever tell you how persuasive you are?"

McLaren snorted. "Cut the soft soap. You want to help or not?"

"What kind of survey are you going to prepare?"

"It makes a difference?"

"On the way I dress, yes."

McLaren sighed. This was turning out to be more complicated than was necessary. His gaze fell on a photo of Gwen, her husband and their dog, a standard sized poodle. "Pet ownership. Dog food and such. Bring Lafayette along. It'll add authenticity to the thing. Pick me up in an hour. She's seen my car." He rang off and started creating a list of poll questions.

"You look very nice," he said later, after Gwen had picked him up. He turned in the seat to pet the poodle sitting behind him. "Hi, Lafayette. Ready for your big role?" Repositioning the clasp on Gwen's necklace, he added, "Perfect, in fact."

"Enough like a pollster, then." She flicked a piece of lint from her gray suit jacket.

"Yeah. Here's a clipboard with the list of questions. And a can of dog food. Give it to Eva for participating in the survey. People love getting free stuff."

"Where'd you get a can of dog food?"

"Jerry brought a couple dozen cans when I dogsat Lafayette last spring, remember? And here's a badge I made for you." He tossed the can onto the back seat, then angled the name badge with 'Noah's Care' printed across the top toward her so she could see it. The cardstock rectangle was encased in a transparent plastic nametag holder. He leaned to his right and pinned the name badge on Gwen's jacket lapel.

"What's it say?"

"Marian Joseph. Your company is Noah's Care, by the way."

"Mary and Joseph? Are you kidding? I already sound like a phony."

"*Marian*," he enunciated. "Not Mary And. Anyway, no one looks at nametags. Besides, Eva will be looking at your dog and trying to keep hers calm."

"*Calm?* What's she got…a Doberman?"

"A boxer. Don't worry. You'll do fine."

"I'm glad one of us thinks so. Where am I going?" She slowed the car as it neared the end of the village.

"Chesterfield." He gave her the address.

"What's with your get-up?" She eyed McLaren's dark blue colored shirt, cotton twill trousers and the clipboard he carried. A baseball cap of the same color, enlivened with a nondescript embroidered logo on the front, perched on the back of his head.

"Camouflage. If anyone sees me, I hope I'm mistaken for a workman."

"Reducing the suspicion of your prowling about their back garden. Super. How are you going to do this? Did you think that far ahead?"

"You'll let me out at the top of the street. I'll walk down a bit, then cut across the back gardens. You park a few houses up from Eva's."

"So it looks like I'm polling the street, I know."

"Then you and Lafayette go up to Eva's house, and when she answers, you engage her in the poll. I'll slip into her house through the back."

"Slip into her house is a euphemism for burglary, Mike. Don't you care about getting caught?"

"I won't get caught if you do your part well enough."

"Thanks for the warning."

"Give me three minutes once I'm inside, Gwen. You can engage her for three minutes."

"Sure, but one slight problem besides you getting nicked. How do I know when to start marking time?"

"Time it from when you drop me off, then. Make it five minutes total by your watch. You can break off the survey when the five are up. I don't dare risk giving you a vocal signal."

"Her husband or kids won't be home? No maid to worry about spotting you?"

"I'll have to chance it. Anyway, I'm just going into the bedroom."

"Oh, cuts your chance of discovery way down, then." She shook her head, her mouth screwed up. "What about burglar alarms?"

"If she's home, it won't be turned on. Especially not if she answers the door."

"Which is why you don't want to do this at night."

"Not with a damned alarm ready to announce my presence."

"Well, I hope you've thought it all out. If not, I'll bring you flowers on visiting day."

"Just talk loudly when you're questioning her. I need to know when you start."

They drove the rest of the way in silence.

McLaren had no trouble gaining access to Eva's back garden, but he found himself sweating as he walked up to the back of the house. Breaking into Charlie Harvester's house had been a snip compared to this. He waited until he heard Gwen's voice before trying the back door. It opened.

Once inside, he eased the door shut and stood in the utility room. No alarm rang, no one rushed into the room to see what had happened. Eva's dog didn't even investigate. Only Gwen's and Eva's voices sounded in the otherwise stillness.

He glanced around the area. It was perhaps ten by fifteen feet, with another door on the opposite wall from the back door. A coat rack, umbrella stand, small wooden chair and metal baker's rack took up one of the solid walls; a washer, clothes dryer and small shelves occupied the other wall. A basket of clothes sat on top of the washer. McLaren searched through the contents for the pair of Firetrap jeans. Nothing. Next, he looked in the washer and clothes drier. They were empty.

He tiptoed to the doorway. Gwen was still talking, asking about the dog's exercise routine. Good ole Gwen. He'd have to do something nice for her when this was over.

McLaren glanced down the hallways. There were two of them, each coming from a different side of the house and meeting at the vestibule leading into the utility room. He tiptoed a few feet down one hall before stopping. It seemed to lead to the front of the house, for Gwen's voice was decidedly louder in this hallway. He eased back to the vestibule and hurried in the opposite direction, toward what he hoped was the bedroom wing.

Evidently, he had guessed correctly. The hall was carpeted in the same creamy color as the front rooms and held three closed doors. He crept up to the nearest door and, after listening with his ear against the door and hearing nothing, opened it. The room evidently was a guest room; no personal items ornamented dresser or night table tops. The second room mimicked the first and McLaren moved on. He struck pay dirt at the end of the hall and eased into the room, shutting the door behind him.

The room didn't match Eva's penchant for gold and white tones. Instead, the walls, bedding and upholstered chairs were done in shades of lilac and blue. The old English style furniture was about as far from the front room's modern minimalism as one could get. Maybe Eva's husband had insisted on the romantic look here.

Two large closets on McLaren's left were adorned with full length mirrors on their outside panels, and McLaren jumped as he crossed the room, momentarily startled by the reflection of the blue-costumed worker. He laid the clipboard on a nearby chair and opened the first closet door.

Obviously Eva's things, he thought, looking at the line-up of clothes. He glanced at the garments as he pushed the hangers apart, noting every bit of clothing in the long line. There were no jeans.

The husband's closet was as packed with clothes as Eva's, but the jeans hanging there were a different brand. McLaren closed the doors in disgust.

Were the jeans at the dry cleaner's? Had she loaned them to a friend? Did she even wear jeans? Had he zeroed in on the wrong person?

He was making for the door, ready to end the hunt, when he heard the click of the doorknob turning. He froze, glanced at the closet, then ran to the four-poster bed. He squeezed himself beneath the bed frame just as the door opened.

McLaren flattened himself against the floor and held his breath. From beneath the edge of the duvet he saw the person's shoes walk into the room, hesitate slightly, then move straight ahead. Making for one of the dressers, McLaren thought, and was rewarded with the sound of a drawer opening and closing. The shoes—sensible, sturdy, and highly polished—moved slightly to the left and went up on their toes.

A muttered "Damn" crept into the silence, thin and high toned. The lower portion of black trousers and hands came down quickly on the blue carpet, and the toes of the shoes dug into the plush pile.

McLaren tried to scoot toward the other end of the bed, putting more space between himself and whom he assumed was the maid. He pressed his cheek into the carpet and inched his head backward. His flesh stung as he squirmed out of her line of sight and he felt his chest rub against the bottom of the mattress. As the maid's fingers grasped the edge of the duvet his hand found a piece of fabric at his shoulder. He pushed it in front of him, glad of the carpet that silenced any noise. Punching it up in front of his face, he prayed every prayer he knew and waited.

Barely two feet from McLaren's face the fingers enlarged into a hand that crept farther underneath the bed frame. He swore silently, perspiration rolling down his face and collecting around his shirt collar. An exasperated "Hell" shot nearly into his ear as the hand patted the carpet. The edge of the duvet lifted and an eye seemed to stare at him.

Slowly, the nose, right cheek, ear, chin and mouth presented themselves to McLaren's nervous gaze. A hand swept a long strand of dark hair behind the ear, then rested on the carpet, supporting the upper torso as it bent lower.

McLaren inched his fingers behind the bundle of fabric, keeping hold of it with his teeth as his hand came to rest against his chest. He waited, not daring to breathe, hoping all she saw was darkness.

The edge of the duvet dropped but not before the light illuminated a small silver glint nearly touching McLaren's left elbow. He grabbed the earring and carefully placed it within a few inches of where the woman's hand had been. Seconds later, the duvet's edge stirred. Another portion of the bottom of the dresser presented itself to McLaren's view, and the searching fingers again crept beneath the bed frame. He snatched his hand back as her fingers slid over the earring.

After the hand retreated from view and the door closed behind the maid, he let out his breath and muttered a prayer of thanks. He lifted the duvet's edge, prepared to drop it should he need to. No one else appeared to be in the room, yet he counted to fifty before moving. He would have liked to have stayed where he was for several minutes, would have liked to make sure that the maid didn't come back. But he'd lost track of time during the earring hunt and didn't know if Gwen was still at the front door or had left. Eva might come into the room any moment.

He pushed the fabric from his face and into the room. He wriggled out from beneath the bed and stood up. No one was there. As he glanced at his feet he nearly collapsed in astonishment. The fabric that had shielded him under the bed was a pair of Firetrap jeans. A button was missing.

Why would Eva hide them? Did they have telltale petrol stains on them? Was she waiting for the case to die down before she risked washing and wearing them? Were they even hers; perhaps she was hiding them for a friend.

He held them at arm's length. They seemed to be Eva's size, though he wasn't certain. He stuffed them under his shirt, sprinted down the hall and out the door, and ran from the house as fast as he dared.

"You seem to have eaten a very large lunch,"

Gwen said when she picked him up on the main road. She poked McLaren's usually flat midriff. "Raid the kitchen while you were there?"

"Comedy is not your forte." He rubbed Lafayette's head. "Any problems?"

"None. How about you? Unless you call your sudden pregnancy a problem."

Ignoring her remark, McLaren took off his cap and leaned back in the car seat. He laid his left arm across his forehead. "Damn, I'm sweaty. If nothing else happens until bedtime, it's still a lovely day."

"Cryptically meaning you found what you were after. Is that how your cheek got hurt?"

"Why? What's the matter with it?" He angled the rearview mirror toward him and looked at his face.

"Hey! I'm driving. I need that." Gwen repositioned the mirror and glanced at the traffic behind her. "Red and raw. That's what's wrong with it. What did you scrape it on? I can't believe Eva did that. She was talking to me the whole time."

McLaren ran his fingertips across his cheek. He winced. "Bloody hell, that hurts. I guess it happened on the rug."

"The rug?"

"Beneath the bed."

Gwen shook her head and passed a slow moving car. "I won't ask. God knows I'm dying of curiosity, but I won't ask."

"I was hiding from someone. Probably the maid. Eva strikes me as the sort who'd have a maid. She walked into the bedroom and I had to hide."

"Eva?"

"The maid."

"Well, wear your battle scar proudly. At least you got what you went for."

McLaren opened his mouth to retaliate, then stared at his sister. "Bloody hell. I left the clipboard in her bedroom."

****

Gwen dropped McLaren back at his house, told him not to make a career of burglary, and waved goodbye as she drove off. McLaren showered and changed clothes before heading to Dan Wilshaw's house.

Dan was vehement about the pot. Janet didn't take drugs. It wasn't part of her culture. She had strict rules for her employees, whether the trio or her catering company. She did not tolerate drugs or drinking; if you overstepped the line, you were fired.

McLaren got a different story from Ian. He said Janet tolerated pot, but taking anything harder put you in jeopardy of your job.

Helene said she never saw Sean or anyone come to work stoned; she didn't believe Janet took drugs. "I don't know about her musicians," Helene said, "but there was never a hint of drug taking connected to the catering employees. You might want to ask Tom. He was her boyfriend at that time, so he might know something. 'Course, his statement might be colored slightly. Break-up and all that, you know. I don't know if I'd really put much stock in what he says. Jilted lovers are sometimes quite bitter, aren't they?"

Tom Murray admitted he could have placed the bag of pot under Janet's couch, but he didn't. "You've got your time wrong," he said, clearly irritated with the early morning visit. "We broke up in June. What you're talking about happened in September. And how would I have planted it? I didn't have her house key any more."

"You could've had a duplicate made."

"Why would I want to break into her house? To stash pot under her sofa? Why? How would I know it would be found?"

"It would be found if she was dead in suspicious circumstances. The police routinely search the home of a murder victim."

"You're daft. Anyway, I don't take drugs, so I wouldn't know how to get any. And anyone who really knows Janet would know she doesn't smoke that stuff, so what would have been the point?"

That *is* the question, McLaren thought as the door closed behind him.

Still, a suggestion of revenge clung to the secreted marijuana. No fingerprints on the bag did, too. Whoever hid the pot didn't want it traced back to him, and that strongly suggested Janet's killer. For, to make sure the pot was found, there had to be a crime large enough to involve a complete police investigation. That large crime was murder.

So it came back to who wanted Janet dead. He sat in his car, re-reading the list of names and the notes he'd made beside each one. Only Stuart, Sean and Ian had the obvious motive of anger, but motive didn't always present itself so blatantly. He rang up Nora, asked if he could see her, then drove back to Buxton.

"I have them here," Nora said as McLaren entered her house. She led the way to the dining room table and switched on the chandelier. The shoebox bulged with bank statements and canceled checks. "Is this what you want to see?" She stood beside the chair, looking up at him, her voice hesitant, as though she wanted a passing mark.

Smiling, McLaren pulled out a chair for Nora. "Smashing." He sat down and pulled out the statements nearest to him, then paused. "You are certain you don't mind me doing this? It's not idle curiosity about Janet's finances. I thought I might get a different slant on the case. Money is one of the major motives in crimes." He eyed her, assessing if she understood.

Nora nodded and squeezed his hand before standing up. "There's a reason for the saying that it's the root of all evil. You go on. I don't mind if it helps you find my daughter's killer." She told him she'd bring him a cup of tea and disappeared into the kitchen.

McLaren had finished his tea before he found what he wanted. He laid a dozen statements side by side on the table and read the items carefully. After writing the information in his notebook he went over to Nora.

She had been reading but laid the book on the sofa and looked up at him. "Did you find what you wanted?"

"I believe so, yes. Did Janet ever mention anything to you about the rating of her catering company?"

"The rating?"

"How quickly it received such a superior ranking, if she had to ask many food or restaurant critics to review her menus. That sort of thing."

"She never said anything to me. I admit I was more interested in her singing. That seemed to be where her true talent lay, in my opinion. But I think she would have said something if she'd been struggling for recognition for her catering company. It's not easy getting noticed, no matter if it's a book or CD or painting. I would have heard if she'd been frustrated by the lack of notice for her company." She angled her head to avoid looking into the sunlight. "What did you find?"

"Withdrawals from her current account, each month for a year, up until the month of her death. A consistent amount, never varying. Does this suggest anything to you? Did she always go to a casino, perhaps, or bet on dog or horse racing, or give to a charity?"

Nora shook her head. "That wasn't Janet. Oh, she gave to one charity, but that was always in December. I know that for certain because we always joked about our yearly gift to this animal rescue shelter. Other than that, no. I can't imagine why she'd always withdraw the same sum each month. Was it a lot?"

"One hundred pounds."

"Lord! That's over a thousand pounds a year!"

"So she wasn't helping a friend, perhaps, who'd fallen on hard times, or paying off a new car."

"She had the same car for several years. And I never heard of any friend or employee that she was helping."

"Had she a bookkeeper or financial adviser?"

"Yes. A bookkeeper. Do you want his name? You already know him, though."

"I know him?"

"Dan Wilshaw."

"Her pianist?"

"He also kept the books. Janet thought it easier to keep it in the group. If there was any question of finances, Dan was right there to answer. Too, they'd just started up, and I doubt if she had the cash to hire a proper bookkeeper. Dan did fine in case you've forgot."

She gave McLaren the address. "How does this information about her finances help you?"

"As you said, Nora, money is the root of all evil." He reboxed the sheets of paper and replaced the lid on the box. "Would you like me to put this back for you?" he asked, calling from the kitchen. He set the tea things on the worktop as Nora came into the room.

"I'll see to it later, thank you. You didn't have to bother with the teacups and such, Mr. McLaren. I would've got to that."

"I'm sure you will, but my mother taught me to clean up after myself."

"She sounds like a brilliant woman. And you're a very polite person, if I may tell you that."

"She'd be glad to hear that, thank you."

"You're so relaxed and confident. Did you get that from her?"

He laughed. "I don't know if many people would tell you that I'm relaxed, Mrs. Ennis. It's something I've had to learn. And I still struggle on certain days to attain that."

"Due to your police career?"

"Yes. There's a lot of stress connected to that job. You have to find a way to lose that stress or it will take its toll."

"If you won't take offense—not that you seem to need it now, but you might in the future—" She stopped, perhaps unsure if she was overstepping the boundary between client and employer.

McLaren urged her to continue.

"Janet had a place she'd go to when she needed to relax. She loved her singing career, but it, too, could be stressful. She'd go to this small cottage for a weekend or a few days, to unwind and think and write songs. She'd watch the birds gather at the feeders and sketch them. She loved it there, so peaceful and close to nature." Nora took a key from a ceramic box on the coffee table and gave it to McLaren. "She'd like for you to have the house, I know."

McLaren stared at the key, then at Nora. Her eyes smiled at him. He sputtered, "I can't. This is entirely too much, Mrs. Ennis. I can't pay you back."

"More than Janet wanting it, *I'd* like you to have it. You seem to understand her, to like her. I know you two would have been great friends if you'd met." She gently closed his fingers over the key. He could feel the smooth metal lying on his palm.

"Mrs. Ennis—"

"The cottage needs to be lived in, Mr. McLaren. It needs to be loved as Janet loved it. Things…and people, too…fall apart if they're not loved. I don't want to see something that my daughter felt so strongly about deteriorate and fall into ruin. You're the man to do that."

"But Mrs. Ennis—"

"Now, not another word. Janet and I want you to use and own the place. For as long as you like. Until the end of time, if you can. Please, Mr. McLaren. For her sake." Nora's eyes pleaded with him to accept the gift.

He nodded, suddenly feeling Nora was right. He believed Janet would have liked him to stay in her cottage. McLaren nodded again and kissed Nora on the forehead. "Thank you, Mrs. Ennis. It's just what I need."

"Lovely. It's just outside Kirkfield. Closer to Thorpe than to Kirkfield, actually. Here." She wrote the address on a piece of paper and handed it to him. "Do you know the area?"

"My girlfriend lives in Kirkfield."

"Good. That's settled. It was meant to be." She opened the front door and stood there while he crossed the room. "You needn't worry about anyone else being there. Janet owned it. No one else has a key. You use it whenever you wish, Mr. McLaren, which I hope is quite often. I-I'm thrilled someone she would have liked will be looking after it. It's like keeping it in the family."

He paused on the front porch, his mind still trying to make sense of it. He thanked Nora again and said he'd keep the cottage in mint condition.

"I believe you will, Mr. McLaren. Oh, and you will let me know what you find out about those monthly payments, won't you?"

He heard the door close and the deadbolt click into place as he stepped off the front porch and walked to his car.

*****

For the next few hours he talked to other owners of catering companies. Many were reluctant to speak so personally to him, but Janet Ennis' name proved to be an Open Sesame, and they revealed their secrets. In every instance they uttered the same person's name.

But blackmail didn't necessarily link to murder. If anything, it was usually the blackmailer who was murdered. And if he were correct in his conclusion, Janet wasn't the blackmailer.

He rang up Dan, made an appointment for early afternoon, then stopped for lunch. The Coach House chippy on Buxton's High Street had seen its weekday lunch peak and McLaren found a table. Nicely warm, the restaurant held the aromas of fish and chips and vinegar. McLaren ordered plaice, chips and a slice of homemade pie. He took out his case notes but instead of reviewing them he sent a text message to Dena, asking if they could meet for dinner.

A woman and man sitting across from him were talking, their voices barely audible, their heads nearly touching as they bent over some sheets of paper. A working lunch, McLaren thought, about to dismiss the couple. But the woman's coppery hair drew his attention. She sat in a shaft of sunlight that seemed to ignite the redder strands. That plus her blue eyes shone with a joy of life. The man seated next to her seemed to share that same passion, for although it was evident they were supposed to be talking over the information on the pages before them, his eyes never left the woman's face. Despite his gray hair, he looked to be the same age as her—mid-thirties, perhaps. And despite the woman's ten or fifteen pounds of extra weight, the man evidently was deeply attracted to her.

McLaren caught the name Simcock and assumed they were police officers. Not many other people in Buxton would know who the Constabulary's detective-superintendent was. He abandoned his speculation as the waitress set his lunch before him.

Twenty minutes later he was back in Dan's living room.

****

"You said on the phone that you needed my help." Dan peered at McLaren, his eyes dark in the shadow of afternoon. "How?"

McLaren settled back in his chair and briefly

related odd monthly withdrawals from Janet's bank account. "I know I have no authority to delve into this, and you have no obligation to tell me, but I believe that these monthly withdrawals may very well be connected to Janet's death. It might help with my investigation."

Dan's eyebrows rose, betraying his curiosity. "This is highly irregular, I assume you know."

"Certainly. But Janet's mother doesn't know anything concerning her daughter's finances. The only reason I'm asking is because I believe it'll point to Janet's killer." He handed one of Jamie's business cards to Dan. "Jamie Lynch is a police detective with the Derbyshire Constabulary. You can complain to him if you hear that I've overstepped any boundaries you set up, or if I've done anything unethical. I realize you don't know me, aside from our few talks, but I swear that this information will go no further than between you and me."

Dan took the card. He picked up the phone receiver and punched in the number of the police department's sectional headquarters in Buxton. When he asked to speak to Jamie Lynch he was told Jamie would be in the following morning and was there a message Dan would like to leave?

"No, that's all right. I'll catch him up later." He hung up and nodded. "Okay. I'll let you know about the finances."

"Did you know about these monthly withdrawals?"

"Yes, though Janet hadn't asked me specifically if she had the money to back the withdrawals. It wasn't my place to question her every purchase, but I did advise her on some matters."

"Was this one of them?"

"Yes. I knew what she was doing. I admit at first, when she told me about it, I was not for it. She wasn't a pauper, but she wasn't wealthy. She had a good, steady income from the catering business and from the trio, but that didn't mean she could spend freely."

"And these withdrawals…why did she need the same amount each month?" He looked at Dan, stealing himself for a revelation about blackmail.

"She gave it to Sean Fallon."

McLaren's eyebrow shot up and he leaned forward. "Sorry?"

"Sean Fallon. The former catering employee. She gave him money."

Having recovered some of his composure, McLaren said, "Those statements extend past the date when Sean was fired."

"Correct. His position was terminated in May, if I remember correctly."

"Janet died in September. Four months later. Had this to do with his inclusion in her will?"

"You know about the will, then."

"Yes. Mrs. Ennis showed it to me. He's mentioned in it. Isn't that rather odd that she'd keep an employee she'd terminated not only in her will but, evidently, continue handing him money? If what you say about the monthly withdrawals is true…"

"It's true." He drew a cigarette from the pack on the table and lit it. "It's all quite simple, really. As I mentioned, Janet had a huge, loving heart. She knew how hard it was to get established in a career. Not just in the arts, but in anything striking out on your own. Janet knew Sean had aspirations of becoming a chef and opening his own restaurant one day. Due to Sean's criminal past she knew it would be hard for him to get a loan to set up his business. She wanted to help him with his dream. She included him in her will. Yes, I know she fired him," Dan added as McLaren opened his mouth. "But I think that was anger speaking at the moment. She wanted to make amends."

"So she wrote him into her will. If she felt so bad about firing him, why didn't she reinstate him later?"

"She was thinking about it and had decided in September to ask him back."

"But she died before she could do it," McLaren finished.

"Fortunately she left him in her will, hoping that would help him. But she had a more immediate solution. She also wanted to give him money now, before she died—hopefully at a ripe, old age—so he could actually get his restaurant off the ground. She withdrew the monthly sums from her bank account and we set it up in an account for Sean. I held off paying it to him until I learned he was making noises in that effort. I knew he had a job as a chef, but my informant hadn't heard of him talking about his ownership dream. Perhaps that's still in the works."

"Then, the money from the will is to come later, to provide him with security to back his restaurant when it's finally going."

"That's what I understand. The money now, the money Janet was withdrawing monthly, went into the fund that Sean is to get the minute I hear he's actually working on his restaurant. Money to finance his dream, you might say." Dan took a puff on the cigarette and flicked the ashes into the ashtray. "Is that what you wanted to know?"

"That just about does it, yes. Thanks." McLaren started to stand up.

"Janet gave money to someone else, Mr. McLaren. Do you know about that, or have you the information already?"

McLaren sat down again and looked at the man in astonishment. "Helene Brogan, perhaps?"

"Not at all. Her father."

"Her father!" Stuart Ennis' hatred for Janet rushed back at McLaren with all the volume he'd previously heard. McLaren leaned forward. "You're certain about this? *Stuart* Ennis?"

"Oh, yes. Quite certain. It had been going on for nearly a year. A monthly cash payment of one hundred pounds."

"Do you recall the starting and ending dates of this?"

Dan got up, padded into another room, and returned with a ledger. He took his seat and flipped through the pages. When he paused at one, he read the entry. "It ended six years ago and, as I said, ran for just a year. So it started seven—"

"Have you any idea why Janet gave her father money? Was he disabled?" McLaren didn't think so, for the man had seemed fit enough raking his leaves.

"The man appeared to be healthy, at least the few times I saw him. No, Janet wanted to ease her father's financial burden and thought the extra hundred pounds a month would help."

"What financial burden did he have?"

"It was no secret, at least from Janet and me. Her half sister, Constance, had medical bills. Janet was helping her father pay them."

"And why did Constance have medical bills? What was wrong with her?"

"Oh! I thought you knew. She'd been in a car crash and ended up in a coma. She died in the hospital."

"Car crash?"

"Yes. Her boyfriend had been driving. He was unharmed. Sadly, that sometimes happens, doesn't it?"

"Do you remember the boyfriend's name?"

"Sure. He was also a member of our group. Ian O'Connor."

McLaren got up, none too steadily, and thanked Dan.

"Any time, Mr. McLaren. Anything to help Janet."

"I think you can help her now by locating Sean and giving him that money."

"He's ready to plan his restaurant, then?"

"More than you can imagine." He left with Dan's voice following him out the door.

****

McLaren walked around Buxton, trying to think through the puzzle of names and motives. If Janet's half-sister, Connie, had died six years ago at the age of nineteen, and Ian was now in his mid twenties... They'd have been the same age while they were seeing each other. And they were dating at the time of the car crash. If Ian had been driving, that might explain his anger, but six years was a long time to hold it. Still, McLaren knew of fiancées who mourned the death of their intended for years, the anger at the world too great to let go.

Had Connie introduced Ian to Janet, or was it the other way round? McLaren passed The Sun Inn, crouching along the High Street. The group had been together little more than a year but fell apart tragically on Janet's death five years ago. So the group had been born slightly after Ian and Connie began dating. Not that it made much difference in the case, but McLaren liked to have his facts straight. He sauntered back to his car and drove to Stuart Ennis' house.

****

"You back again?" Stuart growled on opening the door and seeing McLaren standing on the doorstep. "What's the matter—you forget where you put your brain?"

"I'd like to talk to you for a minute, Mr. Ennis." McLaren forced politeness into his voice, determined not to antagonize the man or let his own feelings explode.

"Fine. But I don't want to talk to you. Clear off." He started to shut the door but McLaren put his hand on its edge and pushed it open. "Please. Just one minute. It's about Connie and Ian."

Stuart's mouth opened and his jaw quivered. He grabbed on to the edge of the door and stared into McLaren's eyes. "Y-you know about them?"

"Yes. In a rather roundabout manner, but I know about them."

"What do you want? Money to keep quiet? Nora doesn't know about Connie. I don't want her to know. It was an indiscretion, it happened just that once. I-I don't have much money. Connie's medical bills wiped me out." He stopped, his gaze on McLaren, perhaps judging what the man meant to do.

"Mr. Ennis, I'm not here to blackmail you. Whatever you did is between your conscience and God. And Nora, if you eventually tell her. I'd just like to ask if you know why Ian disliked Janet so much. I find it hard to believe it was over his pay. People may grumble that they're not getting what they think is fair for their work, but it's now five years later and Ian is still angry."

"I think that should come from Ian. If he's still irate—"

"He won't talk to me, Mr. Ennis. I don't want to know life histories or anything remotely private. I just want to get to the bottom of Janet's case, and I believe Ian's feelings may have some bearing on this. Won't you tell me?" He stood there, quiet and patient, watching Stuart's face.

The man sighed, nodded, and said, "Ian was driving the night of the car crash. He walked away with minor cuts and scrapes, and Connie ended up in hospital. She was in a coma for months—nearly a year—and died without gaining consciousness. She and Ian had talked about marriage, 'sometime' when Ian made more money and they could afford a flat."

"So Ian's happiness crumbled when Connie died, and he blames Janet, for some reason, for this."

"Yes. I'd never seen two people so much in love. He lit up when he saw Connie. You could feel the electricity flow between them, they loved each other so deeply. He met Connie and just about right away she introduced him to Janet. He was looking for a job in the music field and Janet was looking for a bassist. So…" He shrugged and smiled weakly at McLaren.

"And you, if you don't mind me asking?"

"Me…what?" The older man's watery eyes turned slightly defiant.

"Divorcing parents aren't that uncommon when

something tragic happens to a child. I can understand why you and Nora parted ways when Janet died. But why do you so obviously dislike Janet? When I asked you earlier about her, you spoke of her as though she was the vilest thing on earth."

"Not what you'd expect from a father, eh?"

"No. You needn't answer, of course, but I'm curious."

"Am I still a suspect in her death?"

McLaren flashed a smile and shrugged. "I can't answer that until I know why you feel so strongly about Janet."

"Depends on my motive, then, as to where you place me. Well, you can lump Ian and me in the same group, then. Connie was my love child. I would've done anything for her. I adored her mother. Nora and I ran out of love in our first year of marriage. Consequently, I never had much feeling for Janet. She reminded me of Nora and the mistake I'd made with the marriage. Oh, I know, I could have divorced Nora that first year, but I needed a wife and family to make my career look good. Luckily, I wasn't home that much, so I didn't have to endure the home life. I guess I just never really got over Connie's death, and then the following year Janet died. It-it's just too much for me. But no, I didn't kill Janet. I didn't care that much about her one way or the other. And don't you have to either love deeply or hate greatly to commit murder?"

McLaren walked back to his car as Stuart slowly closed the door.

****

Janet's cottage was little more than five miles north of Ashbourne, between the main artery of the A515 and the River Dove. McLaren took the smaller B road north of Thorpe and soon located the stone get-away. Nestled in the undulating land of Dove Dale, the cottage merged into its surroundings. Gray stone, slate and dark timber came together in a one-storey building. Pines and oaks stretched their boughs over the cottage roof, and spent mums huddled around the foundation. It must have looked wonderful in the morning sun, McLaren thought as he walked to the front door. The plants were nothing more than withered deadheads and brittle stems, and dull, brown leaves carpeted the pathway. They crunched in the quiet and McLaren wondered if he were startling anyone.

Despite the cottage's general air of vacancy, the key slid easily into the door lock. He turned the tumblers and a satisfying 'click' released the catch. The door hinges squealed as he pushed open the wooden door, and he stood in the threshold while his eyes adjusted to the gloom.

Scents of dusty fabric and moss assaulted him. But the stale air of shut up, lifeless space wasn't there. Had Nora been here recently, opening windows and infusing the cottage with love and care? He drew in a lungful again and closed the door as though concerned someone would see him.

The main room spread out before him. Mainly a sitting room, it held secondhand furniture, an electronic keyboard and speaker, and a small, used filing cabinet. Two doors flanked the fireplace and took up most of the back wall. McLaren opened the right-hand one first. It led to a small bedroom holding a twin-sized bed, chest of drawers and an upholstered chair. An empty blue vase, a lighter blue ribbon tied around its neck, waited for a small bouquet. A tiny bathroom fed off this room. A bar of lavender scented soap sat in the soap dish and did its best to freshen the still air. Behind the other door lay the kitchen. One of its windows was broken.

McLaren's police training automatically took over and he remained in the doorway, surveying the room. Shards of glass littered the linoleum flooring and a large rock sat in the midst of the debris. The back door stood open, letting in the sunlight and the aromas of dry leaves, moss and the river. He went back through the front room and outside, then walked around to the kitchen door. No obvious footprints showed on the ground and nothing like a snagged piece of fabric or drops of blood adorned the broken window. Remaining outside at the doorway, he peered into the room.

Neither the door nor the floor was damp. Either the intruder had broken in after last night's storm or any water had dried by now. But muddy footprints should have showed up on the floor if this had happened after the storm. After any storm, he corrected himself, for he had no idea when this had happened. Even so, if the door had been open for any length of time, there would be signs of animals throughout the house. Bird nests, perhaps, and scat from foxes or squirrels or rabbits. Mice trailings, certainly, but that would occur if the door had stood open or not.

He re-entered the house by the front door and looked around each room. There were no indications of nesting animals, no beer cans or cigarette ends or drug paraphernalia to indicate the house was used as a party place. The forced entry was recent.

He went over the rooms again, this time looking more closely. He opened drawers, looked under the sofa and bed mattress, peered behind frame pictures on the wall. He even searched under the chair and sofa cushions and flipped back the scatter rugs. Nothing seemed to have been tampered with.

The filing cabinet in the front room looked to be in its original order. No manila folders stood at crazy angles, everything appeared to be filed alphabetically. So what had the intruder wanted? Merely to search for money?

Remembering stories from his grandmother, McLaren went into the kitchen. A set of ceramic containers sat at the back of the worktop, against the wall. McLaren angled the canisters toward him and ran a mixing spoon through each one's contents. No wad of money presented itself, no key gave up its hiding place.

He opened the fridge door. The electricity had been turned off and the appliance's interior smelled musty and unused, but it was empty. He shut the door, frustration mounting.

Back in the front room, he took the books from the bookcase and leafed through their pages. Nothing fell out, nothing was crammed between pages. What's more, nothing sat behind the books. So either the intruder had found what he wanted or there had been nothing to find.

He dusted his hands off on his trousers and stood in the center of the room, letting the silence wash over him. Janet had found a gem of a refuge. A perfect place to think and unwind. A place to write songs with only the river and the wildlife to criticize her efforts.

He picked up a cushion, put it back on the sofa, and sat. When Nora had given him the key he'd had no intention of using the cottage. But now that he was here he was slowly reversing his decision. The quiet suited him, suited his moods. If he got away every so often, mended his temper, would Dena be grateful? Would the fact that he had a retreat to repair his bad disposition be music to her ears?

Music... He looked at the electric keyboard in the corner. Nora had mentioned Janet wrote music. He hadn't known that. Nothing original appeared on her CD. Had she been writing for a while, compiling songs for a second CD, but time ran out on her?

Curious, he went over to it.

A large rectangular basket near the instrument's feet held a sizeable assortment of sheet music. He emptied the contents onto the floor and read each title. They were all standard tunes sung by other artists, spanning seventy or so years. He flipped casually through the music, noticed Janet's penciled phrasing marks or notes, and returned the music to the basket.

Behind the basket, a spiral-bound notebook of manuscript paper leaned against the wall. Maybe this held the music Janet had written. Hands shaking, he grabbed the notebook and sat on the floor. The notebook was rubberbanded lengthwise and widthwise, a substantial lump in its center. A lump that spoke of something wedged between the book's pages. As he opened the book, a cassette tape, several newspaper clippings, small sheets of paper, and a small envelope fell out.

He looked at the sheets first. They consisted of one or two short paragraphs, hand written and signed, apparently, by the writer. Each entry was in a different handwriting. He sat in the half-light, his eyes skimming the pages, trying to understand what he read.

They were testimonies by the same caterers and restaurant owners whom he had talked to today. Each entry was notarized and dated. The earliest one came from six years ago in January; the most recent had been written in May five years ago. They all stated that the named, noted food critic had sought 'donations' to her pet charity. In return, she'd be certain the owner's business got a glowing recommendation in her newspaper column.

As he read further, he noted that the payments were made on one of two dates, which he thought odd. Was the blackmailer collecting for a specific item, needing the money at a specific time? He set the papers aside and turned to the clippings.

As if to strengthen Janet's investigation—for what else could it be?—the newspaper articles sang out the special qualities of each business. All reviews were dated after the notarized accounts.

McLaren picked up the cassette tape; 1 September was written in black marker on the front of the cassette. A few weeks before Janet had died. He got up, his heart racing, and took everything out to his car. He shoved the tape into the car's cassette tape player and turned up the volume.

It was a conversation between two women. Most likely face-to-face, both voices sounded equal in volume. One voice, presumably Janet's, held the same quality as the singing on her CD. The other voice must have been the blackmailer's. McLaren stopped and ejected the tape and looked again at the case. Beneath the date in smaller printing were the women's names. McLaren put the tape back into the player and listened.

The first voice was urgent, demanding yet not

angry. A quiet threat lay beneath her words and tone. She reminded Janet that several of her competitors had already signed up to donate and they were being blessed with a great review and increased business. Didn't Janet want the same prosperity? All it took was a yearly contribution.

Janet's first reaction to this was laughter. When the other woman reminded her rather sharply that damage could be done by a very poor review, Janet replied that she had no intention of giving to any charity. The woman could write what she wanted; one review meant nothing.

The recording stopped with the blackmailer stating that accidents sometimes occurred and wouldn't it be a shame if something happened to Janet's business?

McLaren sat in his car as the tape clicked off. His mind raced in tempo to his galloping heart rate. If the woman had tried and failed at blackmail, had she made good on her threat? He locked up the house and drove home, wondering how he could prove it.

****

Dinner wasn't the multi-course meal he had fixed in July. For one thing, he had used too much of the afternoon at Janet's cottage. And he wasn't in the mood to cook something elaborate. He should have done, for he loved Dena and wanted to please her. But the afternoon had been wearing and he hadn't the energy. Dena would have to like the cidered chicken, broccoli with sour cream, and pan haggerty.

He showered and dressed in gray trousers and light blue shirt, aware of the time slipping away. The table was set, the chicken was simmering, and the potato and onion slices were frying when the doorbell rang.

McLaren glanced at the clock, pulled the tea towel from his shoulder and jammed it over the oven handle, and sprinted to the door. He smiled and pulled Dena inside.

"You're gorgeous," he whispered, his lips against her brunette hair. She wore it down; it brushed her shoulders and smelled of lavender.

"You're not bad yourself."

"Thank you for coming on such short notice." He gave her a leisurely kiss.

"When have I ever turned down a free meal?" she said as he released her. "Smells terrific. Chicken?" She followed him into the kitchen.

"Yeah. I hope that's okay."

"I'd eat bangers and mash with you, Michael, and love it."

He finished the meal and got it onto the table while Dena lit the candles and poured the wine.

After the meal, as they sat in the front room with their coffee, she asked how the case was going.

"I'm making headway." He held his cup on his thigh.

"But not enough and not quickly enough. I know that tone."

"I thought I had a super lead today, but I'm damned if I can figure out how to pursue it. Maybe I'm too old for this. Maybe I've been out of the job too long. I can't seem to wrap my brain around any of it."

Dena took his cup and set it on the table. Holding his hand, she said, "Free advice and a shoulder, for what it's worth."

"You'd be bored to death in one minute if I let loose."

"That's what you need, to let loose. I'm all ears.

Go ahead."

"Is your linen blouse wash and wear?"

Dena smoothed a wrinkle from the pink fabric. "Even if it weren't, you're worth the price of a new one."

After he related his afternoon, he said, "I don't know. I never will understand people. Ruth Wilshaw has a good job. Why does she need to resort to blackmail?"

"Michael, I thought you knew about her."

"What's to know? She's married to Dan Wilshaw, who was Janet's pianist and bookkeeper. She's a food critic. What else is there?"

Dena kissed his hand. "That's what comes of going round in your circles compared to mine. And I don't mean that disparagingly."

"What's your high society, jet set know about Ruth Wilshaw, then?"

"Not that much, but we know Eva Lister."

"Eva?" His mind conjured up a photo of the woman—elegant, expensively dressed, large house. "Did she get Ruth's advice about the catering for her daughter's wedding reception?"

Dena rolled her eyes and patted McLaren's hand. "No, dear. You're not getting this at all."

"Do you know Eva?"

"Never met her, but I know *of* her. She married Lister—some say for his money—but her own bank account was never too shabby. She was Eva Mills before she married. Her daddy owned Mills Computer Solutions. He made his fortune years ago. His children grew up rich and spoiled."

"Children? Who else besides Eva?"

"Her *sister*. Ruth Wilshaw."

McLaren started, his leg hitting the coffee table and nearly upsetting his coffee cup. "Are you serious?"

"Don't look at me like that. Why would I make it up? It was in the society and appointments pages awhile back when Eva married Lloyd."

"Sorry, I missed it. I don't read the society and appointments pages."

"Maybe you should. See what you're missing? Anyway, I thought it odd at the time of Ruth's marriage. You know, Ruth marrying for love, not money. Marrying a struggling musician and living on his income."

"Ruth didn't have a trust or something from her parents?"

Dena shrugged. "Maybe her dad got angry over her choice of husband. Going against the family standards," she added when McLaren looked puzzled. "Instead of looking for someone rich or with an impeccable lineage or in line for a CEO position in a company, she followed her heart and chose the person instead of the bank account. Maybe he kicked her out of the family. Or the will. It happens, you know."

"Yeah. I know."

"Anyway, she must really love Dan to give up the rich life. Because evidently that's all history. I don't see her at the club or track anymore."

"Pity." He said it with more cynicism than he'd meant and quickly said, "I guess you're right, though, about her marriage."

"I'd always assumed she would have married into exalted, rich circles, like Eva did. Just shows you that you can't discount what love will do."

"I never have." He drew her close and kissed her. "Thanks."

"For the information or the kiss?"

"Both." He leaned toward her again but she got up.

"I hate cutting the night short, Michael, but I have to be at the rescue center early tomorrow."

"Saturday morning tour?"

"We've got three groups coming, the first one at eight."

"Those are usually good for donations, aren't they?"

"Yes. That's important, of course, for any non-profit organization, but it's crucial for building public awareness. Most people don't know much about tigers, or know how critical their status is. It's estimated that they will be extinct in twelve years if nothing is done to stop poaching and destruction of their habitat. Can you imagine that, Michael? Twelve years! That's indecent! It'd be a crime if that happened, they're such magnificent animals."

He nodded and tried to recall a recent newspaper article on a case of poaching tiger parts. It had happened in Buxton, of all places.

"If I weren't the trusting type, I'd wonder what was going on." Dena picked up the jeans lying across the back of the chair near the front door. Her index finger and thumb gingerly held the jeans by the waistband. "Or do I need to ask?"

"I think they're Eva Lister's."

"You think? Was Eva here?"

"No. I got them from her house this morning."

"You just walked up to her door and asked for a clothing donation."

"Would've been easier." He related the search for the jeans, giving her all the details and the near miss of being discovered beneath the bed. He noticed her valiant attempt to keep a straight face in the way she kept scratching her nose or rubbing her upper lip. Anything to cover the laugh that threatened to erupt. He finished his narrative in a rather gruff voice. "I assume they're hers. If I need to, I can have Jamie run them through the lab."

"And they will prove…what?" she said, recovering her composure.

"Hopefully that she's my arsonist."

"You mean, for Janet's case?"

"No. The person who set the fires in my drive and tool shed. I'd like to find that bas—" He stopped, realizing what he was about to say. "I'd like to find that…person."

"Hopefully not to beat into a pulp."

"I don't know. It depends how I'm feeling." He smiled, easing her fears, and draped Dena's jacket around her shoulders. "Don't worry, dear heart. I've never hit a woman."

"Glad to hear it. But the jeans and the missing button seem awfully suspicious, don't they?"

"They do to me."

Dena grabbed her shoulder bag and McLaren opened the door for her. They stepped outside and Dena slid her hand into his.

"I need to install a lamp by the drive," McLaren said as they walked from under the small patch of light at the front door. "Wait till I get a torch. You can't see."

"No need, Michael. I can. Besides," she added as his arm slid around her waist, "if I trip, I'm taking you down with me. Who's that, over there by my car?"

Chapter Twenty-Four

A shadowy figure did indeed stand near the boot of Dena's car. McLaren shouted and the figure bolted down the drive and onto the road. Calling to Dena to stay where she was, McLaren gave chase.

Later, he would say it had seemed liked a replay of the previous night, but without the fire. He dashed up the road, his heartbeat as loud as the thud of his shoes on the asphalt. The ribbon of black curved ahead of him and occasionally threw back fragments of moonlight where the trees thinned a bit. He paused, catching his breath, avoiding the silvery patch. Nothing moved in the darkness. He jogged a few hundred yards farther and paused once more. No sound came but his own ragged breathing.

He considered going even farther up the road when, to his right, the snap of a tree branch cracked the quiet. He spun around and entered the wood.

The night closed around him, inky black and smothering. He pushed through the clumps of thistles and crashed past tree branches that reached for him. He ignored the scrapes and cuts on his arms and neck and charged on.

At a moss-draped tree stump he stopped. His fingertips dug into the spongy covering, supporting him as he leaned forward and listened. He'd been incautious during his pursuit through the wood, his need to catch the person greater than the desire to employ guile. But now he waited for a sound to direct his hunt. He stood by the tree, aware of the evening chill, and fought the near panic rising within him. He had to get out of the smothering darkness.

The road lay to his right, hopefully not many yards away. He turned and inched past the tree stump groping his way through the gloom. Branches and twigs cracked, a log rolled downhill, leaves crunched underfoot. McLaren didn't care about the noise; he needed to escape.

He emerged from the wood where the road bent. To the right, his porch light gleamed through the swaying tree branches. Why was he rushing about like a flaming berk? What was he trying to prove, either to himself or to Dena? Did he really believe he could find a man who was determined to stay hidden?

The trees on both sides of the road were tall and crowded together, brambles and cast-off leaves ankle-deep. Moonlight broke through the meager leafy canopy at irregular, infrequent intervals, but jet-black pockets still clung to the deeper recesses, harboring who-knew-what. McLaren swallowed and turned his eyes to his porch light.

He'd taken several steps toward the light when Dena called to him. Her voice floated upwind, wrapped in the scent of pine needles and dry leaves. He yelled a response and dashed back to her.

She met him at the foot of his drive, a torch in her hand. The brilliant light illuminated the gravel and her shoes. As McLaren jogged up to her, she handed him the torch. "I got it from the kitchen," she said, her words coming quickly. "I saw him. He doubled back.

Ran through the front garden and south, across the field."

He shouted his thanks at her, rushed across the lawn and into the open.

The land stretched ahead, open and bright in the moonlight. He vaulted over a low stonewall, exhilarated by the space. The beam of the torch swung in wide arcs ahead of him, picking out thistles and grass tufts and logs. He charged around them, the soft plod of his shoes on the earth a bass line to his unspoken chant. "Got to find him, got to find him, got to find him…"

At the crest of the hill he paused. The vista sprawled exposed, the tawny grasses and light gray stone walls silvery streaks beneath the dark sky. No shack or stand of trees offered a hiding place for the intruder. Which way should he go?

If the man had come this far, he could be huddled behind a section of wall. If he had gone just far enough to convince Dena of his route across the field, he might have doubled around and was even now back on the road.

McLaren swept the light ahead of him, playing it back and forth over the ground. It was a useless pursuit. He was leaving Dena unguarded.

He turned toward his house, cursing himself for a fool. They had seen the man near Dena's car; had he wanted to harm her? If so, McLaren had just given the git an excellent chance.

He misjudged a dark spot in the soil and stepped into a small depression. He went down on his knee and grabbed it in pain. The night seemed to gather about him once more as he shook off the first wave of unconsciousness. He shook his head, grabbed the torch and stood up. Swearing loudly, he tested his knee. Nothing seemed broken. He jogged down the hill.

Dena greeted him at the corner of the house, asking if he'd seen anyone. Noticing his uneven gait, she put her arm around his waist.

"I knew I should have gone with you," she said as they walked over to the front door. "What happened?"

"I never found the bastard."

"No, I mean *you*. You're hurt."

"Oh, nothing much. Just didn't see a two-storey deep pit grabbing my foot." McLaren tried to sound nonchalent but his voice was edged in concern. "You didn't see anything else, I take it."

"Not a thing. I think you scared him off."

"At least I'm good for something."

"Where *have* you been, Michael?" They had stopped at the front door and the porch light illuminated the scrapes and cuts on his arms. Dena's hand went to the doorknob but McLaren pulled her back.

"It's nothing. I've got something to do, first." He went to her car and shone the torch beam over every inch of its exterior. Then he got on his stomach and flashed the light along the car's undercarriage.

Dena joined him and stood by the boot. Looking at him wriggling around the car, she said, "What are you doing?"

"Just checking."

"Obviously. But for what? And why?"

He had completed his circuit, got up, and dusted off his hands and clothes. Walking over to her, he said, "That man was here for a reason, Dena. He was standing next to your car."

"So you were checking to see that everything was

all right," she finished.

"You didn't want me to?" His voice came out of the darkness, close to her ear. She nodded and murmured her thanks.

"I know it all happened quickly, but did you notice anything about him? Bulk of his body or perhaps an estimate of his height as he passed next to the corner of the house?"

She shook her head, apologizing that she knew he wanted a lead, something tangible so he could track this phantom, but she couldn't help. "I'm sorry."

"That's okay, sweets. I saw him, too, and can't say what he looked like."

He unlocked and opened her car door for her when she said, "Do you think my car was second?"

McLaren paused with his hand on the door handle and stared down at her. "Pardon?"

"We saw him at the boot of my car. It's parked behind yours. Maybe he tampered with your first, then was going to do something to mine, only we came outside too soon, before he could get to both cars."

McLaren gave her a nod, then searched his car as he had hers. At the back, under the rear bumper, he located something. He stood up and shone the torch beam on the object.

"What is it?" Dena asked, peering at his open palm.

"A transmitter," he replied, his tone between anger and awe.

"What's it transmitting? Who put it there? You?"

"I think my friend the arsonist put it on my car, and it's transmitting the route I drive every time I'm in the car *and* where I live."

"Where you live?" Her eyes widened and she

grabbed McLaren's hand.

"A good way my fire bug could find my house."

"But when did he put it on?"

"Early on in the investigation. Monday, probably."

"And Monday…when could that have been done?"

McLaren stared at the road, blacker in the contrast of the torchlight on his palm. "At one of the houses when I talked to someone. Maybe at the pub. Yeah, the pub." His voice trailed off as he recalled that day. "The man I was to meet there was late in arriving. He could have attached the transmitter then. Wouldn't take but a few seconds."

The tiny device was a round, plastic case attached to a small collar. The whole thing weighed probably half an ounce. It had been duct taped to the underside of the bumper. He peeled the tape from the pet collar, knowing the tape would be excellent for holding fingerprints, and laid it and the transmitter on a flagstone.

"I've seen those on wildlife shows," Dena said. "They give out a signal that a hand-held receiver can pick up. That's how they track—" She stopped, aware she was about to compare McLaren to a wolverine or moose.

"Yeah," McLaren finished. "These are smaller, I'd bet, than your grizzly bear transmitters. But they're good for pets or children." Or even Alzheimer's patients who might wander off. He wondered if Nora would ever get to that stage. "They have several frequencies, so you can choose a specific channel for your broadcast. The range isn't that great in town, but here, in open country, it could be around a mile."

"No wonder he could track you. How'd he know it

was your car, though?"

"That's no mystery. He just had to wait on the street, watch me park and leave the car. I couldn't have done better if I'd had a sign in the window displaying my name and address. Bloody hell."

They stood in silence for a while, each mentally playing out a scenario. McLaren cursed his stupidity and finally said, "Well, this isn't helping your early evening. Give me a minute to grab my keys." He ran into the house and emerged moments later with his jacket and keys.

"What are you doing?" Dena asked as he helped her into her car and then trotted around to his.

"Making sure nothing happens to you. I'm following you home."

"Michael, that's not necessary. It's an hour round trip for you."

"I'd rather spend the petrol and the time and know you're safe than to worry for thirty minutes. Don't speed." He got into his car, started the engine, and fell in behind her as she drove through the night-wrapped wood.

****

The trip to Kirkfield was uneventful and McLaren unlocked Dena's house door for her. He stepped inside, switched on the lights and walked through the house to the sound of Dena's protestations.

"I appreciate your concern," she called, taking off her jacket. "But it isn't necessary. Really." When no answer came, she said, "Michael? You still here?" She'd headed for the kitchen, when he walked into the front room again. The door closed with a secure thud. Dena whirled around. "God, Michael, you scared me!

Don't do that!"

"Sorry."

"I thought you were in the kitchen."

"Yeah, I was. But I went out the back door and checked out the rear garden and then walked around the house."

Dena shook her head. "No one lurking in the shadows, I assume. No smoke and mirrors."

He glared at her, his arms across his chest.

Grimacing, she said, "Sorry. I know you're concerned. I don't mean to take it as a joke."

"After July's little episode you think I'd take any of this as a joke?" His arms dropped to his sides; a question shone from his eyes. "You think I'm that indifferent?"

"No. Of course not. I didn't mean to suggest that. I'm glad for your caring, Michael. Thank you." She kissed him, pressing herself against him. When they broke apart, she asked if he wanted a cup of coffee.

"To cool me down?" He smiled and gave her a quick hug. "You wanted an early night, remember? I don't want you blaming me tomorrow morning that I stayed too long. One more thing, though." He checked out the remaining rooms in the house, opening closet doors, looking beneath the bed and behind the sofa. He walked through the garage and pronounced that clear, too.

"Thanks." Dena squeezed his hand and kissed him again.

"If this is my payment, I'll be over every night to make a sweep through your house."

"Out." She pushed him toward the door.

"First she offers me coffee, then she shows me the

door."

"*Out*. My early night is fast turning into a normal night."

He bid her sweet dreams to the sound of her light laughter, and waved as he drove off.

****

McLaren parked just down the street from Dena's house and pulled out his mobile. He punched in Jamie's phone number and thought of the evening's events while he waited for the phone to be answered. Jamie was a terrific sounding board; he'd help sort through the mess.

"Mike!" Jamie's voice cut through McLaren's contemplation. "What's going on, mate? You need something?"

"Can't a bloke ring up a friend to chat?"

"Not at this hour. Something's going on."

"This hour? Why—what time is it? Did I wake you?"

"It's just on to nine."

"Glad to hear I didn't interrupt your beauty sleep. You need it."

"Funny man."

He paused, not certain how to bring up the subject. When Jamie asked what McLaren wanted, he answered, "You able to meet me now?"

"Sure. At the usual?"

Glancing at his watch, McLaren said, "No. Meet me halfway, if you don't mind. It'll save time."

"Halfway—why? Where are you?"

"Kirkfield."

"Oh, right. Well, how about Buxton? Take us both about twenty minutes or so to get there. That all right?"

"Sure. Where?"

"I don't care. One spot's as good as another. The Sleeping Fox?"

"Super. First one there grab a table and the drinks."

"That's an old trick, Mike. I'll put out an alert with the lads to look for a car traveling under the speed limit along the A515. Get there on time or you'll buy the next *two* rounds." He rang off before McLaren had a chance to comment.

****

McLaren had time to think on his drive to the pub. The only logical opportunity anyone could have planted the transmitter on his car was at the pub on Monday. And the only people he talked to there were Myles and Ian. Had either of them a reason to threaten him with arson? Perhaps the more pertinent question was, had either of them taped on the transmitter as a favor to someone? If so, that just about included everyone associated with Janet.

He sang along to "There Is A Time" as the countryside rolled past. Night lay across the land but it held no fear for him now. He moved through it, the car's headlights cutting apart the frightening blackness, wrapped in the isolation of a traveler proceeding across the topography and not one with the land. A brook or pond sparkled when the moonlight lay just right upon the water, a quick glint of silver light as he moved past the otherwise dark water, but the bulk of the expanse slept immobile and shadow-shrouded. He glanced at the sky as he passed the turn off for Monyash. The stars winked knowingly, white-hot in the inky region, yet silent as the grave.

The car tires sent gravel splaying as he drifted onto

the verge. He jerked the wheel to the right and the car regained the tarmac. What the hell was he doing? Keep your eyes on the road, you berk. You'll do Dena no good if you wind up in hospital or paralyzed.

Was he any nearer the solution of the case, he wondered? He had suspicions but nothing Jamie could take to court. And he was no closer to knowing the identity of his own arsonist after tonight's mishap than he had been Tuesday night.

All of it had to be tied together, that was the one obvious thing he had. Would Nora recall anything else from Janet's past that could give him a lead? He turned off the CD, now in no mood for music. The whole thing depressed him: Nora's condition, her belief in justice, her struggle to be taken seriously by the police. McLaren slammed his fist onto the steering wheel. Damn everyone who dismissed her, who kept her dangling for five long years. Damn Charlie Harvester for his contempt and ridicule of her.

McLaren was still fuming when he got out of his car at The Sleeping Fox. He slammed the car door and jammed the key into the lock with a recklessness that belied his usual care with his car. He thought about going home, ringing up Jamie and canceling their talk. He was in no mood for polite conversation but Jamie would end up angry for being dragged away from home.

He strode across the car park, dodging slow-moving couples and families, his gaze fixed on the local. Several yards from the front door, he stopped. Charlie Harvester was leaving the pub.

The anger and injustice of last year, mixed with pity for Nora, roared into life. He closed the gap between them in several swift strides. The unfairness raced back to him, and for a few moments, McLaren was back in the Staffordshire CID. It was a June night. He drove to the pub owned by his seventy-year-old friend. Harvester, the senior investigating officer for the case, was there, looking into the pub break-in. And arresting McLaren's friend for assaulting the burglar. Their personal history had never been good—more like ice and fire. McLaren, the hard-working, popular officer, always came out on top despite the influence and assumed hand-up Harvester garnered with the help of his high-ranking daddy. The struggle and competition never diminished, whether in police training or in the job. McLaren lived with it, feeling the tension and hatred grow. Years of hatred that simmered beneath polite conversations and flashed smiles erupted that June night in McLaren's uncontrollable anger. With Harvester's men watching, McLaren flung Harvester into a convenient rose bush. Harvester's rage and embarrassment exploded, cooled only when McLaren resigned from the police.

McLaren didn't consciously relive the details; he didn't have to. They were a part of his personality now. But seeing Harvester before him, the man responsible for his elder friend's arrest and Nora Ennis' contemptuous treatment, awakened his feelings and their history. Yet, he wouldn't confront Harvester, he vowed. He wouldn't let Harvester win this psychological and emotional war.

Stopping a yard away from the man, McLaren took a deep breath, aware of his racing heartbeat. No matter what happened, he would not create a scene. He would not expose his wound to Harvester. Forcing a smile, he called out, "Always a pleasure seeing you again, Harvester."

Harvester turned his head, startled by the voice. He smirked and hesitated in his stride. "I could say the same about you, McLaren. So, I hear you're employed…elsewhere now."

McLaren laughed. "Yes. I've never been so happy." He smiled again, assessing the man. Harvester had added some weight since their last meeting, and his hairline had begun to recede. He looked older than his thirty-eight years, the lines around his eyes more pronounced. The tops of his hands had aged, dry and veined. A slight stoop suggested itself in the roundness of Harvester's shoulders and the forward thrust of his head. All in all, not a man who looked to be in his prime. The change fueled McLaren's determination.

Harvester inclined his head at McLaren. "So glad to hear it. May I ask what's caused this flowering of elation?"

"You know how some cases just speak personally to you? How the victim's joy or despair becomes your own?"

Harvester stared at McLaren. He cleared his throat, as though about to speak, but McLaren rushed on.

"I've met the most engaging woman. Nora Ennis. Despite five years of unhappiness I believe some very good news is around the corner for her, and that after all that's happened to her, the old fashioned ideal of justice is still obtainable."

Harvester blanched and swallowed, staring into McLaren's eyes.

"Well, I won't keep you any longer, Charlie. Just wanted to say hello for old times' sake."

"Glad you did," Harvester squeaked. McLaren reached the door before Harvester could think. "Please give any of our…mutual friends…my best. Night." He walked toward his car, his car key jangling in the quiet night.

"How you kept your cool is beyond me, Mike."

McLaren tore his gaze from Harvester's retreating back. Jamie stood beside him.

"Never let your enemy know what you're thinking, Jamie. Or let them believe they have you rattled."

"Fine, if you can do it. You *seem* to have done it. I wouldn't have guessed you two hated each other's guts. You seemed quite matey when I came up on you. You been taking a correspondence course on acting?" He smiled, conveying it was a joke to lighten the tension that was still palpable, but McLaren seemed not to hear.

McLaren shook his head. "What a nasty piece of work he is." He bit off the words, now that he could release his anger.

Jamie's hand landed on his friend's shoulder. "A lot of us agree with your assessment, if that makes you feel better."

"A piece of shit. Nothing more."

"Come on, Mike." Jamie guided McLaren toward the far end of the building.

McLaren muttered another uncomplimentary remark as Harvester's car turned onto the High Street. He tried to shrug off Jamie's hold but Jamie's grip was too firm.

"Not until you've calmed down." Jamie tightened his grasp on McLaren's forearm.

"The man's a—"

"I'm sure he is," Jamie cut in quickly as parents

with children walked past them. "What's the problem tonight?"

"Isn't seeing that man reason enough?"

"This smacks of something more than merely running into Harvester again. And you rang me up to talk, so something was already eating at you. What is it?"

McLaren sighed deeply and went limp. Jamie released his holds and the two men sat down on a bench at the edge of the square. "Oh, nothing specific, everything specific."

"That clears it up just fine."

"You know my history with him."

"Sure. But tonight's confrontation seemed more recent in origin."

"Yeah, I guess it is."

"So, what happened?"

McLaren recounted the evening's event and his anger over Nora Ennis' treatment. "None of this would've happened, *none* of it—Nora's years of smashed hopes, ridicule, shuffled around from cop to cop, the arsons at my place, Dena put in jeopardy... *None* of it if Harvester had followed up on Nora's plea to reopen the case. He's treated her shamefully and set all this in motion. And for what good? Not a bloody thing. It's been a waste of time and emotions and jeopardized lives. The man ought to be kicked off the Force. What an excuse for a human being." Having released his anger, McLaren sat on the bench, his forearms on his thighs, staring into the night.

Jamie leaned forward so he was shoulder to shoulder with his friend. He didn't reply immediately, but let the sounds of the night wash over them. A family and two dating couples passed them before Jamie said, "I totally agree."

A miniature poodle yapped at them as it trotted past. The dog's owner pulled on the leather lead, admonished the dog and apologized to McLaren and Jamie as he hurried by.

When McLaren's silence continued, Jamie said, "You've done what Harvester has repeatedly failed or refused to do, Mike. *You* took Nora Ennis at her word, believed enough of her story to investigate when Harvester couldn't even get up out of his chair. The coroner's verdict was open, leaving some doubt about the whole bloody incident. You went ahead, reviewed the various reports, talked to people. Everything Harvester should have done if he was any kind of decent cop. Or human being. No, Mike. You've every reason for feeling as you do. And I think that makes you the better person."

The quietness of the night welled up between them again, with McLaren gazing into the distance. Somewhere behind them a mobile phone rang and was answered by a giggling teenager.

Jamie waited until a motorcycle had traveled down the High Street before saying, "You want that drink you talked about earlier?"

The question startled McLaren. He pulled his thoughts from Dena and Nora and turned toward Jamie. "Sorry?"

"Man, you must be somewhere else. You hear anything I just said?"

"Sure. Every word."

"I doubt it but I'll let it pass. You want to go inside?" He nodded toward the pub.

"If you don't mind…"

Jamie nodded. "'Course not. We'll make it another night, then." He stood up, ready to walk with McLaren back to their cars. McLaren remained seated.

"Nora gave me Janet's cottage. *Gave*, as in I own it now. I went there today. It was like walking into a cathedral. I was where she lived and wrote music and walked through the wood. How many fans—whether they're into music or books or sports or whatever—get to wander around their idol's house, let alone be granted the gift of keeping it?"

Jamie looked at McLaren as though wondering where this was leading.

"I was thrilled to be there, *am* thrilled to have it. But I wasn't in awe of her. She was a great talent and could've been even greater, but I felt no hero worship of her while I was there." Did Jamie understand? His support was important. His condemnation would be devastating.

Jamie patted McLaren on the shoulder. "Yes. It's kinda like finding out Father Christmas was really your dad all along. It's a shock, maybe a disappointment because your fantasy has died, but you still love your dad and you still love Christmas."

McLaren got to his feet and walked with Jamie into the pub.

Chapter Twenty-Five

Harvester parked his silver Jaguar sports car in his garage, got out, and locked the car's doors. The car had been a present from his dad, a Chief Constable when Harvester had gone through police training, and it had turned a lot of heads—in envy and in contempt. There'd been no way he could have afforded the car as a probationary officer; there was still no way he could afford to buy a car like this now. So he took extra care of it, being certain the doors were always locked, even in his garage, and regularly seeing to its maintenance. He patted the right rear wing as he walked past the car—almost as absent mindedly as he used to pat his wife—stepped outside, and locked the garage doors before entering his house.

The aromas of his cooked breakfast assaulted his nose the moment he walked through the back door into the kitchen. Lunch had been hardly more than a snack: a bag of crisps, a cup of weak tea, and a piece of cake leftover from an officer's retirement party. Plus, he had worked late, missing his tea. The beer and packet of pork rinds in the pub would've helped allay the hunger he now felt, but he'd hardly touched them, so intent was the conversation he'd had with a friend. Consequently, he was now ready for something more substantial. He took off his jacket, hung it on the back of a chair, and put a piece of cod in a skillet on the stove. Moments later the fragrance of frying fish filled the air and Harvester changed into jeans, long-sleeved t-shirt, and slippers before looking over the day's mail.

In addition to the usual circulars and junk mail, two letters caught his interest. One was from a friend—a colleague, more accurately—in Edinburgh, and the other letter was from his son. Harvester wandered into the kitchen, sliced up some cabbage and an apple, mixed them with a little sugar, pepper and butter, put them on the stove to cook, and sat down to read his letters.

His son, Emory, had written from school, turning the English class writing assignment into a letter for Harvester. Emory lived with his mother, Harvester's ex, in Bolton. They had moved there after Dagmar's divorce from Harvester, nine years ago. She seemed to be getting on fine—a good paying job in the city's museum, a boyfriend, and a house. Emory, Harvester read, turning over the sheet of paper, wanted Harvester to come up for Christmas. Or at least St. Nicholas Day.

Nice thought, but Dagmar probably would have something to say about that. He read on. 'I want to be a police officer, like you, Dad. When you come for Christmas, you can tell me what I need to do to be one.'

Harvester smiled at the naïveté of his eleven-year-old. If it were only that easy, a few lessons. He glanced down the hallway, half expecting to see into his bedroom. If he still had his helmet, he'd bring that along, give that to Emory. Or would it be better to discourage the boy? He'd die if anything happened to Emory while in the job. Society was becoming more violent. You saw it all the time on the television. Criminals didn't care if they hurt officers or not.

Respect, in general, was just an archaic word in the dictionary. It barely meant anything to some police officers, either.

He gathered the letter into his palm, crushing the paper. He didn't need to look any further for an example of that than last June. The burglary at that pub in Staffordshire. The disrespect shown in front of his men. McLaren.

Harvester uncurled his fist, letting the crumbled paper drop to the floor. He uttered an emphatic "Damn." McLaren, in Harvester's opinion, was the poster child for disrespect. For arrogance and lawlessness and smugness, too. The room shimmered and grew darker until everything dissolved under an image of McLaren's face. McLaren's face…shouting at Harvester, red with anger after the rose bush incident.

Harvester picked up his son's letter. He placed the pages on the kitchen table and smoothed the paper flat. *That's* the sort of thing to which Emory might be subjected. Smart mouth criminals, even disobedience from his own colleagues. What a way to earn a living. There must be something else Emory could do.

Harvester snapped his fingers. A smile crept across his face. There was something else *he*, Harvester, could do. Something to get back at McLaren for the defiance and egotism he'd shown that long-ago night. Something so remarkable that it would ensnare and humiliate McLaren. A payback for last June. And for tonight's confrontation outside the pub.

But it would have to be cleverly laid, this trap. So convincing that McLaren would not hesitate to become involved. And harsh enough that he would know what had happened to him and who had perpetrated it. And why.

And, perhaps, roping in that bloody mate of his, the git who had stood by McLaren last June and again tonight. *He* was begging for a rap on the knuckles or a slap, too. Or something worse.

Harvester grinned, already enjoying the virulent revenge and imagining McLaren's disgrace. But his smile soon faded. He leaned back in the chair, his mind a confusion of images and words. What in the hell could he do to entrap McLaren? What would seem so real, so dire that McLaren would jump into the situation without thinking? And where? Somewhere where it wouldn't be evident that Harvested had anything to do with it. Revenge was sweet, but it had to be planned well in order to succeed. He'd get no second chance to publicly ridicule McLaren.

He abandoned the scheme for the moment, stirred the vegetables and flipped the fish, and returned to the table.

The letter from Derek Parry, Harvester's police colleague in Edinburgh, tried to fill in Harvester on five years of life. The topics were confined to one or two sentences apiece, but the feelings rambled on much longer. Harvester sighed with the tone of a man who's heard the same excuse from his teenager once too often. He skimmed the pages of handwriting, and wondered why he was reading this. The meal in the skillet was under control and he had little else to do but wait for everything to cook. He poured a glass of wine and resumed reading the letter.

Bus trips to Culzean Castle, fishing with his new rod, the money spent on keeping his car running, problems with starlings and voles, teeth problems, thinning hair and gaining weight, his wife's sister moving in with them…

The back of the last page killed the groan that was welling up in Harvester's throat. His colleague wanted Harvester to visit him.

Derek had just joined a shooting club and would Harvester be interested in coming up for a long weekend to do some clay pigeon shooting? They could also do a bit of archery or fishing, depending on when Harvester could make it. If not now, winter was good. The Christmas/New Year week was nearly overflowing in Edinburgh with concerts, ghost walk tours, festive lights displays and such. Or there was always skiing in the highlands and climbing. And Hogmany wasn't to be missed. Edinburgh seemed to be the center for the rowdy New Year's Eve street party of drinking, noise and singing. Did any of this sound interesting?

The pages sank to Harvester's lap as he gazed at the calendar on the wall. Was it a sign that he should do this? Bolton, where his son lived, would be more or less on the way to Edinburgh. If he left early enough…

And if he thought hard enough…

Harvester dished up the fish and cabbage, got a pen from the pencil holder, and sat at the table. His food turned cold as he leaned over his son's letter and listed his ideas for his revenge against McLaren.

Chapter Twenty-Six

The fire wasn't big Friday night. No sirens or blue lights interrupted the quiet; no police tape cordoned the crime scene. Consequently, it hadn't made the news on the telly. But a mention in the local newspaper, nearly buried on page fourteen, jumped out at Sean.

His tea grew cold and his cereal turned soggy as he bent over the page, focused on the article.

A fire at a residence on Derwent Road might've turned into a tragedy Friday night if not for the family's dog.

"He started barking and wouldn't stop," homeowner Robert Brogan said. "He woke us up, so I figured something was wrong. I followed him into the front room. That's when I saw the fire on the driveway and ran outside to put it out."

A pile of rubbish, evidently brought by the arsonist and dumped onto the drive, burned long enough and intense enough to spread to a wooden planter, two deck chairs, and a wooden garden gnome.

The Brogans poked through the debris Saturday morning. They found nothing at all useful to tell them who the arsonist was or why the fire was set. "I was all for calling the police, Helene," Brogan said, "but my husband said we'd be wasting their time. He laughed it off as a teenage prank."

"We've the dog," Mr. Brogan said, "and the

314

burglar alarm for the house. We're fine. I'm thankful we caught the blaze before it caused more damage. We'll keep the gnome since it's only scorched, but we'll have to replace the chairs and flower box."

"My mother gave me this gnome as a birthday gift," Mrs. Brogan said. "I'm glad it wasn't destroyed. It means a lot to me."

Picking up on his wife's sentiment, Mr. Brogan said, "We obviously can buy another gnome. It's the link to the gift-giver that's important. That connection can't be replaced. It's frustrating, this wanton destruction, but I'm not overly concerned. It's probably a one-time thing." He excused himself from this reporter to ring up his insurance agent.

Mrs. Brogan is not as confident about the incident as her husband...

The phone rang, momentarily startling Sean. He shook off the scene and set the paper aside. Helene's anger underscored the last sentence he'd read.

"Think you're pretty cute, don't you?" she snapped in response to Sean's "Hello?"

"Helene?"

"Don't pretend you don't know who this is any more than you don't know what I'm talking about."

"I *don't* know what you're talking about. What's going on?"

"That fire you set last night."

"*I* set? Look, Helene, I'm getting bloody well tired of you accusing me of everything and anything inconvenient, or that you think will boost your bank account. Now, lay off."

"Just don't think you can get away with it, Sean. The dog's going to be outside at night from now on.

I'm giving you a warning, which is more than you deserve. Now, you've one more day to come up with the money, or I go to the police." She drew in her breath, and it sounded to Sean as if it were an effort to regain her composure. "I think you've just locked yourself in jail and thrown away the key, darling. Arson on top of murder. Not exactly leading the life of a reformed criminal, are you?"

Sean summoned his courage from the depths of his soul. "I don't think a blackmailer, no matter how amateur or experienced she is, would phone the police to grass on the person she's blackmailing. So I suggest *you* think *that* over."

"But—"

He rang off. His day and future looked a lot brighter.

****

McLaren woke Saturday morning with a reluctance bordering on desperation. Besides being stiff, his head reverberated with the clanging of a hammer inside his skull. He sat on the edge of his bed, his feet on the cold wooden floor, and thought again about the evening. Charlie Harvester was enough to bring on any headache, but the phantom skulking around Dena's car and the subsequent race over the countryside had definitely impacted him physically. What a way to start the day.

He showered longer than usual hoping the pelting of hot water on his lower back would ease the stiffness from his muscles. When he had dressed in navy blue trousers and a blue-and-red print shirt, he wandered into the kitchen and made a pot of strong coffee.

As the coffee brewed, he sorted through the items

from Janet's house. He had spread them on his dining room table last night but now, after he'd had some time to let the information and possible significance of the find perk in his brain, he wanted to look at everything again.

Beneath the sheaf of newspaper clippings lay the small envelope. He hadn't opened it yesterday, his attention on the tape recording. But now he slit open the top and extracted photos and pieces of folded paper.

The handwriting appeared to be Janet's, for she had titled the first page "Connie and me. Loving sisters." Janet filled the pages with brief paragraphs of outings she and Connie had shared, birthdays and thoughts of their futures. The dates between entries were rather far apart, but considering that Janet might not have been able to always meet up with Connie—due to catering or concert dates, and getting away from Nora—that didn't surprise McLaren. And considering the twelve years' age difference between the two girls...

He leafed through the photographs. Janet and Connie shared the same intense, brown eyes and slender build. But Janet's hair was brunette, and Connie was a redhead. Certainly a dead giveaway to her parentage, he thought as he remembered Stuart's reddish eyebrows.

A more recent photo showed Janet, Connie and Ian, the script on the back declaring 'Me, Con and fiancé—another first for Ian.' McLaren flipped the photo to the front, staring, not trusting his eyes. Hadn't Stuart Ennis said Nora didn't know of Connie? If so, how had Janet come to know her? He turned the photo over hoping for some scribbled information, but the back was bare. He looked at the picture again. A happy group, all smiles. Probably taken near the time of the car crash, for the three were leaning against a red Ford Ka. A section of a low stone wall ran across the left side of the scene. Ian held a key toward the photographer. His new car?

Behind the car, her face and shoulders just visible, smiled Nora. McLaren nearly dropped the photo in astonishment. He peered closer at the face, took the photograph into the kitchen and looked at it under the light above the sink. Yes. It was Nora. Her hand rested on Connie's shoulder. He couldn't mistake Nora even with her dark hair and youthful complexion. Perhaps she had grayed after Janet's death. Losing a daughter and an almost-daughter within a year or two of each other might do that.

He leaned against the edge of the table, his mind racing. Why would Stuart lie about Nora not knowing about Connie? If Nora knew about Connie, why hadn't she mentioned Connie to him? Because Connie had no connection with Janet's death, obviously, but wouldn't she have been mentioned just as a piece of information? And if Stuart wasn't lying, was Nora keeping her knowledge from Stuart? Why wouldn't she tell Stuart that she knew about his daughter?

He poured a cup of coffee and returned to the dining room. He sat, still staring at the photo, and set the mug on the table. Janet must have known about Connie fairly early on in Connie's life, for there were several photos of Janet and baby Connie. Which parent had told Janet about Connie? Did it matter to McLaren's investigation?

Maybe it mattered only to Nora. Maybe losing Connie, the child who might have been hers, spurred her into needing to have Janet's death resolved. Nora knew how Connie had died, most likely. She now needed to know how Janet had died.

But if Janet and Nora were in the picture, who was the photographer?

McLaren tucked the photo inside his wallet, poured the untasted coffee into the kitchen sink, and left his house.

****

"Yes, I took the photo. Six or so years ago. I'm amazed I can remember." The vicar of St. James the Apostle Church in Temple Normanton held the photo up to the sunlight and looked carefully at the faces. He abandoned poking the small fire in the wire incinerator when McLaren walked up, and set the stick on top of the stone wall. Within the incinerator, the dry leaves, stalks of the summer garden and the castoff twigs and boughs crackled noisily. The flames burned bright yellow and red in the sunlight. The air smelled of autumn and reminded McLaren of long ago campfires and leaf raking. A tongue of fire curled upward, as though reaching for the yellow-leafed branch overhead. The smoke billowed white and translucent on the downwind breeze, and he thought momentarily of the fires set at his house. They, too, had produced smoke. Smoke that clouded his vision and obscured items usually in plain view…

"I'm glad you can remember," McLaren returned, trying to keep his voice unemotional. He shifted his stance, and his shadow shifted into the smoke. One murky element mingling with another. Was that indicative of his progress in the case?

"The recollection of them is clear, if you're

concerned that I may be confusing them with others." The vicar nodded, his gaze still on the photo. He was dressed in baggy-kneed tan trousers and an ill-defined long knitted waistcoat. A brown corduroy cap sat low over his forehead, as though anchoring his flyaway hair. He smiled, nodded, and returned the photo to McLaren. "We're a small village, as I told you on your previous visit, but even without a multitude of residents I'm certain of these people and the occasion. That's Connie Long, in the center. Her boyfriend, Ian. And her friend Janet Ennis and then Janet's mother."

"Were the four of them close friends, do you know? Did you see them here regularly?"

"Janet came quite frequently. For Connie's birthday, though not yearly. Sometimes for Boxing Day. She came more often for that than for Christmas. Perhaps she and her mother lived too far away to come more often."

"How about Ian?"

"He played bass with some sort of trio. I never heard him, but I believe he as well as the group were quite good. Due to his work schedule, he didn't come to the village very often. Connie would go off to see him, I know. I'd see her at the bus stop or walking back to her house and she'd laugh and say she had visited Ian."

"They're together for this occasion, though." McLaren tapped the front of the photo. "Did you take this shot here, next to the churchyard wall?"

The vicar adjusted his glasses farther up his nose and looked carefully at the picture. "Yes. How clever of you to recognize it. Ian got a new car and took the women for a celebration ride. Not all at once, of course."

"When was this?"

"I don't recall an exact date. Months before Connie's accident, if that's what you want to know. In the summer." He angled his head to look at the photo and pointed to a plant at the base of the stone wall. "See? A daylily. That variety blooms in July."

McLaren nodded and returned the photo to his wallet. Shaking hands with the vicar, he said, "Well, you're been most helpful. I appreciate it."

As he turned to leave, the vicar said, "This is important, then. I recall you had asked about Connie when you first came."

McLaren hesitated, assessing what he should tell the man. The vicar was used to confidences shared. In a small village he would have to be tight lipped so no gossip would start. But the man did not need to know about Connie or Janet, or any of the other people in Connie's life. He had known the woman for a brief year or so and had liked her. He didn't need to know she was illegitimate. McLaren cleared his throat and smiled. "It's important, yes. To Connie and to the folks in the photo. Each of us thanks you." He walked to his car, feeling the vicar's gaze on him and the unanswered questions hanging in the air.

****

Saturday morning, Ian O'Connor was marginally more polite to McLaren. Resentment, either at Janet or at McLaren, showed itself in Ian's tone, but he answered the questions, perhaps thinking he'd get rid of the man soonest that way.

"None of us had money falling out of our pockets," Ian said. "Even Janet. She was better off than me or Dan, but I didn't see her moving to an upscale neighborhood or buying a new car. She worked for her money, just like us."

"She didn't have to spend every penny she earned," McLaren countered.

"No. At least, I don't think she did. Dan might've come close to doing that, though."

"Oh? His place is nice but it's not what I would classify upscale."

"The house isn't, but they got a posh car a few months before Janet died and the group broke up. I guess he'd been saving up for it."

****

Could've been saving up for it, McLaren acknowledged, his gaze on his car's CD player. So could anyone. But added to the conversation on the tape he'd found at Janet's cottage, a marriage that fell short of an affluent level experienced from childhood, and the affidavits of caterers and restaurants owners… McLaren rang up Jamie and told him where to turn up for an arrest, nosed his car back onto the road, and turned up the volume on the tape. Maybe he'd sleep well tonight.

****

Dan Wilshaw settled into his chair opposite McLaren. He had offered McLaren a cup of coffee, which he refused, so Dan drank alone and asked what had prompted the return visit.

"Nora gifted Janet's cottage to me." McLaren watched Dan for a reaction. "I hope you don't mind."

"Why should I? It was Janet's, then Nora's, and now obviously it's yours. She can do with it as she likes. I'm glad it will be used, instead of sitting there to rot away."

"Did Janet ever have you over at her cottage?"

"No. It was strictly her get-away. A place she used for writing her music."

"Nice that she had such a spot. Too many of us don't have any place where we can escape our daily grind." McLaren nodded toward a photograph of a tropical cottage on a beach. "Is that one of your favorite spots?"

"Yes. It's not ours outright, however. It's a time-share thing. We fell into a good deal. Ruth found out about it and we jumped at the chance."

"Nice. How long have you had that?"

Dan scratched his chin. "Now that I think of it, it's kind of funny. A bit before Janet died. In the summer. I think June, but I'm not sure. June or July, at any rate. I had it in my mind to invite Janet and Myles for a week the following year, but..." His mouth skewed up and he avoided McLaren's eyes.

"New car, nice time share place. You must've done all right as Janet's pianist."

"I did, but don't forget that Ruth works, too. Her wages contributed to all this."

"And probably other folks' wages, too."

"What? Other folks? What are you talking about? Ruth, do you know what he means?"

Ruth had entered the house during McLaren's last statement. She laid her shoulder bag and keys on the chair and looked from McLaren to her husband.

McLaren stood up and related finding Janet's tape recording, newspaper clippings and the affidavits of several caterers and restaurant owners. "The police will subpoena each person's bank statements, including yours."

"You're round the twist," Ruth said, walking over to her husband. "You're trying too hard."

"You also killed Janet."

Ruth laughed. "Now there you *are* trying too hard. What brought you to this fictional assumption?"

"You're the only person in her immediate group who might know where the sound equipment was in her house. You'd been over there for Christmas parties. But you didn't know that they never rehearsed in her studio because it was too little. A microphone was found in the debris of the fire. Its round head matches the curved indentation on Janet's skull."

"Fascinating."

"I'm not saying you killed her on purpose, but you went to her house that day, maybe argued with her. In talking, you picked up the microphone, followed her outside and into her studio. The argument escalated and you hit her with the mike. Maybe you panicked, maybe you thought to cover the incident. Janet had a small rubbish fire burning. It had been a windy day. Maybe the studio caught fire accidentally. Or you could have spread the fire to the studio. That's something for the police to prove."

Ruth shook her head in amazement. "Incredibly good. You should write fiction. And what's my motive for doing all this? Killers usually have a reason."

"You had a very good reason. You took bribes from restaurants and caterers to give them five-star reviews in your food column in the newspaper. One good review from you and businesses usually flourish. You tried to strong arm Janet into paying you for a great review, except Janet didn't succumb to your blackmail. In your heated discussion you killed her."

"Like I said, great fiction. Besides that tape and clippings, you've nothing else, have you?"

McLaren went to the front door, opened it and motioned for Jamie, who had just driven up in a police car. He waited until Jamie joined them and cautioned Ruth before he continued.

"I believe I do have something else. One of Janet's coats was missing from her house. A blue ski jacket with dark red chevrons on the sleeves. A rather distinctive coat, with a small rip on the right side hip area. I believe you put on the coat when you left the house, just in case someone saw you. You'd then be mistaken for Janet. Shall we look in your closet?" He walked to the hallway before Ruth could reply. On opening the door he saw the coat Nora had described. He pulled it from the closet. "I think we've got all the proof that we need. You want to bet the lab will find yours and Janet's DNA on this coat?"

Ruth's gaze shifted from the coat to McLaren and then to Jamie. She gestured toward the closet, distracting their attention, then sprinted toward the window. McLaren shoved the coat into Jamie's hand, then dashed after her as she pushed the curtain aside and threw her right leg over the sill. He yanked off his jacket and flung it over her head as he lunged for her. Ruth stopped and kicked at him. She tried to shove off the jacket with her free hand, but McLaren sidestepped to avoid her feet. His grip tightened and he yanked the garment around her head, cocooning it, and pulled her from the sill. She screamed and tried to hook the toe of her shoe on the window frame but she slipped free. McLaren slid his hands to her upper arms and, as her legs folded, deposited her on the floor. She lay there, her ragged breathing the only sound in the room.

McLaren removed the jacket and asked if she was all right.

She didn't speak or move for a moment, and McLaren feared she'd hurt herself in the struggle. As he bent, she turned over and stared at him. "I'm fine, though I don't deserve your concern. Nothing hurt but my pride, and that isn't worth much." She hesitated, then accepted his help up and struggled to her feet. "You'd think I'd learn." She glanced at the coat, now back in McLaren's grasp, and quickly dropped his hand.

Dan wrapped his arms around her, murmuring that he loved her, and seemed not to hear her apology or explanation.

"Yes, you're correct in your assumption, Mr. McLaren. That's the way it happened." Her hand went out tentatively to the coat. The sound of a neighbor's lawnmower starting up drifted into the house, and for a moment, Ruth gazed through the window. A motorcycle roared down the street, pulling her attention back to the men in the room. She nodded, her eyes dark with remorse. "I-I put on the coat before leaving her house, though I didn't mean to hurt her. But she was so smug, so sure I wasn't going to follow through with her. I got so angry with her. I hadn't meant to hit her. We'd been talking in the front room and I just idly picked up the mic. I still had it in my hands when I followed her outside. I'm sorry. I didn't mean to do any of it."

McLaren glanced at Dan, who continued his whispers. Jamie had stepped forward, possibly ready for another diversion. McLaren let her comment pass, and instead said, "You planted the pot under her sofa, didn't you?"

Ruth ran her fingers under her eyes, blotting her tears, and nodded. "While she was in the kitchen, yes. I thought I could call the police with an anonymous tip, and that would show her I meant business, that she should think again before crossing me. I forgot it was there when the fire started."

"And the arsons at my place? Just to satisfy my own curiosity."

She went all pink and grimaced. "That was me, or my sister. We both set the fires, at different times. I...we were trying to scare you off the case, but..." She looked at Dan and he squeezed her hand.

"So Eva knew about you killing Janet, then."

"Yes. I'd phoned her to warn her about you so she'd watch what she said. We were going to meet to discuss how to throw you off the track."

"At Carsington Water?" He remembered following Eva around the lake.

"Yes." Her voice colored with regret. "We—She didn't realize you had trailed her there, so she tried to lose you. She didn't want you finding me there and possibly connecting us. She was only trying to help me."

Jamie escorted Ruth to the police car and drove off. McLaren patted Dan's shoulder, then slowly walked to his car and drove to see Nora.

****

When he told her he'd solved the case, she seemed not to know him or know what he was talking about. She sat in her favorite place by the window and looked out at the gathering dusk, letting his words flow over her without any acknowledgement. McLaren paused halfway through his narrative, wondering if she comprehended anything he said, wondering if he should leave. But he told her everything, neither expecting a response now or any questions. Her eyes had the veiled look of her mind being somewhere else.

McLaren finished his account and took the photo from his wallet. He looked at it once more before laying it on the table. The four people were so happy, so confident about the future. Who could have guessed that within a year two of them would be dead? He glanced at Janet and felt the now-familiar rush of blood to his cheeks and the increase of his heart rate. She'd been such a beauty, so talented. Damn the waste of such genius.

Looking at Nora, he paused by the front door. Nora remained in the same pose, her attention on some faraway object. As he opened the door, she turned toward him and smiled.

"Thank you, Mr. McLaren. For me, Janet, and Connie."

He nodded, kissed her cheek, and closed the door behind him. His satisfaction stayed with him through the ride home.

****

Later that afternoon, McLaren walked to the stereo and reached for Janet's CD. A lot of emotions were packed into each song; he wasn't ready to immerse himself again in them. Not right now, at least. He put on a recording of Chopin nocturnes and sat on the sofa. He thought of Janet as the music washed over him. Janet had been found in the center of the room, implying she had been unconscious and not known about the fire. He nodded, finding peace in that knowledge.

He rang up Dena, needing to get the passions untangled. Ruth's act had devastated the members of Janet's group and her catering company, affected Ruth's sister and possibly her brother-in-law, and of course Nora. So many lives that would never be the same due to Ruth's anger and greed. He tried to make sense of the tangle of emotions. Like a shadow in the smoke—vague, haunting, lurking, but there, nonetheless. He whispered a prayer for Janet, Connie and Nora, then relaxed his mind. Right now all he cared about was Dena and the love they shared. He smiled at her photo as Dena's voice came to him over the phone. He would grab her love and keep it as an island while the world tilted around them.

Epilogue

Sean picked up the phone receiver, his heart racing. Should he call the police or just let it go? After all, nothing much had happened. A wooden flowerbox and two chairs burnet, a wooden gnome scorched. It'd only been a small fire on Helene's drive… He glanced at his wife's photo, the glass front brilliant in the sunlight. What would happen? A fine—jail time? His mouth went dry as he thought of the consequence. After all, Kathryn hadn't really done much damage. She'd just been trying to help him, to scare off Helene from her blackmail attempt… The angry buzz over the phone line annoyed him, reminded him he had to do something. He mentally tossed a coin and slowly eased the receiver back onto its cradle. The silence wrapped him in comfort.

****

Charlie Harvester let the newspaper sink onto the breakfast table. He hadn't read past the front-page article's headline and first sentence, yet he knew what the entire story would say. Knew the tightening in his stomach would grow to a full-blown knot, that the pressure behind his eyes would develop into a migraine. He stared at the far wall, unaware of his surroundings and the urgency of the whistling teakettle. The article's first sentence swam before his eyes. *A mother who wouldn't let her daughter's death investigation die found justice yesterday when ex-cop Michael McLaren solved the five-year old murder case.*

Harvester struggled to his feet, tipped the paper into the dustbin, and glanced at his wall calendar. "Wait until December, mate. My Christmas gift to you."

A word about the author...

Jo Hiestand discovered the joys of Things British on a month-long trip to England during her college years. Since then, she has been back nearly a dozen times and lived there during her professional folk singing stint. This intimate knowledge of England forms the framework of the McLaren Mysteries. In 1999 Jo returned to Webster University to major in English. She graduated in 2001 with a BA degree and departmental honors. Jo is a member of Sisters in Crime and Mystery Writers of America. Her cat Tennyson shares her St. Louis home.

Visit her at http://www.johiestand.com